"How are you ___?" Running Wolf asked.

His voice resonate ___
through her like the ___
her clasped hands to her chest, ___
to hold on to her courage.

"Snow Raven."

"That is not a name for a woman." He frowned as he swept her with his gaze. "But it suits you, for you are not like any woman I have ever met. You are causing trouble, you know. No one knows what to do with you. Some say you will steal a horse and run, but then we would catch you and you would die."

She squeezed her eyes shut at the images now assaulting her mind.

"Ah," he said. "So you *do* feel fear. For a time I thought you were immune to such emotions."

She looked at him now. "A warrior does not admit to fear."

"But a woman does. She cries and uses her tears to gather sympathy. Yet you do not."

"Would that work?"

"It would make you less interesting. And you are very interesting."

"I do not want your interest."

He laughed. "Then you should not have unseated one of my warriors."

AUTHOR NOTE

From the moment Snow Raven came charging into my first scene on her white horse I have been in love with this character. My heroine is the daughter of a Crow chief and is bright, stoic and brave—even after being captured by her enemies. At first she wants only to survive until she is rescued. But when faced with the needs of her fellow captives she grows into a warrior, forgoing her own happiness to win their freedom.

My hero, Running Wolf, is the war chief of his Sioux tribe and an enemy to the Crow people. Running Wolf is at first intrigued, then confounded, and later fascinated by the captive Snow Raven. They both resist a love that will cost them all. He must lead his people and protect them from their enemies, while she must try to bring her people home. What chance does love have when pitted against duty?

I had a wonderful time writing about two Native characters who lived on the North American Plains in a time after the Spanish and before the Americans came to challenge their dominance. The research for this story was a joy—especially learning all I could on earning coup feathers. When I discovered that a woman could become a warrior I was thrilled.

If you would like more details on this story be sure to visit my website for *Behind the Story*.

And if you enjoy my story please let me know with a review on Goodreads or Amazon. You can sign up for my newsletter at jennakernan.com. For extra insider information visit my Facebook page or follow me on Twitter: @jennakernan

RUNNING WOLF

Jenna Kernan

MILLS & BOON

Published in Great Britain 2015
by Mills & Boon, an imprint of Harlequin (UK) Limited,
Eton House, 18-24 Paradise Road, Richmond, Surrey, TW9 1SR

© 2015 Jeannette H. Monaco

ISBN: 978-0-263-24794-7

Harlequin (UK) Limited's policy is to use papers that are natural,
renewable and recyclable products and made from wood grown in
sustainable forests. The logging and manufacturing processes conform
to the legal environmental regulations of the country of origin.

Printed and bound in Spain
by CPI, Barcelona

Award-winning author **Jenna Kernan** writes fast-paced Western and paranormal romantic adventures. She has penned over two dozen novels, has received two RITA nominations, and in 2010 won the Book Buyers Best Award for her debut paranormal romance. Jenna loves an adventure. Her hobbies include recreational gold-prospecting, scuba diving and gem-hunting.

Follow Jenna on Twitter @jennakernan, on Facebook or at www.jennakernan.com

Books by Jenna Kernan

Mills & Boon® Historical Romance

Winter Woman
Turner's Woman
Wed Under Western Skies
'His Brother's Bride'
The Trapper
A Western Winter Wonderland
'Fallen Angel'
High Plains Bride
Outlaw Bride
Sierra Bride
His Dakota Captive
Western Winter Wedding Bells
'The Sheriff's Housekeeper Bride'
Gold Rush Groom
The Texas Ranger's Daughter
Wild West Christmas
'A Family for the Rancher'
Running Wolf

**Visit the author profile page
at millsandboon.co.uk for more titles**

For Jim, always.

Chapter One

Snow Raven raced her gray dappled mustang, Song, along the lakeshore, her horse's powerful muscles rippling with each long stride. She loved how she and Song moved together, how the air rushed against her face and lifted her hair. Her father said that riding was the closest that a person ever came to flying.

This was the very reason Raven did not wear her hair in twin braids like the women of her tribe, but neither did she quite dare to wear it as her father and brother did. The warriors cut their forelock short and used grease and pitch to make the hairs stand up as stiff as a porcupine's quills. Instead, Raven made her own style and had wound narrow braids at her temples and wrapped them in ermine that was decorated with shell beads and quillwork like the men. The rest of her hair she left loose and as wild as the mane of her mustang. Her dress was also a mixture,

shorter than a woman's, made from a single buckskin like a man's, but for modesty and comfort
she wore both loincloth and leggings beneath.

Raven wore a skinning knife about her neck, as
most females in her tribe did, but she also carried
a deerskin quiver from the six-point buck she had
felled when she was eight. Within, metal-tipped
arrows waited, ready. She carried her strung bow
looped over her back. The taut string, fitted between her breasts, revealed her curves.

Raven knew that more than one woman ob-
jected to her hunting, but they never said so to
her face and they did not turn down the meat. As
for the men, her position as the chief's daughter
insured that she had no shortage of suitors, just
a shortage of suitors who interested her. Hunting
and riding were more appealing.

Now she sought to catch her older brother,
Bright Arrow, who had somehow managed to
leave camp without her knowing. His stealth was
only one of the qualities that she admired. Up
ahead the party of warriors turned at the sound
of her approach. There was Little Badger, Turns
Too Slowly and her brother. Little Badger grinned
with pleasure at her appearance, but her brother
did not. In fact, he did not even slow his big blue
roan stallion, Hail. It was only now, when she
drew close, that she saw her brother did not carry
his bow, but his lance. Were they raiding already?

"I could have shot you," said Turns Too Slowly, realizing belatedly that he had not even reached for his bow.

"What are you doing, Raven?" Bright Arrow asked, his voice so stern he reminded her of their father, Six Elks.

"I thought you were hunting elk," she said, already aware of her mistake.

Her offer was met with silence. Finally Turns Too Slowly spoke.

"This is no hunt."

"We are scouting for Sioux," said Little Badger.

Her eyes widened and excitement and fear rolled in her belly until they were blended like berry juice in water. She had not seen a Sioux snake since the attack when she was only seven.

"Have you seen any?"

Her brother raised his hand, halting Little Badger, who was about to answer.

Her brother's scowl deepened. "This is their territory. It is wise to be certain we are alone. If they are here we must prepare to fight."

Was that a yes or a no?

"Did Father send you?"

"Go home, Little Warrior." Her brother now made her childhood name sound like an insult.

She stayed where she was, toying with the leather fringe on the pommel she had made with the help of her grandmother, Truthful Woman. "I will help you scout."

"You will not."

Since word had come of the raids against their people by the Sioux, he was not so forgiving of her insistence to leave the camp.

"I can track game better than Little Badger and hear better than Turns Too Slowly," she said, unable to keep the belligerence from her voice.

"And ride better than all three of us, I suppose," said Turns Too Slowly.

"Yes."

Turns Too Slowly gestured toward camp. "So prove it by riding that way."

Her brother was more to the point. "Do you know what they do to female captives?" he asked. His voice held a note of irritation. She knew. The enemy would disgrace her, take her freedom, give her all the hardest work and worst food. Still, she lifted her chin. "I am not afraid of the snake people. I would kill them first."

"Brave words, but better still, ride home where you are safe," he said. His tone changed, now quiet, respectful with just a note of desperation. "If you are here, I have to worry over your safety."

She wished they could stay in their mountains instead of moving east into the territory of the Sioux with the endless grass. But the whites had built a fort and then sickness had taken so many. Her father, their chief, had moved them here, thinking it better to face an enemy they could see.

She looked over her shoulder at the way she had come. Back there she knew the women were tending cooking fires, gathering wood and gutting fish caught on the trawl lines. She looked forward at the blue lake glimmering through the trees and the forest thick with brush.

Her heart tugged, whispering for her to ride.

"We will take you back," he said, turning his horse.

She did not want to be escorted to camp like some wandering child. She could take care of herself. Hadn't she killed a deer, elk and pronghorn? Hadn't she skinned them and dressed them and carried them home over her horse's withers?

Bright Arrow did not wait for her to reply but pressed his horse forward.

As he passed her, he said, "You'll be safe there."

She did not want to be safe. She wanted to be a warrior like her brother. His hands were tough and smelled of leather, instead of stinking of fish.

"I'll take her," said Little Badger.

Bright Arrow eyed his fellow. "And leave us one weaker?"

She suspected that this was not the only reason her brother said no. Ever since Bright Arrow had caught Little Badger trying to put his hand up her dress, he had not left any of his friends alone with her. It was just as well. She liked the sensation of a warrior's touch, but would not let anyone lift her dress. She was a woman of virtue, not some Sioux captive to be used by anyone.

Still, her stubbornness had limits. She would not leave her brother with one less warrior on her account, especially if the Sioux were near. But with the sun streaming through the yellow leaves and the wind still blowing warm as summer, it was hard to think of danger.

"Have you seen any Sioux?" she asked.

Her brother shook his head.

"Then, I will find my own way home."

Before he could object, she wheeled about, urging her horse to rear before bounding off the way she had come.

She heard the sound of hooves beating the ground behind her. A glance back showed Bright Arrow in fast pursuit with his comrades close behind. He was an impressive sight at full gallop, with his long hair streaming out behind him and the fringe of his saddle, sleeves and leggings all fluttering in the wind. His breastplate, made of a series of cylindrical white beads, beat against his chest with the rhythm of his horse's hooves.

In his hair were tied the two notched eagle feathers he had earned stealing horses and facing the Sioux in battle. She wished women could earn such honors, but although she could ride and shoot and throw a lance, she would never have the chance to earn a feather with an act of courage—kill an enemy, sustain a wound, steal a horse. Women did not do such things.

A woman's courage was quiet and went unsung. There were no feathers for bearing a child or making a lodge. Yet she still dreamed of the ceremony where her father, the chief, presented her with a coup feather.

Behind her, Bright Arrow leaned low over his horse's neck trying to catch up. They never would. Song was too fast. There were no two better riders in the entire Low River tribe than her and her brother.

It seemed that all the warriors would accompany her home, which was very bad, because it meant that Bright Arrow planned to speak to their father. She needed to get there first. She needed to explain that she loved the scent of the wind and hated the stench of fish. He would listen. Since her mother's passing, he always listened.

Raven lowered herself flat to her horse's neck and gave Song her head. They fairly flew over the ground.

As she tore over the animal trail, she noticed a tan-colored lump lying in the path. A fawn, she thought as Song snorted and jumped the tiny obstacle. Raven gaped when she saw that the carcass was a village dog with one arrow sticking from its ribs. At a glance she recognized that the fletching on the shaft was not like the ones of her people.

The hairs on her neck rose.

Raven opened her mouth to scream a warning to her brother, but another scream filled the air, farther away, one coming from their fishing camp. Her brother straightened in his saddle and then did something she had never seen him do. He slapped his open hand on his horse's broad muscular shoulder. The horse lunged forward as Raven slowed.

"The camp!" she yelled.

"Run," shouted her brother as he surged past her with Little Badger and Turns Too Slowly on his horse's flank. Raven wheeled her horse to flee but then thought of the women, caught between the lake and attack. Song seemed to know her mind before Snow Raven did, for her mare raced after the other horses. They broke from the trees into chaos. The men in the village were fighting from the ground as mounted warriors ran at a gallop through the camp, upsetting cooking kettles and trampling lodges. She saw that they were Sioux by the cut of the enemy's war shirts and because they wore their hair in twin braids, like a Crow woman.

Her brother gave a whoop and charged, drawing the fight to them while giving the women and children time to flee in the opposite direction. The Sioux were outnumbered, but they were mounted and had the advantage of surprise.

Snow Raven drew up at the woods, calling to the women, telling them to flee in this direction where there was good cover. Raven watched in horror as she saw two of the Sioux break away from the fight to follow the retreating women.

She saw her old grandmother hobbling along at an ungainly trot. Truthful Woman had raised Snow Raven since the time of her mother's death, but could no longer run because she was bent and her joints were puffy and stiff. With each moment her grandmother fell farther behind, the Sioux in pursuit.

Was that their aim, then, to take captives? Or was this a fight over territory, as her brother had said? Either way they could easily kill her grandmother on their way to the younger, more useful captives.

Raven pressed her heels into her horse's flanks and gave her first war cry. She swung her bow over her head and reached back for an arrow. The lead warrior dressed in a red war shirt trimmed with long strands of trophy hair grabbed Truthful Woman by the multistrand shell and bead necklaces that circled her throat. Raven vowed the redshirt would not harm her grandmother, though he was upon her already. Truthful Woman was dragged backward against her enemy's horse. Her hands went to her windpipe and her face turned scarlet. The warrior shook his hand, further strangling Raven's grandmother.

Snow Raven screamed again and notched her arrow, but was too close to shoot.

She dropped her bow and rammed his horse with hers. Song's muscular chest collided with the other horse's flank, causing the beast to skitter sideways. The necklaces broke away in the Sioux's hand and Truthful Woman dropped to her knees choking and gagging.

Snow Raven launched herself from her saddle onto the warrior's chest. The thud jarred her teeth as they toppled together from his horse.

Raven landed on top of the warrior. The jolt robbed the wind from the man's body and gave Raven the moment she needed to draw her skinning knife and lift it above her head. Today she would send this snake to his ancestors and take her first war trophy. The warrior's wide eyes stared up at her as she thrust, preparing to lodge the knife into the center of her enemy's throat.

Running Wolf met the charge of the three mounted Crow warriors. The fourth had halted at the tree line, the dapple-gray horse dancing with power and nervous energy. His gaze lingered a second. There was something amiss about the rider. He forced his attention back to the large Crow leading the charge on a big blue roan stallion. The feathers in his hair spoke of his opponent's bravery.

Running Wolf lifted his lance to strike. Today they did not carry the coup stick used to mark bravery, but weapons to kill, for the Crow had invaded their territory. His opponent lifted his shield. Running Wolf saw the symbol of a red arrow emblazoned on the hard rawhide. It was good medicine, he thought as his opponent deflected his thrusting lance and he made his own thrust. Running Wolf twisted in his saddle to avoid the iron spear tip and lost some of his momentum. His spear did not pierce the shield or his enemy, but slid harmlessly away.

His men engaged the other three warriors with cries and blows. Running Wolf wheeled to have another chance at the leader, but as he turned he saw the warrior on the roan horse leap forward. The Crow gave a high thready cry.

Running Wolf engaged the first man again. This was the obvious leader. It was not difficult for one war chief to recognize another. His opponent shouted directions to the men on the ground, who quickly fell back behind the horses.

Running Wolf lifted his lance and thrust again, and his enemy deflected, but not quite enough, for the spear tip sliced deep into his opponent's shoulder muscle, cutting a gash in the Crow's shield arm as the horses moved past each other again. The warrior threw his lance to the ground. It stuck upright and quivering as he yanked his tomahawk from his breechclout and swung at Running Wolf's head.

Running Wolf flattened to his horse's back as the metal ax head flew past him. He straightened and swung the pole of his lance like a club, striking his foe across the back with enough force to unseat him.

The Crow warrior did not stay down long but kept hold of his horse's mane as he fell, then used the ground to vault back onto his moving horse. He and his men dropped back to stand between their women still fleeing for cover and Running Wolf's men. They took a defensive stance. Retreating, delaying, giving the women time to escape. Nearly all had disappeared into the woods. Even those carrying small children now darted like shadows beneath the mighty pines.

Only one old woman remained, limping along like a wounded elk before a pack of hungry wolves. Red Hawk pursued the old Crow, but for what possible reason Running Wolf could not imagine.

Running Wolf had made his orders clear. Destroy this camp. Steal the horses and go. He recalled now Red Hawk asking about captives and his reply—only if the taking would not slow their escape. But despite his orders, Red Hawk had

left the fight to pursue captives and now lifted
an old woman by the throat, dragging her beside
his spotted horse.

A blur of movement drew Running Wolf's eye.
The small warrior on the gray mare leaped from
the galloping horse right at Red Hawk. The force
of the collision carried Red Hawk sideways to
the ground. Running Wolf wheeled toward the
downed warrior and saw the flash of a small iron
skinning knife. He frowned at the strange choice
of weapon as the pieces fell into place.

The small figure pinning Red Hawk was not
an undersized warrior, but a woman.

A strangely dressed woman warrior.

She straddled her opponent as masterfully as
she had straddled her mount just moments before, only now she lifted her blade. Beneath her,
Red Hawk had lost his wind and writhed inef-
fectively, still clutching the old woman's white
beaded necklaces.

Running Wolf let out a war cry. The woman
hesitated, giving him time to reach them. He
raised his lance as the warrior he had challenged
gave a second war cry. Running Wolf was not
distracted as he used the flat side of his lance
to knock the knife from the woman's hands. He
reached down and hoisted her up onto his horse's
withers, capturing his first prisoner. He whooped

and pulled his horse up until it balanced on its hind legs.

Red Hawk rolled onto his hands and knees and vomited. The others reached them as the Crow warriors followed the women into the woods where the fighting would be difficult. All except the one who had fought Running Wolf.

He remained, blood running from his arm down his mount's shoulder. Still he charged again, but this time he met eight of Running Wolf's men and was forced back. Was this the woman's husband? Was that why he made such a suicidal charge?

Yellow Blanket struck the man with his club and the warrior toppled from his horse, sprawling on the ground, as limp as a tanned buckskin. Yellow Blanket captured the warrior's horse, giving a yell as he turned to go. It was a wonderful prize.

Running Wolf held the struggling woman down across his horse's withers as he glanced about the ruined camp. They had toppled the tepees, trampled the racks of drying fish and stolen their horses. Their work was done.

Pursuing the fleeing tribe would only increase the chances of fatalities as his men no longer had the element of surprise and there were many places in the forest for the sneaking Crow to ambush them. He called a retreat.

Red Hawk stood and pointed to Running Wolf's prisoner.

"That one is mine. I took her."

"You took a handful of beads. This one is mine."

So he pointed at the blue roan.

"The horse is mine, then."

Yellow Blanket looked at the reins of his captured horse that now rested in his hand. Older and more experienced, he had only to lift a brow at Red Hawk before the man fell silent.

Yellow Blanket looked at the beads in Red Hawk's hand.

"Those are yours."

Red Hawk's face went scarlet but he held his tongue. Yellow Blanket had been war chief and his bravery was without question.

"Were you unclear on your war chief's instructions?" asked Yellow Blanket. Running Wolf appreciated the man's assistance. It was difficult to lead a man older than you, especially when he felt he should have been Yellow Blanket's successor. But he was not. The council had chosen Running Wolf.

Red Hawk shook his head.

"Then, why were you chasing old women instead of driving away their horses as you were told?"

Red Hawk looked at the strings of broken

beads in his hand. He stuffed them into a pouch at his waist. The warrior woman's gray horse pawed the earth beside Red Hawk and then lifted its head to sniff its mistress.

Weasel brought Red Hawk his horse.

"Let's go," said Running Wolf. His prisoner wriggled and tried to lift her head, but he pushed her back down with one hand planted on her neck.

What kind of woman was this who fought like a man?

The raiding party rode toward home, with great commotion. The woman spread across his thighs tried to throw herself headfirst off his lap, but he held her easily. She was small, even for a woman, making her act of unseating Red Hawk even more impressive.

He had never taken a captive but now wondered if he could keep this one. He liked the feel of her warm, firm body against his thighs, and her clothing and behavior had him both troubled and intrigued. He did not understand why she acted as she had, but he did know that she had the heart of a warrior.

Still, keeping her was not entirely his decision. True, their chief, Iron Bear, was generous, often leaving the spoils of their efforts to each warrior to keep or distribute as they saw fit. Running Wolf found himself holding the wiggling woman more tightly and recognized with some shock that the thought of giving her up filled him with a selfish, grasping need. It was perhaps the best reason of all to give her away.

He straightened in his saddle, lifting to a stand in his stirrups. He heard her gasp as she slid from his lap to wedge into the gap between his legs and the saddle's high horn. She pressed her hands against his horse's side to keep from tumbling headlong to the ground. Still fighting, he realized. Fighting for the old woman. Battling Red Hawk. Resisting capture and now struggling to survive. She was brave, this enemy warrior woman.

Did that mean she had earned her life or a swift death?

He pulled her upright and settled back in his seat. She curled against him for just a moment and sagged as if in relief. He stared down at the curve of her bottom and the short dress that had hiked up.

Was she wearing a loincloth?

He had seen a woman wear leggings in winter, but never a loincloth.

He rested a hand across her lower back and felt her muscles stiffen in protest. But she did not struggle. Perhaps she waited for her chance to plunge his knife into his heart. He added *patient* to her list of attributes.

Running Wolf stifled his rising need, fighting that deep empty place in his heart. He struggled to resist the whisper of desire for this woman. No. His father had died at the hand of a Crow. They were his enemy, and that included this small temptation. His duty was to his ancestors, his chief and his tribe.

He told himself that he would not covet this woman even as his hand tightened possessively about her.

Chapter Two

Snow Raven bounced with the steady lope of the black-and-white stallion. Each landing of the horse's front hooves jarred the warrior's muscular thighs against her stomach and breasts. She saw at close range the blue war paint along the horse's long elegant leg. Handprints for kills, bars for coups and hoofprints for horses stolen in raids and, the last, a square. He was the war party leader. This man was impressive by any measure. She stared at the heavily beaded moccasin. The cut and decoration were more reminders that he was Sioux.

If only she had followed her brother's instructions, she would be safe in the woods right now.

And her grandmother would be dead.

Her grandmother would have preferred that, Raven knew, rather than see her only granddaughter taken and debased by the enemy.

Raven had enough of lying across the warrior's lap as if she were some buffalo blanket. But when she tried to push herself up, he shoved her back down.

How long they traveled like this, she did not know. But when his horse finally slowed from lope to trot to walk, she was sweating and nauseous.

Her captor ordered a halt to check on the injured and called for his men to report to him. His accent was strange. Their languages were very similar, but his speech was faster and more lyrical than that of her people. His voice seemed almost a chant.

He captured one of her wrists. She tried and failed to keep him from securing the other. Before she could stop him, he had dragged her up before him and plopped her between his lap and the tall saddle horn made of wood covered in tanned buckskin. He used his other hand to loop a bit of rope about her joined hands and wound the rope around and through her wrists, binding her.

She had lost her skinning knife, her bow and her dignity. But she had not yet lost her pride or her virtue. That would come later, at her arrival to camp. She knew how Sioux captives were treated by her people.

Her band currently had no captives because her father killed all the Sioux he could, including women. But she had seen the female captives at the larger gatherings and winter camps when all the tribes of the Center Camp Crow came together. The women wore buckskin dresses soiled and torn, their hair a dusty tangle and their eyes hollow. She had even tossed an insult or two in their direction. Now she would be on the receiving end of such derision. The hatred between their people was old and strong. Everyone she knew had lost someone to the constant fighting and raids.

Once with the Sioux, she would get little food and might die of starvation or exposure. But that was not the worst. Dying was preferable to being soiled by a Sioux snake. Unless she had a protector or was lucky enough to be adopted, any might take her. This warrior who captured her or one of his tribe.

Raven shivered, vowing to take her life before submitting to such indignities. But what if she was not able to kill herself? There were ways to prevent her, deny her even the freedom to die. Her head hung. Should she try to stay alive and wait for her father and brother to come? Or should she try to end her life at the first opportunity?

Where was the warrior she pretended to be? *She* would know how to face her fate. But if she were a warrior, her destiny would be far worse. Male captives had to endure a slow death by torture designed to test their bravery. She might be roasted over a low fire or have bits of flesh cut from her body.

Some small part of her wondered if that end might be preferable to hers. She had always prided herself on her virtue. Now she realized it was already gone.

She did not wish to die. But she did not wish to live like this. She had saved her grandmother's life and, in the process, she had lost her own.

Running Wolf halted the raiding party after a long run. The open plains hid a spring of sweet water for the horses and riders. Here they could rest and the Crow could not sneak up upon them.

Their raid would remind the Crow that they had ventured too far from their place and into the Sioux territory.

The woman before him made no sound. She did not weep or beg. Instead, she sat still as a raptor, watching his men dismount and stretch their tight muscles. If he did not know better he would swear she was counting their number and measuring their strength.

Running Wolf looked back and wondered if their enemy would follow. His party had taken only one captive. Then he thought of the look in the eyes of the warrior when this woman was taken. He would follow. Running Wolf knew this in his bones.

He called to Weasel, asking how many horses they had taken.

"All" came the answer.

Running Wolf smiled. Weasel was a very good thief. He must be to sneak past village dogs and the boys watching the horses and to do that in full light. Running Wolf's first raid as war chief and they had not lost a single man. He complimented Weasel's skill and then dismounted.

His captive threaded her hands in his horse's mane and he had the flash of precognition. He grabbed her with both hands as she kicked his horse's sides. His horse bolted forward as he swung his captive up and around until she landed before him.

Their eyes met.

He felt the electric tingle of awareness. She was beautiful, no question, with wild hair that streamed about her lovely face in long waves. She had tied a medicine wheel in one narrow braid at her temple. The opposite braid was wrapped in the pelt of a mink, tied with strands of tanned leather and bits of shell. The adornments framed her face.

Her nose was straight and broad, brows high and arching like the wings of a raven. She had dark eyes glittering with emotion, showing her passion even as she stood perfectly still. He dropped his gaze to her mouth. Just looking at those generous pink lips made his stomach jump and his muscles twitch.

He caught a motion to his left and turned to see Red Hawk approach, his expression stormy. Running Wolf was about to speak but Red Hawk lifted a hand to strike the captive. Running Wolf had time only to grip Red Hawk's wrist. The men locked eyes. Running Wolf saw his mistake immediately. He had rescued Red Hawk from this woman and now he had easily stopped his blow. Both acts highlighted that he was the stronger man. A war chief did not intentionally embarrass his warriors. Running Wolf released Red Hawk and the older man fumed.

"What are you doing?" Red Hawk asked, his voice hot with anger.

"I thought you were going to strike my horse," said Running Wolf, and cringed at the stupidity of that. He was not always quick-witted and preferred time to consider his responses. Meanwhile, his captive tugged in an effort to gain release from his grip. He gave a little yank and pulled her back beside him while keeping his focus on Red Hawk.

"Your horse is gone," Red Hawk said. "This one kicked it. Now I will kick her."

"I would prefer you did not. If she is injured, it will be harder to bring her to camp." That response was a little better. But his reaction was worse because just the threat of kicking this captive made Running Wolf's flesh prickle. What was happening here?

Weasel, still mounted, went after Running Wolf's spotted mustang, Eclipse, and captured him easily. Running Wolf recognized that he and Red Hawk had become the focus of the eight other warriors, including Weasel, who returned now holding the reins of Eclipse.

Yellow Blanket intervened. "Water your horses first, then the Crows' horses."

The men moved to do as they were told.

"You should kill that one," said Red Hawk, and then stormed after the others.

Running Wolf felt deflated. It was the order he should have given instead of staring like an owl. His raid had been a great success. The Crow did not even have horses to pursue them. Everyone lived and collected coups, and still he felt lacking as a leader. He knew the reason, the one change since he had ridden out this morning. He looked at the woman.

They made eye contact and she immediately looked away, lifting her chin as if she were above him. It made him smile. She had not lost her pride. That much was certain.

Yellow Blanket remained with Running Wolf, but he let Weasel take his horse. Yellow Blanket wore his eagle feathers today, marking him as a warrior with many coups. Iron Bear, their chief, often turned to him for advice. It had been on Yellow Blanket's suggestion that Iron Bear had made Running Wolf the new war chief.

Yellow Blanket glanced at the captive and then to the place where Running Wolf gripped her bound wrists.

"You hold that one as if you did not wish to let her go," said the older warrior.

Running Wolf felt the truth in the warrior's words but he replied, "She is just a captive."

"Is it wise to tell the men to take no captives and take one yourself?"

"Did you see the circumstances?"

"I did. You could have left her behind. Then she would not be here like an oozing wound in front of Red Hawk. Each time he looks at her, he sees his shame in flesh. She unseated him. Unmanned him." Yellow Blanket looked at the woman. "Who are you?"

She lifted her chin still higher. "I am one of the Center Camp Apsáalooke of the Low River tribe."

"A Crow. Just like any other," he said, and she nodded. "Yet the son of the chief risked his life to save you."

Pain broke across her expression but she mastered it swiftly. Running Wolf narrowed his eyes as suspicions clouded his thoughts. Who was she to this man, the one Running Wolf had fought and bested to claim her?

Yellow Blanket glanced to Running Wolf. "Did you not recognized their war chief?"

Running Wolf gave a shake of his head. He had only seen their new war chief at a distance. But Yellow Blanket had scouted their village prior to this raid.

Yellow Blanket posed the woman another question. "How did you learn to fight like a warrior?"

This she did not answer. "I am an Apsáalooke woman, like any other."

"You do not dress like any other. You do not ride like any other. You do not speak like any other. I have taken many captives. They wail. They cut their hair. They rub ash upon their face and then they live or die in our tribe. They never meet a warrior's eye and would not think to speak to one as an equal. Yet this you do. I do not know what you are, but you are not a woman like any other."

This took the stiffness from her spine. She glanced across the waving grasses, toward her camp, now in ruin. Was she thinking of the warrior sprawled facedown in the dirt?

Yellow Blanket turned to Running Wolf. "She can ride as well as any man here. She carried a bow, so assume she knows how to use one. How will you keep her from stealing a horse and riding home?"

"She will not know the way to go."

Yellow Blanket's look said he thought differently, but he said nothing.

"What would *you* do with her?" asked Running Wolf, already regretting his question. If one did not wish an answer it was better not to ask.

"I would let her go. And I would bet my first coup feather that she makes it to her camp before we reach ours."

Running Wolf felt his fingers tighten on the woman's wrists. A wellspring of defiance gurgled inside him. Yellow Blanket's words were wise, but he knew he would not take his advice.

"It is a war chief's duty to earn the respect of his men. You have lost one warrior today. I do not know how you will fix what has passed between you and Red Hawk. But I do know that keeping this woman will make that harder. Red Hawk's wife is the sister of our chief. He has influence."

"I will think of something."

"You know that her life will be worse at our camp. If you care for her, do not bring her there."

Running Wolf pulled the woman closer to his side.

Yellow Blanket sighed, recognizing, Running Wolf suspected, that his words were wasted. "You have taken her. But our chief will decide her place. Will he choose to give her to the one who took her, a young single warrior? He is ill but still wise. He has spoken of you in high regard and believes you will be a great leader one day. All leaders must choose what is best for their people over what is best for them." Yellow Blanket pointed at the woman beside him. "She is beautiful, but she is the enemy. Remember who you are and what she is."

"She is just one woman."

"White Buffalo Woman was just one woman, too," said Yellow Blanket, referring to the supernatural prophet who gave them their most sacred rituals and had turned the first man who approached her into a pile of bones.

"Perhaps I will give her to my mother."

"Throw a wildcat in with a dove and you will have a dead dove."

With that, he turned and joined the others at the spring.

Running Wolf watched him go, feeling a cold uncertainty in his belly. He stared down at this woman, wanting to know her secrets, wanting to see her body. The need to possess her was strong, and that was proof that Yellow Blanket's words were true.

It was unmanly to want to possess anything.

A warrior had a generous heart. He shared what he had with his family and his people. And up until this moment, Running Wolf had never wanted anything badly enough to do other than what was wise and what was expected.

"Will you let me have a horse?" she asked.

He scowled at her now.

"You could just cut my bonds."

"No."

Her shoulders sank. Then she gathered up her courage from a well that he feared had no bottom.

"I *will* be trouble." It was a promise, an echo of Yellow Blanket's words. But he would not be threatened by a captive.

Weasel returned, leading two horses, his and Running Wolf's warhorse, Eclipse. On his face was that sly grin he wore when he was up to no good. He led Running Wolf's horse behind him and extended the reins between him and his captive.

"Who is riding?" he asked, and his grin widened.

Running Wolf did not rise to the bait but accepted the reins. "I thank you for watering Eclipse."

"Do you think she is as good at wrestling as she is at flying from a galloping horse? Because I am a very good wrestler." Weasel lifted his eyebrows suggestively.

Running Wolf felt the sharp squeezing grip of ownership across his middle. This was bad. He managed a half smile and again made a sloppy comeback.

"You might end up on your back like Red Hawk." Running Wolf cringed at his words. First, they had insulted a fellow warrior. Second, they had reminded Weasel of Red Hawk's embarrassment.

"I would not mind being on my back beneath that one." Weasel grinned.

Running Wolf reached out to cuff him and Weasel dodged the blow easily.

Running Wolf leaned down and yanked a hank of grass from the prairie and offered it to his captive.

"Rub down my horse," he ordered.

She held the grass in her joined hands for a moment. Then she lifted her bound hands and let the grass fall from her fingers like rain.

"You may take my freedom. But you will not take my spirit."

Weasel's twinkling eyes widened as he stifled a laugh and looked to Running Wolf for his response. They faced off for a long moment. She lifted her chin and angled her jaw as if offering that long vulnerable column to him. He could kill her; her eyes told him that she knew this. Was that what she wanted?

"You know, that one is crazier than I am," said Weasel.

"Would you die rather than obey?" Running Wolf asked her.

"Yes."

"Do you wish to die?" Now he found himself holding his breath.

"I do not. But neither do I wish to be your captive."

"Things are getting more interesting," said Weasel.

Running Wolf scowled and Weasel laughed and returned to the warriors, likely to tell what he had witnessed. Having a captive who would not obey was bad. Dangerous, even. He should punish her right now, but he found the prospect distasteful and thought on Yellow Blanket's words again. If he did not punish her, she would not work. If she did not work, the others in the tribe would see she suffered. But they would see she suffered in any case. The best thing for her was for him to follow the advice of Yellow Blanket.

But he did not. Instead, he pushed her to the ground and bound her feet. Then he left her in the tall grass, leading his horse away so he could join the others.

As he chewed on hunks of dried buffalo and drank his fill, he watched the waving grass around his captive. When the grasses fell still he went to check on her and found that she seemed to be asleep. He returned to the group to find

Weasel asking to see the trophy that Red Hawk had captured. Red Hawk's face colored. Running Wolf sensed an impending fight. Weasel loved to wrestle nearly as much as he loved to steal from the Crow. It seemed he had directed his energy from the captive to Red Hawk.

Yellow Blanket told Weasel to watch the horses, diffusing the impending quarrel. Red Hawk showed the strands of long tubular beads that came from the French traders. The multiple strands were separated with circular shells that had come from the clay river people far to the south. The necklace was beautiful, but why Red Hawk had wanted it was beyond him. It was a woman's adornment and of no use to a warrior. Perhaps it was for Buffalo Calf, his wife. He didn't know and didn't ask.

Instead, the men counted the horses and argued over which was the best. Running Wolf was the only one to like the mare that his captive rode. She was sound and strong and seemed to have good confirmation. Of course, no warrior would ride a mare into battle. But for hunting and traveling, the dapple gray would be useful, especially in the snow, when she would all but disappear. Of course, it was up to the chief to divide the horses among those who won them and those that needed them. He wondered who would get the big blue roan ridden by the son of the chief of the Crow. Yellow Blanket, he decided.

The men now set about haltering the horses and tying them in strings for the longer trip home. They broke into teams and he paired with Big Thunder, his best friend. Big Thunder had an overlarge mouth and intent eyes. Big Thunder wore a series of four bear teeth about his neck in a necklace nearly identical to the one Running Wolf wore, for they had come from the same hunt and the same bear.

Big Thunder threw a rope over a large buckskin and Running Wolf quickly fashioned a halter from another rope woven of buffalo sinew.

"Do you remember how we trapped that bear?"

Running Wolf nodded, focusing on tying the halter to the string of ponies already assembled. "It was hungry."

"There is more than one kind of hunger, my friend."

Running Wolf's finger's stilled and he glanced up at his friend.

"Be careful with that one or she may end up wearing your claws about *her* neck."

Chapter Three

For a time, Snow Raven wiggled in the grass like a snake. Then she stopped, saving her energy. The bonds were tight and well tied. Chewing on the rawhide at her wrist had only made her teeth sore. The sunlight warmed her face. Insects buzzed about her and grasshoppers leaped from one grass stalk to another.

She pictured the village as she had last seen it, from the withers of the warrior's horse. Her brother sprawled bleeding on the ground. She squeezed her eyes shut against the terrible image. Was he alive? Had they killed him because of her?

He had asked her to run. She had disobeyed. Had she traded her grandmother's life for her brother's? Snow Raven began to weep. She wept for the lodges toppled like trees before the whirlwinds and for the family she had lost and the brother she had endangered. Shame devoured her. She could live with her capture if she knew he was alive. But to be responsible for the death of her brother was a stone in her heart. She did not think she could bear it.

Her tears washed her cheeks and dried in the sunlight. Snow Raven curled into a ball, encircling her pain as she waited. After a time she realized she was alone, and so she relieved herself in the grass. Then she stood to see where the men had gone. She could hear them, of course, but it was not until she stood that she saw they had taken the forty horses and roped them into five strings of eight. Song, her mount, was there with the others, second in the line behind the black-and-white stallion belonging to the one who had taken her. Running Wolf, that was what the older warrior had called him. He had a wolf on his shield, as well. Wolves had strong medicine.

She found him easily. He stood with the others, but seemed unlike them. Was it his carriage or his size? This was her first real opportunity to look upon him. He stood twenty paces away with the others, and she noted first that he was broad across the shoulders and narrow at the hip. He moved with an easy grace and confidence of one gifted in movement. It explained how he had plucked her from the ground while on horseback and done so as easily as she might pluck a flower from a field.

She did not make any sound, but he turned to

her and they stared across the distance. Her skin prickled. Perhaps he had been checking her location at regular intervals. He pointed to her horse as if telling her that he had taken that, as well. She nodded. Not knowing if she should thank him or hurl insults at him.

None of the Sioux cut their forelocks, and that was one of many reasons the warriors of her tribe called them women. But this hairstyle of the Sioux was not feminine in the least. In fact, she found the look of all the warriors elegant and masculine.

Running Wolf wore his long black hair in twin ropes wrapped in the pelts of beaver and tied with long strips of red cloth. His war shirt was decorated in elaborate bands of quillwork in red, green and white. The shirt was not stained with colored clay like the other men wore, but remained a natural tan color with long fringe at the arms and the side seam. Grandmother said the fringe took the rainwater away from the seams, but it was also for show. Over this shirt he wore a breastplate made of a series of long cylindrical white trade beads punctuated with red glass beads and round brass beads. The breastplate could deflect an arrow, if it was not shot at close range.

About his strong neck was a cord of tanned leather threaded through five bear claws. Each claw was separated by a red bead. She could not see his leggings or moccasins but had seen both while hanging over his saddle like a dead buck. Beneath his war shirt, she knew he wore his medicine bundle. All warriors did. Inside were the sacred objects that helped protect him. Each warrior was different, so each bundle was different and private. Her own brother would not even tell her what lay inside his, but he was never without it.

The warrior started toward her, his stride long and sure. He had the confidence of leadership. Were he not the war chief, she was certain that he would have held some other position of authority. It was clear that all respected him, even the older warrior, Yellow Blanket, who had advised him to let her go.

Running Wolf continued forward with such intent aim that she thought he might better be called Stalking Wolf.

He stared at her with fixed attention so that for a moment it seemed as if the rest of the prairie did not exist. She met his gaze, noticing the fine strong angle of his jaw and the broad chin. His elegant nose bisected his symmetrical features showing flaring nostrils that reminded her of a horse at full gallop. His brows peaked in the center as if she was some puzzle he must solve. She liked the shape of his eyes and the way that they were bright and dark all at once.

He drew closer and she noticed something

else—the buzz of energy that seemed to shimmer between them, like the waves of heat off rocky places in the summer. The tension began in her belly and pulled outward until she had to clench her fists against the need to lift her arms in welcome. He would not let her go free, and for one ridiculous moment she was glad.

This made no sense. He had captured her. She should spit at him or hurl insults or weep and tear her hair. Instead, she stood and stared like a lovesick calf. He had captured her. Was that what made him different than other men, or was there some other reason for the tingling sensation of her skin?

Would he really keep her or would he turn her over to someone else? In her tribe, her father let the warriors keep what they captured and distribute possessions as they saw fit.

He stopped very close. She had to tilt her head to look at him. He frightened her, this wolf of a man. But she also wondered if her fate would be better with this man than with any other among his warriors. Certainly it would be better than with the one who tried to strike her. The one she had knocked to the ground.

She smiled in satisfaction at the memory and heard his intake of breath.

She knew the possible fates that awaited her at his village. She knew that her test of endurance had only just begun. She lifted her bound hands between them, but kept herself from laying them on his chest.

"How are you called?" he asked.

His voice resonated in her, rumbling through her chest like a roll of thunder. She pressed her clasped hands to her chest, squeezing tight to hold on to her courage.

"Snow Raven."

"That is not a name for a woman." He frowned as he swept her with his gaze. "But it suits you, for you are not like any woman that I have ever met. You are causing trouble, you know. No one knows what to do with you. Some say you will steal a horse and run, but then we would catch you and you would die. Some say they would like to ride you as you rode that gray mare."

That prospect frightened her more than death. She did not want to be debased and used in such a manner. She squeezed her eyes shut at the images now assaulting her mind.

"Ah," he said. "So you do feel fear. For a time I thought you were immune to such emotions."

She looked at him now. "A warrior does not admit to fear."

"But a woman does. She cries and uses her tears to gather sympathy. Yet you do not."

"Would that work?"

"It would make you less interesting. And you are very interesting."

"I do not want your interest."

He laughed. "Then, you should not have unseated one of my warriors. Who was the old woman?"

"My grandmother, Truthful Woman."

"She will not be happy at your sacrifice."

"She raised me and I love her. I could do no less."

"Apparently you are alone in that, because none of the other women even slowed down. They ran like rabbits."

"That is what they are expected to do. To flee, so the men can fight."

"Yet you did not do so. So you are brave but not wise."

Raven made no reply.

"You can ride and you carry a bow. Can you shoot?"

"I do not think I should tell you what I can do."

"Hunt?"

She found herself nodding.

He smiled and her stomach twisted. His smile was dazzling, bright and beautiful, making him suddenly seem approachable and even more handsome. She gritted her teeth against the attraction. He was a Sioux snake, enemy to the Large-Beaked Bird people.

"I like to hunt," he said. "I once brought down an elk with seven points."

"Nine," she said, and then pressed her joined hands before her mouth. Why had she told him that?

"Nine? I have never even seen an elk with nine points."

"Because you stay in the grasses instead of venturing into the mountains."

He nodded. "That is true, because this is Sioux land." His smile was gone. "You left your mountains and ventured into our territory. We cannot allow that, Snow Raven. Your chief knew this and still he put your people in harm's way."

"My…chief is wise and brave." Had she almost said her father? She must stop and think before she spoke. It was a skill all warriors cultivated. Yet she went blathering about with the first thing that popped into her head.

"Brave, yes. Just as you are. And you must continue to be brave when the women in my village welcome you."

She looked at her bound hands. "Will you cut my bonds so I can defend myself?"

"No."

Why had she thought he would?

"Because if you harm any of them, they will kill you."

"So I am to let them beat me?"

"What choice do you have?"

She was about to say that he could prevent it. But she could not bring herself to ask his help.

"When?"

"Tomorrow by sunrise. I will put you on your horse but I will have to tie you to the saddle. Do not fall asleep."

"I will not."

He smiled again. "Very good, Snow Raven. Eat this." He passed her a long piece of jerked meat. "Then go to the spring and drink all you can. We ride all night."

He leaned down and untied the binding that held her feet together. She considered kicking him and running, but a glance told her that the other warriors watched the proceedings. They could not see their war chief now as he disappeared from their view into the tall grasses. But she had no chance of escape. The men had all the horses and running about like a prairie chicken was a waste of energy.

She did as he bid her, eating and then drinking. She even walked past the men on her return. Her horse nickered a greeting. She mounted unassisted and waited as Running Wolf tied her bound hands to the pommel of her saddle. She would not be able to drop to the ground and vanish in the darkness. At least the saddle was comfortable.

Her brother had made the wooden shell specifically to fit this horse and Snow Raven's smaller frame. It had a high pommel and high cantle so she could hook her leg over the back of the saddle and hold the front while hanging on the side of her mount. This position was ideal for creeping up on deer. Her brother had taught her and said he used the same position to make it harder for the Sioux to shoot him from his horse. She and her grandmother had made the buckskin covering. She was especially proud of the series of brass tacks decorating the front pommel. Raven realized with some sorrow that this saddle, the buffalo-skin saddle blanket and the horse were no longer hers. She, herself, was no longer hers. From this day forward until the day she died or was rescued, she belonged to the enemy.

Running Wolf finished tying her, giving her enough lead that she could move her hands midway to her face. It was a boon that she did not deserve. She recalled her brother speaking of the capture of Sioux women. They ran behind the horses or were tied like meat behind the saddle. They were given no food and water. Until this moment she had seen nothing wrong with such treatment of enemies.

The party set out through the long grass. Raven already missed the forest they had left behind. She paid close attention to the path of the sun. She did not know how the warriors knew the way to their tribe, for the grass looked much the same in every direction. All about them was high buffalo grass and scrub brush and more grass. Rolling hills that stretched out to the setting sun.

They passed a large mound covered with prairie dogs that chirped and clucked and vanished at their passing. They flushed grouse but none of the men shot at the retreating birds. She saw pronghorn in the distance moving away from them. She glanced forward to see Running Wolf glancing back at her.

"Do you wish you had your bow?" he asked.

"Yes." Oh, yes. But she would not use it on the pronghorn.

He lifted a brow as if trying to gauge her intent from her reply.

The Sioux continued until the receding light made riding too dangerous. It was easy for a horse to step in a hole and break a leg. The men dismounted, ate and drank. They walked and stretched and relieved themselves. Running Wolf allowed her down to relieve herself, as well. She was glad for the darkness but still embarrassed. He said nothing to her as she remounted and he tied her back to the saddle. But his hands lingered longer than necessary over hers and his thumb brushed the back of her hand in a secret caress. His touch did strange things to her skin and the speed of her heart. How could so small a gesture make her feel so much?

Her reaction shamed her. This was the enemy of her people. The man who had unseated her brother and destroyed their fishing camp. She straightened in the saddle and looked down her nose at him.

The corner of his mouth quirked and he walked away.

The men gathered in a circle to talk and wait for the moon to rise enough to make travel possible. She listened to them repeat tales of their exploits. The men seemed to have forgotten about her and she again considered trying to turn the entire line of eight horses. She knew Song would respond to the pressure of her legs, moving in any direction she chose. But what would the stallion do? Would he turn and walk beside her mare? She weighed her chances.

She had the darkness in her favor, but the line of horses would make travel very difficult. She did not know the way to go in the dark and there was no cover on this open prairie. She recalled Running Wolf's promise—that if she ran, she would die. But the darkness was tempting, so tempting.

Soon Hanwi, mother moon, rose in a perfect orange ball of light. Running Wolf rose from the circle of men and the others followed suit. He came to her with that slow, confident step, sweeping through the tall grass. He stopped before her and rested a hand on her right foot, which was still sheathed in her beaded moccasin and stirrup. His grip was strong and possessive.

"Perhaps brave *and* wise," he whispered.

Chapter Four

Running Wolf looked back frequently throughout the night. He did not know if he expected his raven to fall or fly away. But she did neither. He once caught her looking back over her shoulder at the way they had come. But most often she sat straight and relaxed in the saddle as if she was more comfortable astride than with her feet on the ground.

Seeing her straddling that horse filled his mind with a series of sensual images that made riding exceedingly uncomfortable. Even the chilly night air did not lessen his insistent erection.

Running Wolf did not have a wife, though he needed to see to that soon. He had several women who had made their interest known. He did not favor any especially.

As the light of morning streaked across the sky, they reached the river above camp and made the ford.

By the time they arrived at camp and the women began to call, he was irritable beyond his recollection. Boys, roused from their sleeping skins, hurried out, some without their breechclouts because they were in such a rush to see the warriors returning triumphant.

Soon the stolen horses were being paraded about the center of the village, and those warriors who had families were greeted by their relieved wives and excited children. He saw Red Hawk give his wife the string of beads and shells that had caused Snow Raven to return to protect her grandmother and resulted in her capture. As the horses circled, Snow Raven stood tall and proud despite the insults hurled at her.

Running Wolf's mother, Ebbing Water, made her way to her son to congratulate him on leading his first raid. She was a solid woman and still very useful. He did not know why she chose not to marry again after his father's death ten winters past, for she was attractive for an older woman and more than one man had made his interest known. His father had died in battle and his mother held a simmering hatred for all things Crow.

"I see you bring a captive," said Ebbing Water. "Who took her?"

"I did."

She did not hide her shock. "You?"

"She is in your care until Iron Bear decides what to do with her."

She smiled. "I know what to do with her." Ebbing Water drew out her skinning knife. Running Wolf was out of the saddle and standing in front of his mother before she had time to turn.

"I do not want her scarred."

She lifted her brows. "She is an enemy."

"No."

Ebbing Water studied her son for a long moment. He tried not to shift or fidget under her scrutiny. Did she recognize that he found this captive beautiful...fascinating? Mothers could tell such things with just a look. His mother made a noise in her throat and then turned toward Snow Raven.

Running Wolf had to force himself not to follow. What came next was for the women. The men would only bear witness.

Ebbing Water shouted louder than the other women and called the men to halt the horses. She walked to Snow Raven and quickly sliced the cord that tied her to the saddle. Running Wolf knew how stiff and sore his captive must be. Unlike his men, she had not been allowed off her horse since he'd tied her there late last night.

So when Ebbing Water dragged Snow Raven to the ground, his captive lost her balance and went down. That was all it took for the wolves to close in. The women circled her as the men led the string of horses away.

He heard the curses and saw them spitting on his captive. He watched the vicious kicks and hoped Snow Raven was wise enough to roll into a ball and protect her head. Some women brought sticks to beat this Crow woman while others used their fists.

They tore at her war shirt and ripped the medicine wheel from her hair. They peeled her from her leggings and dragged off her shirt and tore off her moccasins. He could see her seated, knees to chest, as the insults continued and the blows grew wilder.

He did not mean to act.

Even as he called out he told himself to be silent. But still he shouted his mother's name. She looked to him and he shook his head.

His mother stepped between the captive and the hive of women buzzing and striking like hornets. She called a halt and shooed them off. Gradually they left Snow Raven, dressed only in her loincloth, sitting in the dirt. The fur that wrapped her hair had been ripped away with the strands of shells and her face was bloody and bruised. They had taken everything of value. But she was alive.

He watched as she rose, coming to stand with her bare feet planted and her chin up. Her lip was bleeding. So was her nose. Her hair, once so beautiful and wild, was now a mass of snarls and tangles. Her body, which he had so longed to see, gave him physical pain to witness. Her breasts showed scratches and welts. Purple bruises began to show on her shoulder and thighs.

Yet still she stood as if she was war chief.

It made him feel small and angry. Why had she returned for her grandmother? Why couldn't she have run? Then, he would not have this trouble or these confusing feelings.

Ebbing Water grasped Snow Raven's bound hands and tugged her toward their lodge. His captive walked on slim feet, now covered with dust and mud. Her legs were long and smooth and muscular. Running Wolf watched until they were out of sight. Only then did his thoughts return to some semblance of normalcy.

He saw that the horses were watered and then oversaw their hobbling so the new arrivals could graze. They staked the stallions, for they did not want the newcomers fighting with the established leader. That would come in time, for each herd could have only one leader, the strongest. So was the way of the world. Running Wolf must be the strongest if he were to serve his people.

The women had killed a village dog in preparation for the feast to celebrate their return, and he and the other warriors went to the river to bathe away the taint of the enemy. Afterward they went to the council lodge.

The open door of the chief's lodge was an indication that they were expected. Red Hawk called a greeting and their chief, Iron Bear, replied, welcoming them. The illness that wasted Iron Bear's flesh now resonated in his voice, which was so changed, Running Wolf nearly did not recognize it.

When Running Wolf entered, Red Hawk had already taken the place beside Black Cloud, the last in the semicircle of the council of elders and the closest place available to their chief. The elders were all great warriors who now served to help lead their people and no longer went on raids. Still, Running Wolf would not care to fight any of them, for despite their age, they were strong. They formed a half circle, and the returning warriors completed the circle.

Iron Bear greeted each man by name. Their chief was seated by a low fire, though the month of the ripening moon was mild and the days warm and bright. This was the first time that their leader had not come to greet them, and now he huddled beneath a buffalo robe like the old man he had rapidly become.

Iron Bear had once been fierce and feared by all his enemies. Now he was unsteady on his feet and his color was bad. Even his eyes were turn-

ing an unnatural yellow. Still, he led their tribe
with wisdom. But all knew he would not lead for
long. A new leader must soon be chosen.

Across from the old chief sat Turtle Rattler,
the shaman of their people. Turtle Rattler was
much older than Iron Bear but looked youthful
by comparison. True, his face was deeply lined
and his hair streaked with gray, but his color was
a good natural russet. He had ceased his chanting upon their arrival. He wore a medicine shirt
that sported two vertical bands of porcupine
quills. The adornments had been carefully dyed
in green, brown and white before being flattened,
soaked and meticulously sewn by his long-time
captive into a skillful pattern.

Turtle Rattler had worked very hard to restore
the chief to health but confided to Running Wolf
that at night the chief's spirit already ventured
onto the Ghost Road. It would not be long, he
said, for the chief's water smelled sweet and he
had no appetite. He seemed to be shriveling up
before them like a bit of drying buffalo meat in
the sun.

All were seated—the elders across from the
entrance and the youngest warriors closest to the
opening as was proper. The buffalo skin held the
heat and the air was stifling. Many of the warriors
began to sweat in their war shirts, yet their chief
continued to shiver in the warm air.

The coyote staff was passed to Running Wolf. As war chief it was his honor to speak first, and only he would speak until he passed the elaborately beaded staff that held the skull of the clever trickster, coyote. Running Wolf briefly relayed their victory and the number of horses they had taken. He spoke of the brave deeds of his men and the clever theft of livestock, giving credit to Weasel. He considered mentioning Red Hawk's defiance of his orders to take no captives, but he decided this would only bring more animosity between them.

He passed the coyote staff to Big Thunder, who had no such qualms. He relayed what he had seen.

Red Hawk shifted in his place and his expression became stormier. It was obvious that he could not wait for his turn with the talking stick. But as the stick had begun with Running Wolf, he had to wait and wait. He would, however, get the last word. Since it was so hot, many of the men chose to simply pass the staff along. At last Red Hawk gripped the talking stick.

"This woman dresses like a man. She rides like a man and carries weapons like a man. She is unnatural—a witch. She should be killed as quickly as possible."

"Who captured this Crow woman who fights like a man?" asked Iron Bear.

All eyes turned to Running Wolf.

"Ah, our new war chief. That is well."

The chief turned to Running Wolf. "Do you think this woman is a witch?"

Running Wolf did not need the stick, for when asked a question it was only polite to answer. "She could not escape her bonds. She could not fly from her horse like a bird or shift into a coyote and dart into the grass. She is just a woman."

Red Hawk extended his hand. The stick made its journey to him.

"This captive is young. She should be made a common woman. There are many men in need of relief who are yet too young to provide for a wife."

His chief frowned. "The captive belongs to the captor. If Turtle Rattler determines that she is not a witch, then let Running Wolf do as he likes with her."

Running Wolf squeezed his eyes shut for a moment as the relief struck him like a kick in the gut. When he opened them it was to find all staring at him; some looked expectant, hopeful. Did they all want to have their turn with her? The notion filled him with a surging of white-hot rage, and he set his jaw to keep from revealing the strange, unwelcome emotions. Why was it so hard to consider sharing her? She was only a woman, an enemy.

Yet she was more. His heart knew it; his body knew it. Only his mind rebelled.

What was he to do with his captive? How to

keep her safe, exclusively his and still appear the war chief?

Running Wolf opened his mouth to say that he would leave the decision up to Iron Bear. But instead he found himself saying, "I would give her to my mother."

The chief's brow wrinkled. "Your mother has never needed help caring for her lodge, and you have kept her cooking pot full. Why do you think she needs a woman to help her?"

"I will keep her cooking pot full for as long as the Great Spirit allows. But I am considering a wife and so will be leaving my mother's tepee. I am afraid she will be lonely."

"She could take a husband," said Iron Bear. "It is past time."

He thought so, too, but when he'd said as much to his mother, her fury had been like the whirlwinds.

Running Wolf nodded. "If she wishes."

"Now it is time to smoke," said their shaman.

The pipe was lit and passed. The men talked and joked. Everyone wanted Weasel to again wear the headpiece made from the mane of a black horse. Once the roached hair was tied to his head he looked so much like the Crow warriors that Running Wolf was not surprised he had fooled the young boys watching the herd. With meat for the dogs and a costume designed to deceive, Weasel had walked right among the horses of the Crow.

Running Wolf would normally have found pleasure in the ritual of smoking the sacred tobacco and having an opportunity to hear stories of their success retold for the members of the council of elders. But now he saw the stories as an endless delay that kept him from where he truly wanted to be.

Where was Snow Raven and what was happening to her?

Turtle Rattler had kept the men from her, for now, but what about the women?

Finally the men dispersed, but just before he took his leave, the chief called out to him. Running Wolf gritted his teeth at the delay as Red Hawk swept out the circular door. He caught the eye of Big Thunder and motioned his chin toward Red Hawk. His friend nodded and followed after Red Hawk as Running Wolf sat close to the chief, who now extended his hands to the fire.

He motioned to the upright feathers on Running Wolf's head. The eagle feathers each carried a red bar, marking his success at killing six warriors in battle. Had he stopped to kill Bright Arrow by slitting his throat or taking his scalp, he would have earned an additional feather, notched for this new coup. But he had chosen to take the woman rather than kill the man.

"I think Weasel has earned a feather for his stealth."

Running Wolf smiled and nodded.

"And you have led your first successful raid. It is my wish to mark your success with this." He withdrew an eagle feather topped with tufted white downy feathers and the hair from the tail of a white horse that once belonged to Iron Bear. "I will present it formally at the feast, but I wanted to tell you that it was given to me by Kicking Buffalo after my first successful raid."

"I am honored," said Running Wolf, feeling the glow of pride. This was what he wanted, to lead his people. To earn coups with brave deeds. To walk the Red Road as the Creator intended and to bring honor to his people. One day soon he would earn enough feathers to have his own war bonnet, and later, perhaps a coup stick fluttering with a hundred feathers.

"Before you go, I would like to ask you a question."

Running Wolf leaned forward, anxious for some new quest, another opportunity to prove his worth. He was war chief of his tribe, a great honor. But soon the council of elders would be faced with a dilemma. They must choose the chief's successor. He knew he was young, but both Black Cloud and Yellow Blanket had told

him he was being considered. Red Hawk and
Walking Buffalo were, as well.

"Yes, my chief?"

"You say you wish to take a wife. Have you
chosen a woman?"

"I have not." Even as he said this, he realized
he should have reflected on why Iron Bear was
asking this before he answered. A leader needed
to consider his words more carefully.

"The choice of wife is an important one. She
must not only warm your blankets and keep your
fires. She must make your home from the best
buffalo robes you can provide her and she must
be strong to bear your children. Most important,
she must act as adviser. For though many pretend that decisions are made by the council of
elders, we all know that they do not act without
considering the opinions of all and, most especially, their wives."

This was true, so why did Running Wolf feel
a rising uncertainty at the direction this conversation had taken?

"My daughter, Spotted Fawn, is young, but
she is a good woman, modest and hardworking.
And although her mother is gone, she has learned
much from my second wife, Laughing Moon. She
knows what it means to be the daughter of a chief.
Her mother bore me five children, three of them

sons. I believe that Spotted Fawn will also bear her husband strong children."

Running Wolf glanced toward the door. Two days ago he would have gladly taken the chief's daughter. Before the raid he firmly believed that one woman was much like another. One might be comely and another a better cook. But all and all, they were just women.

Now he felt differently.

An ache gnawed at the pit of his stomach. Why had he ever pulled that woman onto his saddle?

The chief continued on, failing to notice Running Wolf's distraction. "I would ask that you consider her for your wife, for I would like to see her wed to a good man before I walk the Ghost Road."

"Your daughter is a virtuous woman. Any man among us would be lucky to call her wife."

Iron Bear smiled, his withered face now as wrinkled as a dried buffalo berry. "Make it soon, son."

Running Wolf nodded and took his leave. What had he just done?

Chapter Five

Snow Raven followed the mother of Running Wolf toward her tepee. The warriors had succeeded in their raid, and that meant a feast of celebration and dancing. If the Sioux custom was similar to the Crow, their deeds would be told by one who witnessed and not the one who performed the coup, for to do otherwise was boastful.

She wiped the blood from her lip and pinched her nose to stem the flow. By the time they had reached the large conical tepee, she had stanched the worst of the bleeding.

She ignored the cuts and the dull ache of the bruised tissue that seemed to cover her body. Even with her focus on her injuries she could not help but still at the sight of the lodge before her. The bottom of the tanned buffalo hide was ringed in a red band. Above this band were drawings of battles. She recognized Running Wolf immedi-

ately from his spotted horse. She circled the conical base with slow, measured steps. Ebbing Water
smiled with pride as Snow Raven leaned forward
to peer at the unfolding story of many battles.

Running Wolf had killed two Crow in this battle using his lance. Suddenly she thought of her
brother again and wondered if he had survived.

She moved along, the ache in her muscles now
reaching her heart. He had killed four in the next
battle and stolen three horses. According to the
next drawing he had captured seven eagles in a
single hunt and also trapped and killed a wolf.
Had that been that his vision quest?

Near the top by the smoke flaps appeared a
wolf again. She knew how difficult a wolf was to
fool, and this feat truly impressed. But all served
to remind her that he was a formidable enemy,
one she could not trust and in whom she would
find no pity. If she where to survive until she was
rescued she must be wise and cautious.

Her father would come for her. He would find
her. But for the Crow to come out onto this prairie, so far from the protection of the other tribes,
was dangerous.

What would her father do?

He must find help among the other Center
Camp tribes, she realized.

She might be here a long while. So she must
be careful that none here discovered that she was

the daughter of Six Elks. If she could only survive until her father came, she would be rescued.
Then she could return again to her life as it had
always been and would be again.

"You see that my son is the most skilled of
hunters. He brings me more furs than I know what
to do with. And he has killed many of the evil
Crow who try to invade our hunting grounds."
She studied the paintings for a moment longer,
and her voice grew sharp. "Enough dawdling.
We have a feast to prepare and you have fuel to
carry."

On the plains, there were no trees, so the people used the dried buffalo droppings for fuel.
Raven wondered if the women expected her to
carry buffalo chips in the nude without moccasins. The answer, she discovered, was yes. When
Raven asked if she might have a bit of buckskin
to cover herself, the woman laughed.

"You must earn your keep here. If you do as
you are told, I will feed you. If you wish a buckskin, perhaps you should kill a buck."

Raven did not ask for a bow and arrow to do
just that.

Ebbing Water gave her a basket and told her not
to come back until it was full. On her first journey past the ring of tepees, Snow Raven paused
to see if anyone was watching her and found she
was alone. Was this some test? A trial to see if

she was stupid enough to run with no weapons and no garments to protect her? She knew she would freeze in the cold rains and starve on the long journey.

That was, unless the wolves found her on foot.

She hoisted the basket higher on her bare hip and turned to search for buffalo chips. It was more difficult to walk barefooted through the grass than she had imagined, and it took some time to fill the basket.

As she walked, she braided the tall grasses into a fine rope. When it was long enough, she looked for animal trails through the grass and set her first snare. Before she returned to the camp she set six more. It seemed from the trails she saw that the jackrabbits were plentiful here.

When she stood from laying the final snare it was to find Running Wolf standing within ten paces of her. She gasped with surprise. No one ever crept up on her before. Had she damaged her hearing in the beating?

Her arms went up to cover her breasts and then she stopped herself. Captives had no shame, and she was not embarrassed of her body. Let him see the bruises and cuts.

"What are you doing?" he asked.

"Your mother would not give me a buckskin. She said if I wanted a hide, I must get my own. So I am." She motioned to the snare, carefully staked and set to encircle the neck of any rodent foolish enough to use this path.

He stepped nearer and stooped to examine her work. "Well laid."

He stood close now and her skin began to prickle, as it sometimes did when the thunder-birds charged the air.

Raven reclaimed her basket and held it between them. He turned to go and she headed after him, walking slowly enough so as not to appear to be following. She did not know if another beating awaited her upon her return. And she didn't know if Running Wolf would prevent one. He had not intervened in the first, so she was doubtful his proximity would help her.

Still, she felt safer with him than alone.

She considered her options. To stay unnoticed she must be submissive and not draw attention. That meant taking any beating.

It went against her very nature.

She was a fighter, and a good one, too. Could she even manage to restrain herself if they came at her again? It had been hard to let them drag her from her horse. It had been hard to curl up like an infant and allow the feet to kick and the hands to claw. But she had done it.

He turned to her before they entered the circle of lodges.

"Stay well behind me. But call out if you need me."

She waited while he moved well ahead of her, anxious to let him go but relieved he would be close enough to come if she needed him.

It was near sunset, and when he reached the first lodge his skin glowed golden in the failing light. Running Wolf disappeared as he crossed into the circle of tepees. She paused to get her bearings and recall where to find his home. She met two women who laughed and called her Buffalo Chips. She ignored them and continued toward Running Wolf's tepee.

Before she reached the lodge, Raven felt someone watching her. She looked about and found who spied on her, thinking it would be Running Wolf again, but instead she found a woman and instantly recognized her as another captive.

She wore a dress that was too short to be proper, a dress that held no elk teeth or quillwork or beading with not even the simplest of fringes across the seam. Beyond this, the dress was patched and ill fitting. Her legs were as dirty as Snow Raven's and her feet were also bare.

She stared at Raven with a hollow expression of one pushed past her limit. Yet still there was a flicker of life behind the dead expression. The woman's mouth turned down at the corners as she looked at Raven. Bringing a new captive to a tribe could upset the order among the other captives. Raven wanted no trouble. She desired only to remain anonymous and to survive long enough to be rescued.

The woman strode forward and spoke to her in perfect Crow without the accent of the Sioux.

"So they have taken everything from you, too."

"Not everything," said Raven.

The woman's brow quirked in a silent question.

"I still have my life."

That made the woman smile and nod her approval, as if Raven had passed some sort of test.

"Yes, if you can keep it. You are too pretty and the men will be after you."

The loss of her virtue was what Raven most feared. Morality was highly prized by her people, except among captives. Their feelings were not considered. That was how it had always been.

Now she was experiencing the opposite side.

She remembered that some of the captives had earned a place. Some had even married into her tribe. She thought of Running Wolf and was horrified at the line of her reasoning. She was the daughter of a chief, the sister of a brave warrior. They would rescue her.

Her head dipped as she realized that even if they did bring her home, all among her people would assume she had been soiled by the Sioux.

The woman spoke again. "You will not last long if you don't gain one or more protectors."

"I can protect myself."

The woman laughed.

"Well, Little Warrior, what about your clothes? How do you plan to earn them?"

"Earn them?"

"Frog went naked for over a moon. They give all of us names. I was called Mourning Dove by my people, but here am called Mouse. They named her Frog for her croaking. There were two of them then, Frog and Fish. Nothing Frog did earned her a scrap. She was old and no one wanted her. Still, she begged to come into each tepee until she found one man who let her in— Turtle Rattler, the shaman. She keeps his fire and says he does not touch her. Fish walked into the snow and died. I did not beg, but neither did I walk into the snow. I took another road and decided that I would have meat and I would have clothing and I would have a tepee of my own. I did what I had to do to earn these things."

Mouse glared at Raven, daring her to say something. Raven knew what Mouse meant. She was a common woman, used by any who wished to spend time with her. The young men in her tribe had such a female, but some widowers and married men also went to her lodge. Raven did not judge Mouse, for she knew she might suffer the same fate. When one was starving and freezing it was hard to say what one would do. Would she choose to stay alive, like Mouse, or die, like Fish?

"I have set snares to catch rabbits." Raven motioned toward the prairie.

This earned another smile from the woman. "They will take the meat and the pelts. But there is no harm in trying. How is it that you know how to do such things?"

"My father…" Again Raven nearly said her father's name. "My father and my brother taught me to hunt and ride."

"Really? You can hunt?"

Raven nodded, not wishing to appear boastful.

"Can you track game?"

"Of course."

"Shoot a bow, use a lance?"

Raven did not like the way this conversation had turned.

"Can you read the land and find water?"

"I have done these things," she offered, "but not on the prairie."

The woman was now glowing.

"There are others, six now that you have come." Mouse paused and her gaze dropped with her expression. "Some have been here two winters. Some four. I have been here four. Little Deer nearly froze to death last winter because she was too young to be a common woman. Little Deer has not yet broken her link with the moon. When she does, they will take her to our lodge."

Four years? Had Raven heard that right? In all that time had no one come for her? Raven felt a little piece of herself die. What if her brother and father could not find her? There were so many tribes of Sioux. Was she like a rock on the prairie, impossible to see unless you stumbled over it?

"I am of the Center Camp Crow, the Shallow Water tribe," said Mouse.

"I am Snow Raven. I am of the…" But before she could speak, Mouse cut her off.

"Also Center Camp Crow, but from the Low River tribe. Your father is Six Elks."

Raven's stomach dropped. Somehow this woman knew her. She could tell the Sioux. Perhaps such information could be valuable. Mouse could trade it for a blanket or food.

"No. I am not."

"I met your mother at one of the gatherings. I danced with her. I ate with your grandmother, Tender Rain, and listened to your grandfather, Winter Goose, tell stories of the Spirit World. He is your shaman."

That had been before he and her mother's mother died of the spotting sickness with so many others. The trappers had come and then the traders and then the many sicknesses. But the spotting sickness was the worst. It was why her father had said they must go. Leave the home they'd had since the beginning of all things.

Raven shook her head. "No, you've made a mistake."

Mouse lifted a fist to her hip. "Why do you say this? You know who you are. I know who you are."

In desperation, Raven told the truth. "But no one must know. Don't you see? My only hope is to remain like any Crow captive. If they know, they could kill me or use me to hurt my family."

"Or trade you and the other captives for some of their own."

"No. I can't take that chance."

The corners of Mouse's mouth continued to sink. "You cannot take that chance? Are you the daughter of the chief of the Low River tribe or are you not? Are you the granddaughter of the greatest far-looking man our people have ever seen or are you not?"

Her grandfather had been a far-looking man, one with the gift of seeing things before they happened. Snow Raven would give anything for that gift right now. Would she live to taste freedom again? Would this woman use her knowledge to dash any chance she had of survival?

"I used to be those things. But now I am just a captive. My life is no longer my own."

"But you still long for freedom. We all do. You could lead us. It is in your blood to lead."

Raven lowered her head, knowing what would happen if she tried. The risk was too great. "If we go, I will lead you to your deaths."

"Winter is coming," said Mouse. "Little Deer will not have enough to eat."

Raven stared at Mouse. "What did she eat the past two winters?"

"Last winter was mild. The one before she stayed with me when I had no men. But this one will be hard and the men will want a woman on cold nights. If she is in my lodge they will take her, too. Snake has a baby. When her milk stops, he will die like the last one."

Raven pressed her lips tight together against the urge to act. None of this was her fault. It was not her place to intervene. But was it her duty?

Mouse's face went hard as she stared at Raven. "You ride. I saw you arrive seated on a horse. We can steal horses and you can lead us home."

"They will catch us and kill us. We must wait for rescue from my father."

"Wait? I hear the warriors boasting. They come to me with tales of great deeds. Weasel tells of stealing all the horses of your village. Is that true?"

Raven lowered her head. "Yes."

"So I ask you, without horses, how will they hunt buffalo? And how will they come for you?"

Without horses, they would be wiped out. Suddenly Raven did not want her father to come for her. The cold dread of certainty took hold of her like an icy wind. Her father must look to his people's survival. He could not waste precious time searching for her.

Mouse waited for an answer. "If he comes on foot, they will kill him."

For the first time she understood, truly understood what she faced.

"He would be a fool to come, and Six Elks is no fool," said Mouse.

Even as she recognized the depth of this cold reality, Raven could not relinquish hope. "He will come."

Mouse snorted. "Do you know that I have a husband and a son? My husband is handsome and kind and loved me very well. Four times seasons have turned, but he has not come for me. Now I still tell myself that he will come, but I fear he has found another. We had a son, Otter. He was four when they took me. If I do not return home to my boy soon, will he even know his mother? I dream of them in my sleep. I think of them when I wake. They are what has kept me alive."

Raven understood now what she had not before. If she was to find rescue, she must find it herself. Something else crept into her thoughts and she straightened.

"How is your husband called?" asked Raven.

"Three Blankets."

Raven stilled at the name.

Mouse continued on, not noticing Raven's shock. "Oh, he is very brave. He had his first eagle feather for slitting an enemy's throat when he was only sixteen winters old."

Raven's hands had gone still, for she knew that Mouse's son had fallen through ice in the river. Raven had been there in the winter camp when his body was brought back to the village.

The following spring, Mouse's husband had been killed on a raid led by Far Thunder, the chief of the Shallow Water tribe. She knew because many of her tribe had gone with them, including her brother. They had told of Three Blankets's brave death and sang at his funeral platform.

Raven opened her mouth to speak but Mouse was talking again.

"Without them, I would have died so many times. They have kept me alive, my husband and my son."

Raven closed her mouth tight.

"I worry that if he learns what I have done to stay alive, he might not want me. But then I worry about hiding the truth from him. What would you do?"

Mouse looked up at Raven, waiting for her reply. Raven held her tongue as dread made her skin prickle.

"What?" asked Mouse.

"I… I am…" She pressed a hand over her mouth and tried to think what to say.

Mouse's eyes narrowed and she closed in. "What do you know of my husband? Has he taken another wife?"

"No."

"Then, why do you look so guilty?" Mouse grasped Raven's shoulders and gave a little shake. Raven met her gaze. The scowl disappeared. She released Raven and stepped back, now protecting herself from the news by folding her arms before her.

Mouse's eyes went wide and her face went chalky white as if she already knew. Her next words confirmed Raven's fears. "What has happened to him?" Her fingers clawed into her hair, holding a fist at each temple. "To my husband. To my son."

Mouse swayed as if the energy to shout had stolen the last of her strength. She placed a hand on the riverbank.

Raven sank down beside her and spoke in a rush, racing to finish as Mouse blinked up at her. She spoke of the raid and the victory and the losses. How her husband was killed in the raid of the Shallow Water tribe and her son in the icy water.

"I am sorry. They are both gone," said Raven.

Tears streamed down Mouse's face and then she threw herself to the ground, curling into a ball. Her cry of agony was terrible to hear.

Raven stayed with her, but she worried that they would be missed and that would make it harder to leave the camp. When Mouse had no more voice to cry she folded into Raven's arms.

"I have no one now. My sister and mother walked the Way of Souls before me. They died in the spotted sickness winter, the same winter that took your mother from you. My mother-in-law hates me."

"She's still alive."

"Moon Rise is a good swimmer. Why did she not save my son?"

"I do not know. I only remember hearing of your husband and son because I spoke to Moon Rise. She now has no son to hunt for her and must rely on the gifts of others."

Mouse stood woodenly and began to walk up the bank.

"Where are you going?" asked Raven.

"To the woman's lodge. Perhaps I will never come out."

Raven stopped her with a hand. "I am still bringing you home."

Mouse snorted. "I have no home."

Raven watched her go and wondered if she had made a mistake. Should she have kept the deaths of Mouse's family secret until they were safely back with the Crow?

But what if they never reached them? Didn't Mouse have the right to mourn and pray for her husband and son? Was it her decision to keep the truth from a wife and mother?

Raven hurried back to Running Wolf's tepee, hopeful that she might sit near the fire.

When Raven reached the lodge, she was received with sharp words from Ebbing Water, who snatched the basket back and sent her to the river to wash the blood from her body. The water stung but she managed. As she was leaving the river, she ran into a group of women who'd come at their customary time to wash. They shouted at her that she could not use this place and must bathe downriver so they did not get the stink of the Crow on them.

Raven hurried back to the tepee and found Running Wolf seated inside. His eyes followed her every movement as she returned to Ebbing Water.

"Can you not cover her?" he asked his mother.

"She must earn her clothing."

"Cover her while she is inside, then."

Ebbing Water gave Raven a blanket. The warm

rough wool scratched her skin and made her cuts burn. But it took away the chill and soon she was not shivering. She smiled at Running Wolf, but before she could offer her thanks he rose and stalked out, leaving a half-finished bowl of stew beside him. She eyed his leavings eagerly as her stomach gave a loud gurgle. She'd had nothing to eat since Running Wolf gave her a strip of dried buffalo last night.

"He does not want you here," said Ebbing Water. "So you will sleep outside."

Ebbing Water turned back to the fire and Raven snatched up the bowl and left the tepee. Had Running Wolf left it intentionally for her?

She sat behind the tepee to gobble down her prize. She knew Ebbing Water would miss her bowl eventually, and placed it just under the base of the tepee, hidden between the outer wall and the inner hanging lining that served to keep out the cold.

In a short time, Ebbing Water left the lodge, closing the flap of hide that covered the circular entrance. Raven knew this was a sign that she didn't welcome visitors or had gone away. Once she made sure she'd gone, Raven retrieved the bowl, wiped it clean and then placed it with Ebbing Water's other cooking things.

Raven was going to leave again, but she spotted the rawhide parfleche box covered with brightly colored geometric patterns. Her grandmother kept pemmican in just such a box. Pemmican was portable and could keep her alive. The mixture of fat and pounded dried meat might even contain some dried Saskatoon berries or wax currents.

Such food was meant for traveling and for the long dark nights of the Deep Snow Moon when hunting was hard and game scarce. It might keep indefinitely, as long as it was kept dry and did not mold. But stealing would get her a beating or worse.

She weighed her options.

A weak, starving woman could not fight and she could not survive the winter. She crept forward, untied the soft leather bindings and then lifted the stiff rawhide lid.

Inside sat the pemmican, but they were unlike the long rolls that her grandmother fashioned. Ebbing Water's food stores looked like flat skipping stones, the size of her fist. They lay one upon the other in no order. Raven wondered if she would know if there was some missing.

She quickly took five and rearranged the top layer to cover their absence. Then she continued out the opening only to find Running Wolf waiting for her. She was caught with the stolen food.

He grasped her arm and several of the pemmican rounds fell at her bare feet.

"So you ride and shoot and fight, and now I find you steal as smoothly as Weasel."

Would he kill her? He could. Captives had died for less. Raven found it difficult to stand—her legs began to shake and sweat popped out upon her forehead.

She pressed her lips together to keep herself from begging for her life, although that was what she wanted to do.

"Would you slit a man's throat with the same ease?" he asked.

When she did not answer he tugged her forward so that she fell against his broad chest and felt again the power of his body.

"Why did I ever take you?"

"I do not know."

He gave her wrist a little shake. "I wish I had killed him."

"Who?"

"Your war chief."

Raven shuttered at the thought of her brother's death earning this man one more eagle feather.

"I would rather have you earn the feather of a gull."

His eyes widened at this and then went hard. He knew what she was saying. The killing of an enemy woman might earn a gull feather, dipped in red paint. She was saying she would rather die than have him kill her war chief. She met his glare, realizing she had never seen him look so angry.

"Why didn't you kill me?" she asked, wondering how she even found enough wind to speak. His proximity continued to make her body quake and her stomach quiver. It must be because he was an enemy and because he had the power of life or death over her. It must be that, for the alternative was too terrible to consider.

"Why?" he asked. "I have been asking myself just that same question since I first saw you. The easy answer is because of the way you dressed. But now you have no clothes and still you intrigue me. It cannot be good for you or for me. Perhaps you are a witch, as Red Hawk says."

That charge was worse than being a common woman. Witches were dangerous. Witches were killed.

"I am no witch," she whispered.

"I believe you. But my opinion does not matter. You must convince Turtle Rattler."

"How?"

"I do not know. But you must or you will die."

He released her and gathered up the food she had stolen. Then he handed it to her. "Are you going to eat it?"

"No. Hide it."

"Then, do it. And come with me."

Chapter Six

The evening breeze brushed Running Wolf's face. How much colder was it on her bare skin? he wondered as he watched her dress with the loincloth and draped buckskin he'd handed her across her shoulders.

"Come," he commanded, and turned and walked before her because it was unseemly for her to walk beside him as an equal. As he went, he listened for her tread and could hear only the whisper of her feet upon the grass. It was better to have her behind him, for then he did not have to look at her perfect form or the angry bruises that covered her skin like the spots on his horse.

When he was away from her he knew what to do. Everything was clear. He would be generous and offer his captive to the one in the village who needed her help the most. Perhaps an old woman whose hands were knotted like the trunks of old cottonwood trees. Or to a young mother who had several children to look after. That would be charitable.

What he would not do was make her a common woman.

The thought of her lying beneath man after man made him sick. With Snow Raven, he felt possessive, and that was not the way of his people.

But when he was with this enemy captive he began to notice the fine curve of her shoulder and how her breasts were high, firm and round. He noticed the way she walked and the subtle sway of her hips that was not meant to be seductive, but still was more enticing than any female he had ever seen.

He led Raven to the tepee of Turtle Rattler and called a greeting. The shaman bid him enter and Running Wolf ducked inside, then motioned to Snow Raven to enter. As he took his place beside the shaman, he glanced at the small frail woman with hair streaked with gray. He had never noticed her before, though he knew she had been here on each of his visits. Now he watched her intently, a captive that he recalled Turtle Rattler had admitted to his lodge on her first winter.

It occurred to Running Wolf that she and Snow Raven might know each other or even be from the same tribe. He had been there at the taking of this woman. There were two, but they had not been taken in a raid, so Running Wolf did not recall the tribe.

After the formal greetings were exchanged, Running Wolf turned to the reason for his visit.

"I have brought my captive," said Running Wolf. *My* captive, he had said. Not *the* captive. Inwardly he groaned.

Turtle Rattler straightened in anticipation. "Bring her in."

Snow Raven did not wait to be summoned, but stepped through the opening, gracefully sweeping into the warm interior and kneeling, closest to the door, as was proper for the one of lowest rank. He was glad that she took this position without him having to tell her.

She sat in the firelight, hands on knees and shoulders back; it was impossible not to be affected by her. Her long hair covered her breasts and the buckskin hid her shoulders and arms, but the smooth skin of her belly and enticing indentation there all provoked his interest. His arousal stirred, and he growled at his body's unwelcome response to her beauty.

She kept her head down and waited to be spoken to. Running Wolf looked at her fingers, long and elegant, splayed upon her strong, bruised thighs, and felt an unfamiliar tug in his chest. He stilled. Lust for a woman was common enough, but this aching at his heart was new, unfamiliar and unwelcome.

She was Crow, so he should feel nothing for her. Running Wolf realized the tepee was suddenly very quiet. He tore his attention from Snow Raven to find both Turtle Rattler and his captive, Frog, staring at him.

His face grew hot.

Was he supposed to speak? One did not introduce a captive. Still, somehow he felt that Turtle Rattler expected this. He had some strange ways. He said he sometimes confused the future and the present because he could often see both at one time.

"This is Snow Raven of the Low River tribe of Crow people and my captive."

Turtle Rattler nodded and waited. Running Wolf felt increasingly uncomfortable. But this time he held his tongue.

"So this is the one everyone is talking about," said the shaman. "Some say you flew off your horse like a spirit. But the one who says this the loudest is the warrior who ended up on his back in the dirt. He has said that you are a witch."

Snow Raven's head came up at this accusation. She parted her lips and seemed to wish to speak but there had been no question and so it would be impolite to reply. She correctly remained silent but her fingers were no longer relaxed, curled into fists upon her bare thighs. She swayed a little but quickly righted herself.

Was she weary from lack of sleep or from this new threat?

Neither of them had slept since the raid, though he was sure many of his men had spent the day in their buffalo robes, while he would not find his until late into the night.

He wondered where Snow Raven would sleep.

"I see a young woman. Not a man. Is that correct?" the shaman asked.

"I am a woman," she replied.

Running Wolf could see the pulse at her neck now beating hard and fast. Surely she knew that if she was denounced as a witch, they would kill her.

"But you also fight like a warrior?"

"I have learned to ride and fight from my father."

"Why does he teach a woman such things?" asked the shaman.

"My mother died after my tenth winter. After that, I preferred the forest to the village. I would not gather berries or cook meals. My grandmother did not know what to do with me. I started following my brother but they would not give me a horse. So I ran after them. I am a good runner."

Running Wolf made note of this, wondering if she might actually escape without a horse.

Snow Raven continued speaking, not noticing her captor's growing unease. "Later I caught my own horse and trained her. That was when my father gave me a bow and taught me how to shoot, track and hunt."

"An unusual education for a woman. What does your husband think?"

Running Wolf leaned forward, waiting for her reply. Turtle Rattler was asking all the things that he wished to ask but could not. To question was to show an interest that he must not have.

But his apparent disinterest was a lie because nothing captivated him more than Snow Raven.

"I have no husband."

So who was the man who protected her? Bright Arrow, the son of the chief. Was this her intended? Had he stood with her wrapped in a buffalo robe before her father's lodge, exchanging secret touches and love words? Now *his* hands were in fists.

The shaman nodded. "And you prefer men, their company, I mean?"

"Yes."

"You are not attracted to women. In other words, you enjoy a man's touch?"

She blushed and dropped her chin in a way that Running Wolf found irresistible. He wanted to move to the other side of the circle and gather her up in his arms. Of course, he stayed where he was. But now he noticed how Turtle Rattler's captive sat, close to the shaman's left and slightly behind him. It was the place of an honored wife. He quirked a brow. Perhaps this lowly Crow did not only keep the shaman's lodge?

Turtle Rattler spoke again. "You are a maiden. Are you not?"

She blinked at him in astonishment and nodded.

"And your horse. It is the gray one you rode in upon."

She nodded again.

"And you have made a dress of rabbit hides, and when someone tried to take your rabbits, you knocked her to the ground. That is why they call you Kicking Rabbit. Is that right?"

"I have not made such a dress."

Turtle Rattler frowned.

"But I have set several traps."

"Ah, well, then you *will* knock someone down. One blow. Not two." He made it sound like a warning.

She stared at him with a mixture of wonder and apprehension.

"What do you say to the charge that you are a witch?"

"I am not."

"That you are possessed by evil spirits?"

"I am not possessed."

Turtle Rattler turned to Running Wolf. "She is telling the truth as she knows it. She is a woman, not a witch. Maybe that is dangerous enough." Turtle Rattler looked back at her. "She is unusual, surely. And I see that her path will not be an easy one. She could have lived like other women but she did not. At first she did this because it was best for her. Yesterday it was best for her grandmother. Tomorrow it will be best for many. But she will face hard choices. Like the one she has already made, choosing her love of another over her own safety. She will do this once more. But ultimately, she will choose the love of her own over the love of her people."

"Never," she said, and then placed both hands over her mouth and lowered her head in shame at her breech of good manners, but too late, for the denial was already spoken.

"Did I say she is spirited? She is." Turtle Rattler motioned for his pipe and Frog hurried to bring him the long pouch hanging from a peg from a lodge pole that held both pipe and tobacco in separate compartments. He spoke to Snow Raven now. "Also, the one you worry over? He is alive and will recover in time."

Her shoulders sagged in relief as Running Wolf's tightened. He knew now who Turtle Rattler meant. The warrior. Not her husband. But he fought for her. Was that the love she would give up to aid her people? He hoped so. He did not want that one to have her.

The shaman said he would be well in time. In good time or in time to come for her?

Turtle Rattler spoke now to Running Wolf. "Take her back to your mother. Tonight I will speak to the people and tell them that she is no witch."

Running Wolf rose and thanked his host and then left the tepee. He had to turn to see if Snow Raven followed for her steps were so soundless. He wanted to ask her about Bright Arrow. But he forced himself to stay silent.

If that warrior came for her, he would kill him. That would make her give up her love. Was that what the old shaman meant?

Night had now come to the sky and the stars blazed bright. The moon that had illuminated their way yesterday now peeked up between two tepees, big and orange, but not quite full tonight.

In the center of the village, the tribe assembled for the feast. The women who had tended the dog all day, roasting it over coals, still labored to turn the carcass. He headed toward the gathering, knowing they would know where to find his mother.

Instead, he was intercepted by Red Hawk. Running Wolf prepared for another battle because this warrior would not be happy until his captive was dead. Running Wolf knew that if Red Hawk touched her, he planned to put him on his back, just as his captive had done.

"What did Turtle Rattler decide?" asked Red Hawk.

"He said she is no witch."

"Still an enemy. We should kill her now. We already have a bed of coals. We could roast her until her skin falls from her body like a horse shedding its winter coat."

"That is not how a woman is put to death."

"She fights like a warrior—let her die like one."

All male captives were tested by torture. It was expected, the ultimate trial of their endurance, bravery and spirit. Women were mostly neglected. They sometimes starved in lean times or were strangled if they were troublesome. But a woman had never been tortured, and that was not going to change tonight.

"I must find my mother," said Running Wolf.

"I can take her to Ebbing Water. I know where she can be found."

"Not necessary." Running Wolf captured Snow Raven's arm and drew her away.

When they were out of earshot she whispered to him, "Thank you."

He led her along until he was sure they were away from Red Hawk. Her thick hair brushed against the back of his hand like a caress. The sensation was arousing. He leaned toward her and inhaled, taking in the tantalizing scent of her clean skin.

"Running Wolf?"

He jumped at the sound of his name. He recognized the female voice and felt his heart sink. He released Snow Raven and turned to see a young girl, not quite a woman, hurrying toward him. She had glossy hair decorated with many strands of brass beads. Her eyes sloped down at the corners, making her look perpetually worried.

She wore her most elaborately decorated dress. The entire top portion was covered with tiny white seed beads, sewn in even rows. Over the dress she wore a series of necklaces, each slightly longer than the last so they cascaded down the slope of her chest. This woman liked shiny, pretty things. Whoever married her would be forever trading for baubles to keep her content.

He recalled with a jolt that her father, Iron Bear, had encouraged him to become one of her suitors and stupidly he had agreed. Now that he was face-to-face with Spotted Fawn he regretted his words. He wanted the chief's favor. He just did not want his daughter.

Spotted Fawn toyed with one long braid as she mooned up at him with shining dark eyes. He could not think of a single thing to say.

Finally she spoke. "I am glad you are safe. Father tells me that you led our warriors with bravery and that we now have many new horses."

"Yes, the horses will be shown tonight."

"And I heard that you have taken a captive." Spotted Fawn eyed Snow Raven with curiosity. Her voice dropped and she grasped his arm, cuddling against him. "Is she dangerous?"

"She is a woman. All women are dangerous."

Spotted Fawn laughed at this. "Buffalo Calf is telling everyone that she is a witch."

Buffalo Calf was Red Hawk's wife and also the younger sister of the chief. Her words had weight. It was likely that her husband had asked her to tell the women, and he knew that if you said a thing, even a lie, enough times, people began to believe it. He thought he must set his mother out to repeat Turtle Rattler's words.

"Turtle Rattler will speak to us all tonight, but he said that she is just a woman. She is not to be touched."

He heard Snow Raven gasp. Only he and she knew that Turtle Rattler had not said that last part. And Running Wolf had not said that those were the shaman's words. He had only made it seem so.

"Turtle Rattler must have a reason for this. I will tell the others what you have said."

His thank-you sounded wooden to his ears. He

wanted to find his mother. Wanted to be rid of this burdensome captive. Wanted to be alone with her.

What was happening to him?

"Will you share a platter with me?" asked Spotted Fawn.

If it got rid of her, he would agree to almost anything.

"Yes."

She grinned, and he saw that her smile was pretty enough. Why then did it light no fire in his belly? Why did he not yearn to touch her hair, her face, her neck?

Spotted Fawn giggled and then skipped away like a child. Her father said she was a woman. Perhaps only her body was that of a woman, for she still seemed more like a child to him.

He faced Snow Raven in the darkness cast by the moon's shadow on the tepee to his right. The murmur of voices came from the center of the camp. Soon the feast would begin, and she must not be there in case the news that she was not a witch caused Red Hawk to cause her harm.

"Go to the place where I saw you set your last trap. Sleep there tonight. Do not come back to my mother's lodge until dawn."

"You trust me alone in the dark?"

"I do not. But I do not trust Red Hawk, either. If enough believe his charge it will go badly for you. Do you wish to die?"

"I have answered that."

He offered her a warning. "Our horses are more carefully guarded than the Crow's."

He knew that her tribe's horses might have been better guarded if most of the men had not been out scouting for sign of the Sioux.

Running Wolf lifted her chin and stroked his thumb along the downy soft skin of her cheek. He wanted to bring her into his arms, feel her full breasts pressed tight to his hard body. Here in the darkness, none would see.

He drew her in. Her soft body pressed to his. He heard her gasp, but she did not struggle. He wished he did not wear his war shirt. It was not the clothing made for holding a woman, but perhaps the right choice for holding an enemy. She stiffened for a moment and then she yielded, resting her head upon his chest. He tucked her beneath his arm and stroked the tangle of her hair.

He pressed his lips to the top of her head in a kiss and spoke in a whisper. "The war chief of the Sioux cannot choose a captive. I do not know what is wrong with me."

"Nor I."

Did she mean she also did not know what was wrong with him or that she did not know why she let him hold her in the night?

She sighed, her breath warm against his neck, her face tipped up to his. He knew that he could kiss her and that she would let him. But did she wish his touch or only wish a protector? The notion that she was willing to use him for his position soured him.

He pushed her gently aside, turned her and gave a little push against her back. His fingers tingled and his flesh itched as he watched her vanish into the night.

If she ran, he would find her.

Chapter Seven

Running Wolf attended the feast and danced with the men and listened to the stories of their latest triumph. Then he ate a great meal and thought of Snow Raven sitting alone in the dark. Was she eating what she had taken from their stores? Was she even now sneaking around their herd trying to steal a horse?

He stood and then sat again. He could not go himself, but he sent Crazy Riding with instructions to see if the gray mare was still with the others. Iron Bear stood to present the eagle feathers. Weasel and Running Wolf were called to the center of the gathering. They stood beside their chief as Big Thunder told of Running Wolf's prowess. For his courage, Iron Bear presented him with an eagle feather with one red spot at the top to indicate he had wounded an enemy in battle, then another for his leadership.

Yellow Blanket spoke of Weasel's skill at fool-

ing the enemy in broad daylight and said that even
the coyote would be proud. Weasel received a
feather for his craft at deception. His friend made
a joke about the way the Crow tufted their hair
like frightened porcupines and everyone laughed.

Running Wolf glanced about the group, searching for his friend Crazy Riding and found instead Red Hawk, scowling at the proceedings.
This warrior came away with a handful of beads,
the shame of attacking an old woman and of
being unseated by a younger one. He received no
feather, though he was the husband of the chief's
sister, while Running Wolf had many feathers and
would soon have enough to make a war bonnet.
Their gazes locked and Running Wolf saw the
fury burning there.

Crazy Riding appeared near Red Hawk and
Running Wolf's attention shifted. He nodded.
Yes, the horse was still there. Running Wolf blew
away a sigh of relief until it occurred to him that
if he were to flee captivity, he might not take his
own horse. After that it was hard to listen to the
stories of famous battles won against the Crow.
He just wanted to go and find Snow Raven and
be sure she had not run.

Running Wolf did not enjoy the feast or the
ceremony or the dancing. He especially did not
enjoy sharing an eating trencher with Spotted
Fawn, whose giggle rang out like hoofbeats on

stone. This was the first time in his memory that he had not savored the sweetness of earning another feather. All he could think about was Snow Raven. Where was she? What was she doing?

He had never thought of what a captive did during the feast celebration before. He had never cared. But now he did and he didn't understand why.

He was just trying to think of a way to leave the circle of men when Red Hawk spoke to the gathering.

"You have all heard of the captive that our war chief brings back to our tribe. Some of you have heard that she is a witch."

There was a collective gasp from the gathering. Clearly some of them had not, despite the efforts of Red Hawk's wife.

"She used her magic to bring me from my horse. Turtle Rattler has seen her. He can tell you."

Big Thunder muttered, "She brought him from his horse by diving on him like a wolverine on a bear. I will tell them."

But Turtle Rattler spoke first. All eyes turned to their shaman as he nodded to Red Hawk.

"I have spoken to this woman and she is not a witch."

Running Wolf's shoulders relaxed.

"But she is still dangerous. Still enemy."

Running Wolf's jaw tightened.

"I need time to seek the answer in the Spirit World on what is to be done. You have brought your concerns to me. I have heard them."

It was a rebuke and all knew it. Turtle Rattler did not like being pushed or prodded like a pack animal and had let Red Hawk know this publicly.

"He deserved worse," said Big Thunder.

Weasel took that moment to leap to his feet and pretend to ride a horse. He was waving something in his hand. Running Wolf peered and saw a strand of beads. Weasel made a full circle and then made an elaborate show of falling to the ground. The warriors who had returned from the raid knew what this was. The village did not. After Weasel had come to rest he lay still for a moment and then thrust the hand with the beads up toward the night sky.

"Red Hawk looks as mad as a wounded bull buffalo," said Big Thunder. "I would not be surprised if blood starts pouring from his nose any minute."

A lung wound would cause the bulls to rage, Running Wolf knew. It was when they were most dangerous.

"Weasel," said Running Wolf. "No more riding now."

Weasel grinned and made his way to Red Hawk, offering the beads. Red Hawk lifted his hands as if he would strike them from Weasel's hand but instead he took them, gripping them so tightly the strand broke. Then he dropped them in the dirt.

"You should become a *heyoka*, Weasel," said Red Hawk, referring to the sacred clowns who taught the people how to behave by doing the exact opposite.

"You don't like my show? Why don't you tell them *I* am a witch?"

Red Hawk rose to challenge Weasel, but Yellow Blanket put a hand on Weasel and asked him politely to tell the story of how he tricked the Sioux again. Weasel now had the attention of everyone. It was usual that another warrior, a witness, would tell the story, and earlier Crazy Riding had told the tale, but no one told a story better than Weasel.

Weasel began, engrossing all in his story. Running Wolf noticed Red Hawk withdrawing from the gathering. His wife, Buffalo Calf, wearing the multiple strands of beads, followed a moment later.

Running Wolf did the same. He had not intended to follow Red Hawk closely. He only wanted to get to the place he had told Snow Raven to rest, and Red Hawk and his wife were between him and his objective. That was the reason Running Wolf heard Red Hawk's words to his wife.

"She is the cause of this embarrassment. If she were not unnatural I would never have been unseated."

His wife's murmured reply was not audible but Running Wolf thought her tone sounded soothing.

"I don't want you to wear them any longer. And I want you to tell the other women to beat her."

Running Wolf paused in the darkness. It was as he'd feared. Weasel's antics had made things worse, and he knew he would not always be there to protect her. Could she protect herself?

He hurried on his way and came to the general place where her snare was set. At first he could not see her, then the silvery moon revealed a spot where the grass was absent, as if a deer slept in the field. He crept forward and found her curled like a child, her joined hands tucked beneath her chin, her arms tucked to her chest. She was shivering. Why had he not given her a blanket?

In sleep, her mouth was parted slightly. Her skin shone bright and pale in the moonlight. Her hair gleamed silver with dew. He paused, finding himself again of two minds. One part of him wanted to wake her and get rid of her before the women found her. But the selfish part wanted to lie down beside her and draw her into his arms. He wanted to feel her soft, pliant flesh pressed to his.

But he did neither of those things.

He did not wake her or join her. Instead, he released the blanket he wore about his shoulders and dropped it over her. If Turtle Rattler deemed her a threat, he would bring her to safety. He wanted her to stay, and it angered him more than all reason to think of her returning to the Crow warrior, especially now that he knew this was the son of Six Elks. But he would not see her sacrificed. For it served no purpose. In the meantime, he would see how much her father had really taught her.

Snow Raven woke to find the moonlight on her face and a red blanket draped over her body. She thought she heard something, but when she sat up it was to find herself alone. She clutched the blanket to her naked breast knowing that Running Wolf had been here, given her this.

She had listened to the drums and the chanting from her place among the tall grasses. She had gone exactly where Running Wolf had told her to go, and this bothered her. Why hadn't she chosen another place in the meadow? She drew the blanket about her shoulders and lay back down in her bed of grass. The wool helped against the chill. Now that the night held the land, the biting flies and mosquitoes had vanished. She wrapped the blanket twice about her and lay on her back, chewing on the pemmican she had taken from his mother's stores.

Raven gazed up at the stars and prayed for her brother's recovery and the safety of her family. Had they reached the Black Lodges or Shallow Water people?

Then she thought of what the shaman had said. Something about hard choices and losing her love and then forsaking her people. He was wrong, of course. She had no love *but* her people. They were one and the same and she would never forsake them. What else had he said? She could not remember. Her eyelids were so heavy now and her brain did not work. She yawned and turned to her side and thought no more.

She slept soundly but woke in the blue hours before dawn to a rustling near her head that ceased the moment she moved. She had fallen asleep with the pemmican still in her hand. Had a mouse smelled the bounty?

Raven gazed up at the fading stars, seeing only the brightest remained. She could no longer see the Sky Road cast across the sky. But the moon shone bright and in the silvery glow she could see her own shadow. The Hunter's Moon, she thought, was a good time for a hunt. Raven ran her traps, finding five long-legged jackrabbits waiting for her. She removed the limp bodies and reset the traps, thinking she might catch another before the dawn broke. When she returned to her place she saw a man wrapped in a buffalo robe waiting there.

She paused and glanced about. There was no good cover here, or anywhere on this plain. One had to run far to be swallowed up in the rolling hills and shallow valleys. How she missed her forests and mountains.

Was this Running Wolf? Even if it was her captor, she did not care to speak to him in the darkness, alone, away from the village.

"Come here," he said, and she knew it was Running Wolf from his voice.

He seemed larger in the darkness, with the moon casting his shadow out before him.

"Where were you?" His voice sounded gruff. Was he angry, or was this just the sound of his voice upon waking from sleep?

"I have been here. Thank you for the blanket."

He ignored her thanks and pointed at her catch. "What do you carry?"

She lifted the five lanky carcasses in answer.

"What will you do with these?"

"Eat, perhaps. Skin them for their coats as I have none of my own."

"You are a captive. You cannot have anything that the people do not give you. You cannot keep them."

"Then, may I keep the blanket?"

"For now."

She offered the rabbits to him. "Now why don't you give them back to me?"

He took the rope holding her catch but did not return them. "You may keep the skins of what you catch. Bring the carcasses to my mother."

Her throat burned as she realized what he had done. He had given her a way to cover herself and a chance to survive, perhaps even feed the other captives. Impulsively she threw her arms about him. She felt his body stiffen and she recognized too late what she had done. The gift he'd offered was great, but why had she embraced him?

She drew back her flaming face. "I am sorry. I only meant to offer my thanks."

His eyes narrowed and then he snorted, a sound that was either amusement or dismissal. She did not know. She only knew that she could keep the skins because of him.

"I will not give you a knife."

That was wise, she thought, but said nothing.

"But you may have a scraper."

She gaped at this and waited for him to think better of the offer. But when he did not, she felt obliged to warn him.

"I could cut your throat with that."

"Will you?"

"I should."

"It was not what I asked."

"No," she whispered. "I will not."

"Why?"

"I still owe you for my life."

"You will not harm my mother."

"Never."

"Come to my mother's lodge at sunrise."

He turned and left her. She took one step after him, realized what she was doing and stopped. Why would she follow a Sioux? He was nothing to her.

But despite her convictions, her body would not rest. She tossed for a long time as she thought of his handsome face and deep rumbling voice that made her shiver even while wrapped in a fine blanket. She could not sleep but lay restless as she recalled the touch of his mouth and the feel of his hard body pressed to hers.

For a captive to desire a warrior was madness. He would likely take what she offered, and if she succumbed, she would earn her place beside the others in the common woman's lodge. She was not a fool, she told herself. She might just as well desire the sun as the war chief of the Sioux.

But why, then, did this truth make her heart ache? And why, whenever he was near, did her body vibrate like the head of a drum?

Chapter Eight

Running Wolf tumbled into his sleeping robe with the scent of Snow Raven still clinging to his skin like honey. Was the blanket keeping her warm? Not as warm as he could, he realized.

He had planned to wake at dawn and see that Snow Raven made it safely to his mother's lodge, but when he finally opened his eyes the golden color of the buffalo hide of the tepee told him that the day was half over. He jerked upright and slid from his sleeping skins, then grabbed one of the blankets and pushed back the closed flap opening. His mother had not wanted him disturbed.

Where was Snow Raven?

He poked his head from the lodge and did not see his mother or his captive. A sick feeling stirred in his empty stomach. What if they had hurt her while he was sleeping? She was his and her safety was his responsibility.

He stepped from his lodge and offered his

morning song of thanks to the Creator. Then he rounded the tepee, going where, he did not know. His mother called to him.

Running Wolf turned to find both his mother and Snow Raven working with the rabbit hides. His mother scraped and Snow Raven tied the hairless leather to a circular hoop of wood with bits of cord.

"Another," said his mother. "She caught another rabbit in the night. Did you say she could have the hides?"

But Running Wolf was no longer listening. Instead, he was looking at Snow Raven and most especially at the purple welt above her left eye.

"Who struck you?" he asked.

She tugged at her hair, pulling the long locks more securely over her naked chest. "I do not know."

"Stand up," he said.

Snow Raven scrambled to her feet.

"Mother, give her a dress."

He waited while his mother ducked into their lodge and returned with a folded garment. "It will be too large."

"She will have one of her own soon." He turned to his captive. "Put it on."

She did, and the two-skin dress hung to her ankles. But it did remove the terrible bruises from his sight. He gathered up his weapons, saddle, blanket and bridle. Then he motioned to her with his head.

"Come with me," he said.

His mother said nothing as he stormed away. He took Raven to the horses and saddled her gray mare. He swung up and reached for her. She accepted his help as she swept up behind his saddle, sitting on her horse's rump.

He rode away from the village, past the boys snickering at their passing. They were so sure what the war chief would do with his captive and they were so wrong.

He rode them far down the river to a flat stretch of sand surrounded by thick cottonwood trees. Then he helped her down, only then noticing the many grass cuts oozing blood. She needed moccasins.

"What did your father teach you?"

"What?" She looked startled and confused and more beautiful than the first time he saw her.

"Riding, shooting, what else?"

"Snares. Tracking, and I know how to throw a lance."

He lifted his bow from his back and handed it to her. "Show me."

She hesitated, her eyes moving from the bow and then to him. "It is taboo for a woman to touch a man's weapons."

"Because you will draw away my power."

She nodded.

"Do you bleed?"

Her eyes rounded and she shook her head.

"Then, if anything, you will add power to them. Take it."

She did, her slim hand circling the smooth surface and hefting the weapon, measuring its weight. No doubt the bow was tighter than hers, and he did not know if she was strong enough to draw back the string. He slung the full quiver across her back.

She glanced over her shoulder at it. When she met his gaze, she was smiling. "Are you not afraid I will shoot you?"

"No."

She notched an arrow, fingering the end. "Why not?"

In answer he drew out one of his knives and hurled it with enough force that the steel tip sank two inches into the trunk of a nearby tree. Raven gaped as he retrieved the weapon.

Her smile was now conspiratorial. "What would you have me hit?"

He pointed at a log on the bank, some twenty paces away. "That."

She drew, sighted and released. The metal tip sank into a knothole that he only now noticed. Had she intended to hit that?

He retrieved his bow and handed her one of

the knives. She did not know how to throw, but she was a fast learner and practiced diligently.

"If I use that on anyone, they will kill me," she muttered.

"Use it only to protect your life."

Next he turned to hand-to-hand combat. Her father had taught her nothing in this regard, and he savored pinning her far more than he should have. Then he showed her how to use the momentum of another's attack to her advantage.

"You are small. So you cannot escape a bigger person, unless you find their weakness." He taught her eye gouges, how to draw back a finger or a thumb, how to drop to her knees and roll clear. How to kick out a man's knee or sweep him from his feet. On this, she had little success. But she did manage to throw him over her head, clumsily at first, but finally with some expertise.

She stood, panting, grinning and streaked with mud. "Why are you teaching me this?"

"So you will be safe."

Her lower lip began to tremble. Her eyes swam as tears welled and then fell over her lower lids, wetting her lashes so they stuck in dark clumps. The bruise above her brow had swelled and the color had begun to creep beneath her left eye.

He felt his own throat tighten at her suffering.

"I do not understand," he said, his voice nearly unfamiliar to his own ears. "You were captured, tied, dragged before the village and did not cry. Why now?"

"Because kindness is harder to accept than blows."

He opened his arms and she stepped into his embrace. He held her as she wept, rocking her as he cradled her head in one hand. Finally her tears turned to sniffles and she drew back.

It was hard to let her go.

"I want you to survive, Little Warrior."

That made her cry again. "Little Warrior," she muttered.

He drew back to look at her, his expression a question. She bowed her head, her hair a mask covering her features. She shook her head and he hooked his finger beneath her chin so he could see her expression.

"I did not mean to bring you more sorrow."

"I know." She wiped her face with both hands. "I have not cried so since my mother crossed the Way of Souls."

She stared up at him with those wide dark eyes luminous with tears.

"Well, past time, then." He took hold of her hand and helped her mount. She let him, though he knew she needed no help. She waited as he retrieved his weapons. Was it the knowledge of how he threw a knife that kept her, or did she feel the same respect for him that he did for her?

He paused a moment, standing by her horse, his hand on her calf muscle.

"You are a very unusual woman, Raven. I am sorry for your capture, but I am also glad to know you."

"And I thank you for the lesson. It is not what I expected."

"Did you think I meant to take your virtue?"

She nodded, her face flushed now.

"I would take it, if you would give it to me."

She looked away. "I cannot."

He drew up behind her and wrapped his arms about her waist. "If I were not your enemy?"

She leaned back against him and let him take the reins.

"But you are. How can that ever change?"

There were ways, he thought, recalling his shaman, Turtle Rattler, and his captive. But for him, taking a captive for his own would carry a heavy cost. One he was not prepared to pay.

They returned to camp to find his mother none too happy over the state of the dress. She sent Raven to clean the mud from the buckskin with white clay, and she studied her son.

"What do you do with that one?" she asked.

He shrugged.

"Be careful, son. A beautiful woman can make a man her captive."

"Do not talk nonsense."

His mother merely shook her head and fed him a hefty bowl of rabbit stew. When he finished, he told his mother to be sure that Raven ate some of what she caught. His mother's reply was a sullen nod.

He went to find Raven, but was caught up instead with the distribution of the captured horses. It seemed to take forever, and when he returned to his lodge he was famished.

The cooking pot bubbled with more rabbit stew, and his mother turned the horn ladle, calling a greeting. Raven sat beside her, tying a rabbit hide.

"Another?" he asked.

"Yes," said his mother. "This one has had a busy afternoon. Three more rabbits and another fight."

He tensed, looking at Raven, who now sat in only her loincloth, her long hair running in parallel streams down her breasts. He could see no new injury.

"Who attacked her?" said Running Wolf, barely able to contain his rage.

"Why don't you ask her who ended the fight, instead of who began it?" asked his mother.

He looked from one to the other.

"She was carrying the rabbits and Buffalo Calf called her a witch. Some of the women began to throw stones. One hit her here." His mother

pointed to the bruise on the back of her hand that
he had not noticed until Ebbing Water pointed it
out. It was blue and puffy and looked sore. "Buffalo Calf pushed her. And she let her, did not lift a
hand or say a word. But when Buffalo Calf tried
to take her catch, this one waited until Buffalo
Calf is tugging with all her might and then just
let go." His mother laughed. "She fell on her bottom in the mud."

Seemed to run in the family, thought Running
Wolf.

"So now she is furious. Spitting mad and as red
as fresh meat. She runs at your captive with her
claws bared. But this one just grabs her by each
shoulder and rolls to her own back with two feet
planted in Buffalo Calf's soft belly. Did you ever
see a buffalo fly? I did." Ebbing Water laughed.
"If Weasel hears of this, there will be no stopping him."

He and Raven shared a conspiratorial smile,
for she had already put into use the lessons of the
day, using Buffalo Calf's own force against her.
He nodded his approval as he spoke to his mother.

"What happened then?"

"Nothing. This one picked up her rabbits and
walked away as if she was the daughter of the
chief. The women are calling her Kicking Rabbit now."

"Will they attack her again?"

"I would not."

Snow Raven continued tying the wet rabbit skin to the circular frame to stretch and dry.

"Nine rabbits. At this rate she'll have her own tepee by the Hard Freeze Moon."

The thought of Snow Raven with her own tepee made him hard so fast that he gasped.

"What's the matter?" asked his mother.

He shook his head and retreated. He was not gone long, but when he returned his hair was wet and freshly braided for he had missed his usual morning bath. Droplets of water glistened on his skin. He cast Raven a long look as he ducked into the lodge. He carried out his tools wrapped in soft leather and sat down with a bit of flint to begin fletching. When he finished, he had a small white scraper. He called Snow Raven to him and pressed the tool into her hand.

"I give you this. See that you remember your promise."

She closed her fist around the scraper and smiled.

Ebbing Water called Raven to her and then sent her to the river for water. Raven ducked into the lodge to collect six buffalo bladders and strung the strap connecting them over one shoulder.

But when she stepped out of the lodge, it was to find Running Wolf blocking her way. She stood, still naked from the waist up and vulnerable to his gaze.

Running Wolf looked at her as he spoke to his mother.

"I wish to have a tepee of my own."

Both she and Ebbing Water knew why a young man wanted a lodge of his own, but only Raven could see the fire of want blazing in his eyes.

Raven's attention flicked to Ebbing Water to realize that his mother could not see her from where she sat.

"It is true, then," she said. "You are courting Spotted Fawn. That is why you bring me a captive. So I will have help here. And you find one who can provide me with meat as well as gathering fuel and water. You are a caring son."

Running Wolf lifted a long strand of Raven's hair and brought it up to brush his lips. Raven shivered at the sensual gesture.

"A man needs a woman," he said.

Only Raven noted that he did not say which woman.

Running Wolf released her hair but still held her with his gaze. His expression told her that it was not Spotted Fawn he wanted.

Once he had a lodge, would she find the strength to resist him?

The next morning one of the village dogs woke Raven with a wet nose to her face. The day crawled by with task after task. She carried water and collected fuel. On that trip she met Mouse again, also gathering the dried buffalo paddies. How Raven missed the wood that lay everywhere in the mountains.

Mouse appeared, looking more drawn than before. She had slashed at her forearms as a sign of her mourning and painted her face black with charcoal.

"How goes it with you?" asked Raven.

"I still stand and I still wish to see the mountains before I follow my husband and son."

"Then, we should go speak to the others," said Raven.

A flicker of life showed in Mouse's eyes and she nodded. "I will tell the others to meet us here at sunset when they are sent to gather water."

Raven left her to return to Ebbing Water's lodge. As she walked she thought of the mountains and felt a longing to see them once more. Would she ever?

At the lodge of Running Wolf's mother, Raven scraped and stretched the rest of the hides. Afterward she worked to pound dried buffalo meat to powder. Several Sioux women passed by and Ebbing Water greeted each by name. They either stared at Raven or ignored her. None threw stones or even insults.

Her stomach rumbled but she was given no

meal until the late afternoon when her work earned one small bowl of rabbit stew. She knew with this amount of food, she would quickly lose weight and grow weak.

Ebbing Water sent Raven to the river again for more water just before sunset as Mouse had predicted. It was the time many captives set about this errand and she went with a slow, reluctant tread, dreading meeting the others.

She moved along in the gathering dusk, taking the trail along the water's edge, following the wide river. She did not find Mouse, so she crossed the narrow tributary and continued on. She heard them before she reached them.

Mouse stood with the others, all women, all overly thin and all dressed in an odd assortment of ill-fitting, poorly made clothing. She had seen some of them throughout the day, but did not know how many captives the Sioux had.

"Here she is," said one woman.

They grew silent as she approached. The circle opened for her and she stepped into the ring. There were five in all. Mouse, looking gaunter than any of them, made introductions. She told her the Crow name for each woman, her tribe, when she was captured. Then she gave her the name the Sioux had given each one and explained that she must use these names or it would cause trouble. Finally Mouse told what each now did here. They were all young, except for Frog, whose hair was streaked with gray. Two had been invited into lodges, one with an old widow, and Frog with the shaman. Two were common women, and Little Deer, like her, had found no lodge and was in danger of freezing to death this winter.

"We were fourteen last year. The cold and sickness took the rest," said Mouse. "We are like the weak elk. It is easy for the wolves of winter to pick us off. But I, for one, want to return my people."

They all looked at Snow Raven. No, that wasn't right. They all looked *to* her. To her for hope, for rescue, for salvation. Her, the woman who had unseated a warrior.

"We want to go home," said Snake, a large-boned woman whose flesh now hung on her. She lifted a bridle. "We have made it from our own hair, but I do not know how to steal a horse." She pressed the bridle into Raven's hand. "We can make more."

"I have this," said the one the Sioux called Wren, and produced a knife with a broken point. "It belonged to Pretty Cloud's husband but he will not miss it."

Then they all laughed.

Wren explained for Raven. "I live with an old widow who has no sons." It was a fate all women feared, Raven knew. To have none to protect or provide for you and have to rely on the generosity of others.

Truly, thought Raven, he would not miss the knifepoint.

One by one, each produced a gift. A rope, a basket, tanned buckskin, a bow, six arrows.

Snow Raven gripped the shaft of the unstrung bow. "How did you know?"

"I overheard Red Hawk say you planned to shoot him with an arrow but were too close."

Mouse gripped Raven's hand. "Will you take them home?"

She looked from one hopeful face to the next. The task they set her was impossible. To steal six to twelve horses without notice, escape and stay ahead of pursuit, keep them from discovery by other enemies and predators. Provide food, locate water and, not to forget, actually find one of the three Crow camps that moved with the seasons.

Raven lifted her chin, finally accepting the responsibility she wanted to shirk. She looked from one to the next. Hopeful faces, wide eyes in pale, thin and weak bodies. They wouldn't survive another winter. That much she knew.

"Yes. I will lead you."

Chapter Nine

Raven moved through the grass under starlight. The moon had yet to rise but each night it grew larger. When it was full, they would go. She had only to choose the best horses for five women who had never ridden before.

It was not difficult to slip into the hobbled herd. There was no watch at night and the dogs now recognized her scent and did not even lift a head at her passing.

She looked from one horse to the next, judging their conformation and gauging their endurance. She needed gentle horses that would tolerate inexperienced riders. As she moved through the herd, past the sleeping horses and a few that were awake and grazing, she kept an eye out for her mare, Song. Finally she gave up and tried a low whistle. She heard a familiar nicker and headed in that direction, reuniting with her best horse. She wept and stroked her mare's neck. Song gave her a thorough checking, searching for the treat of dried cherries that Raven often gave her. Finding none, she returned to grazing.

"Are you ready to go?" she whispered to Song.

Raven hugged her horse's strong neck and then grasped hold of her mane. She did not remove the hobbles on her mare's front feet before she swung up onto her horse. She just sat there for a few moments. Then she lay across her mount's withers, letting the warmth seep into her chilled skin and breathing the familiar smell of horse. After she was warm, she swung back and lay on her back along Song's spine.

"Mother, can you hear your daughter?" she whispered. And again she received no reply.

The horses grazed, some snored and the wind blew through the grasses. Eventually she was chilled and slipped off Song. She told Song to be good before moving back toward the village.

She was nearly out of the herd when she saw a man standing so still she was not sure that he was real.

"It is good you did not go."

She knew the voice instantly. Running Wolf had followed her here. How long had he been watching? The entire time, she was certain.

"I come here sometimes to be with the horses."

He stood so close she could feel his warm breath on her cheek.

"I will not let you go. That means I must protect you," he whispered. "Even from yourself."

She met the cold accusation in his eyes. "I just wanted to see my horse."

"She is not your horse. She is mine and you are mine."

"But you do not want a Crow captive."

"I want you."

He reached for her, dragging her forward and carrying her down to the grass. He rolled her to her back and pinned her legs beneath one of his own. She stared up at him, this man she coveted and could not have. But perhaps in the darkness, where no one could see…

She angled her head and lifted her chin in invitation. He took what she offered, his mouth descending fast as a diving hawk. His fingers laced in her hair, controlling her head as their lips met and joined. He gave a low rumbling growl of need deep in his throat and she answered with a whimper.

She opened her mouth to him, savoring the enticing glide of his tongue along hers. His hand crept up her thigh, reaching beneath the soft rabbit pelts to find her own thatch of hair. The shock of his touch at so intimate a place was enough to startle her from her desire into the realization of what she was about to lose.

She pushed at his shoulders. It took a moment

for him to realize that she meant to escape him. He lifted his head and she saw the hunger flare before his eyes narrowed. Running Wolf was accustomed to taking what he wanted, and right now he wanted her.

They sat up together, side by side amid the grazing horses.

Running Wolf captured one arm and tugged. She fell against his wide chest and he held her tight, controlling her, bending her to accept his kiss. At first she tried to turn away. But he was so strong and his lips were so firm. She let the night hide her shameful wanting for this man and surrendered to what her heart desired.

His tongue glided into her open mouth and she felt the shot of liquid desire shoot through her body like one of her arrows.

He deepened the kiss, his hand moving along her body, caressing first the back of her hand and then the sensitive skin of her palm. He lifted her hand and pressed it to his chest, her palm flat so she could feel the beat of his heart.

Falling into his arms was like falling into a dream, filled with secret desire and the promise of pleasure she did not fully understand. Her body came alive with his touch, and she found herself pressing her breasts tight to his chest, struggling against the need for the pressure of his body to hers.

Just when she began to tear at his clothing, he captured her wrists and set her aside. She knelt before him, panting with need, crazed for just one more kiss.

He released her. She reached and he pushed her hand aside. She recoiled at the pain of his rejection, trying to understand. He stared at her, his gaze hot with need, but his jaw tight with denial. And then she understood. She had pushed him away. Now he showed her that she could not stop him physically and she could not stop him emotionally. He had already won.

She gasped. The lesson he taught was too successful because now she understood that her only recourse was escape. If she stayed she would be his whenever he wished.

"You will come with me now. You will sleep inside my lodge and you will not come to the horses again."

She nodded her compliance as her mind screeched a denial.

"Do as I tell you and I will keep you safe. You will survive the winter at my fire."

"What of your mother and of the chief's daughter?"

"They are my concern. Now come."

In the morning, Running Wolf prayed before his lodge and then bathed in the river with the other men. His body was here with them, but his mind was on Snow Raven and her sweet kisses. She had tried to deny him, but she was inexperienced and it was easy to turn her own desire against her. It had taken control to stop her, almost more control than he had.

His mother had been surprised to see Raven sleeping in their lodge before the entrance. He had told his mother that she would be staying inside from now on. His mother had not argued, but she had made a sour face that told him of her objections without words.

But he was the man now. His father was gone and his mother could do as he said or she could find another man to provide for her. Had she seen his resolve? Was that why she had not argued?

The air was cold as he shook off the droplets of water. Soon they would find the buffalo and, after that, a harvest camp to prepare the meat. Before he knew it they would be heading south for their winter camp.

Running Wolf drew on his loincloth, tying the soft leather at his hip and then adjusting the tanned leather to drape evenly over the band.

"Do you think the scouts will find buffalo?" asked Big Thunder as he dragged the soft, absorbent buckskin over his skin to draw away the water.

"Soon," said Running Wolf, confident in the men looking for signs.

Everyone knew that Running Wolf took more buffalo than any two warriors combined. He was unsurpassed in riding beside a bull and planting his spear into his lung. But he had also perfected the skill of retrieving his lance so he could chase another buffalo. Then he would shoot an arrow into the shoulder to mark the kill for his mother.

The men were now talking about women. This one. That one. They were all the same to him. All but the one he could not claim.

"What about you, Weasel? Do you have a sweetheart?" asked Crazy Riding.

He shrugged. "I like them all."

Crazy Riding turned to Big Thunder. "You?"

Big Thunder's expression was serious but he gave his head a shake.

Crazy Riding now turned his attention to Running Wolf. "My mother says that my uncle heard Iron Bear ask you to court Spotted Fawn."

Running Wolf sighed.

Big Thunder stiffened and his frown grew deeper.

Running Wolf did not like being gossiped about, and he didn't like being told who to court. Actually, until a certain raven had swept into his life, he would have been happy to court Spotted Fawn.

"She is young yet," he said. He thought she was six winters younger. He recalled going on his vision quest when she was still playing with a stuffed leather bear.

Big Thunder nodded his agreement but did not speak. His silence on this topic troubled Running Wolf. His friend usually had opinions on such things.

Crazy Riding said, "You have enough horses, more now with the raid. The buffalo skins for a lodge you could take in one good hunt." Their chief had been generous, giving him five new horses and the captive he had taken, whom he'd immediately given to his mother.

The women of the tribe called him a good son. He wasn't. He was burning with lust for Snow Raven and he was doing all he could to hide his feelings from the others while keeping her from being a common woman. What would Spotted Fawn do if he married her and kept Snow Raven as his own?

Some women would welcome the help of a servant, but no wife wanted to be second favorite behind an enemy captive. Running Wolf knew that, if he took that path, sooner or later Spotted Fawn would hate Snow Raven.

He could not have them both.

Weasel laughed. "If you think she is too young, then wait. But if just the thought of her does that—" he pointed to the bulge in Running Wolf's loincloth "—then you should go see Mouse."

Big Thunder took his leave at this point without another word.

"What's wrong with him?" asked Crazy Riding.

Running Wolf shook his head in confusion as he watched his friend retreat up the riverbank.

"Maybe he likes Mouse," said Weasel.

"Don't be stupid. She's an enemy," said Crazy Riding.

Weasel nodded. "She's pretty, though."

"Skinny, you mean. All bones now. Besides, no Sioux warrior would ever demean himself by choosing a Crow for a wife," said Crazy Riding.

"But he doesn't mind sleeping with her."

"That's different," insisted Crazy Riding. "Every man has needs. Right, Running Wolf?"

"Turtle Rattler has a captive," he pointed out.

"She keeps his lodge. He's too old for that, isn't he? And too smart to have children that are half-Crow."

A call came from the village and a boy ran to the men bathing in the river.

"The scouts are back. They found buffalo."

A cry of excitement broke into the air. The buffalo had been acting differently now that the white man's wagons had made a track across the plains. It made everyone nervous. But their scouts had found them.

Running Wolf walked quickly through the village to find the women already breaking down the lodges in preparation to follow the herd.

Running Wolf was considering which of his hunting horses he would pick. Lately he had been riding Snow Raven's gray horse, Song. The mare was smart, fast and very quiet. He had decided this was his new favorite deer-hunting horse. He tried not to think of the real reason that he preferred this mare—imagining Snow Raven as he had first seen her.

Big Thunder appeared beside him. They both listened to the scouts as they relayed the position and size of the herd. Running Wolf grinned, knowing that Big Thunder enjoyed buffalo hunts best. But Big Thunder just stared at him as if suffering a toothache.

"Will you ride with me?" asked Running Wolf. It was an unspoken promise that they always rode together. But it was still polite to ask.

"I don't know."

Now Running Wolf was frowning. "What is the matter with you?"

"Are you courting Spotted Fawn?"

Running Wolf's eyes widened as he recognized the look in Big Thunder's eyes. It was how he felt much of the time since Snow Raven had appeared.

Suddenly Big Thunder's abrupt departure from
the river made perfect sense.

"You want that one? I have never even seen
you speak to her."

"Our chief has asked *you* to court her."

"He just wants to see her wed before he takes
the Ghost Road."

"But he did not ask me. He asked you."

Before Running Wolf could address this,
someone slipped beside him and clasped his arm.

He stared down to find Spotted Fawn mooning
up at him. He grimaced. What terrible timing. He
glanced to Big Thunder and the two exchanged a
look—Running Wolf's apologetic and his friend's
defeated.

Spotted Fawn tugged at him, demanding his
attention in the way of children.

"A hunt," squeaked Spotted Fawn. Her head
did not reach past his shoulder, and her voice was
high and unappealing. What did Big Thunder see
in her?

She smiled, and he thought she was pretty and
had straight teeth. But having her grip his arm
only made him want to shake her off. She stuck
to him like a burr.

"I will help your mother skin any buffalo you
take. You will need them for a lodge. And you
have many horses, and my father said you could

trade some of those for wool blankets and beads to please his new wife."

She was listing her bridal sum, he realized. He glanced about for Big Thunder only to find he had vanished.

He put his free hand on Spotted Fawn's shoulder to stop her restless bouncing. She stilled and blinked up at him, smiling as if she were already a bride. Running Wolf shivered.

"Where is your shirt?" she said, running her hand over the dimpled skin of his chest.

He forced himself not to recoil. This was not going to work.

"You know my friend Big Thunder?"

Spotted Fawn made a face, and Running Wolf's spirits dropped even farther.

"What about him?"

"What do you think of him?"

"What do I think? I think he *hates* me."

"What?"

"Well, he never speaks to me, and when I try to talk to him he runs away."

"Perhaps he is just shy?"

"He has no trouble speaking to the council."

"Speaking to a woman requires a different kind of courage."

Spotted Fawn's hand paused and then slid away from his skin. He found he could breathe easier.

"Why are you telling me this?"

"I just…" Yes, why was he?

"I thought *you* were courting me." One hand lifted to her hip. "Are you trying to get rid of me?"

"No!" Was he? He must be the biggest fool ever born. If he married this woman, he would surely be the chief's favorite. Gaining his support would go a long way toward winning the votes of the council of elders.

"Why are we talking about him, then?"

"Well, he is my best friend, and I want you to be nice to him."

Her protruding lip vanished and she brightened again.

"I can do that."

"And I will ask him to try to speak to you."

She grabbed his arm again. "Yes. I will do all I can to be friends with your friends. Even Weasel. And you must be kind to Pretty Thrush and Lighting Butterfly."

Running Wolf groaned inwardly but managed to nod. "Of course."

Pretty Thrush was only thirteen and Lighting Butterfly was only one winter older. All were more girls than women. He did not care what her mother said and what ceremony she had completed. He would not be shocked to learn she sucked her thumb at night.

Whereas Snow Raven was lush and lithe and completely self-possessed. She did not cling or

fawn. Well, she had clung last night, but that was
the right kind of clinging. And she was strong and
brave and rode like a warrior. He wondered if she
had ever taken down a buffalo.

Spotted Fawn now jabbered like a mockingbird
about the color of the dress she was making for
herself and how she would decorate it with elk
teeth if he would bring her some. Running Wolf
scanned faces, looking for Snow Raven. Was she
tearing down his mother's lodge?

"I have to get ready to travel," he said by way
of an excuse to Spotted Fawn, and saw that pink
lower lip once more stick out in a very unappealing pout. "I will see what I can do about the elk
teeth."

Her smile was back and he was away from her,
thank the Great Spirit.

Before the sun had reached its apex the tribe
was packed. The horses that were not needed to
carry or pull would follow along. No halters were
necessary. Their instinct kept them with the herd,
and so they followed wherever the others went.

Running Wolf had selected his packhorses
but he substituted the usual brown horse with
white socks for her gray mare. His mother lifted a
brow, but the horses were his. Women did not own
them. Her mother ordered Snow Raven about. It
was clear that, though she could ride a horse, she
was not accustomed to packing one.

"Did you not pack your family's lodge?" he asked.

"My grandmother needed no help. In fact, she insisted on doing this herself."

"What did you do?"

"I gathered my horses and weapons."

"You have horses?"

"No. I *had* them."

"How many?"

"Seven."

Seven horses! That was enough for a bridal payment. What would her family expect a groom to give if she already had seven horses? And why was he even thinking of this? Now he was thinking something else. Who gave her these horses?

"Gifts from your sweetheart?"

"I caught them myself, except one, the foal of my chestnut mare, Drum."

"So you can ride and hunt *and* catch horses?"

"Yes. And now I can also wrestle." She smiled.

"Crow women are unnatural," said his mother, tying another bundle onto the gray mare. Then she retreated to the diminishing pile of their belongings.

Running Wolf stepped closer to Snow Raven and rested a hand over the one she had on the crosspiece of the packsaddle. Her gaze lifted to his.

"One day I will take you hunting for elk."

Her eyes flashed with excitement. It was the first time that his words had made her look truly animated since her arrival and the sight filled him with gladness.

"I can track for you."

He did not say that he could track quite nicely for himself. He was too happy seeing her pleasure. "Have you ever taken an elk?"

"I have. I sewed the teeth onto my hunting shirt."

He remembered now. He also remembered the women tearing that beautiful shirt from her body. He understood all the strands of hair she had tied to the front now, as well.

"The hair locks…were they from each of the horses you have caught?"

"Yes. But I traded some horses for this and that."

"A metal skinning knife?" he asked, recalling the weapon she had tried to use to slit his throat.

She blushed. "I did not know you then."

"Would you do differently if we met today?" Her skin was warm and soft under his. He used his thumb to stroke the back of her hand. She weaved her fingers with his. He cupped her chin and she tilted her head, preparing for his kiss.

His mother dropped her cooking kettle on the lodge poles, making it ring. Raven leaped back from Running Wolf, who turned to meet his mother's glare. Her scowl was as fierce as a mother bear protecting cubs. Snow Raven withdrew behind him, but his mother's attention seemed fixed to her. Then her gaze flashed to his.

"You will never take this one hunting. She is a captive."

Running Wolf knew his mother's moods, and she was furious now. He had protected Snow Raven from becoming a common woman. She had protected herself from the females of his tribe by putting a woman as large as Buffalo Calf on her back. But now that his mother had seen his desire for Snow Raven, who would protect her from Ebbing Water?

"Kicking Rabbit," she said, her voice as sharp as a breaking stick, "go and fetch the blankets."

Snow Raven hurried to do as she was bid. Running Wolf could not keep himself from watching her go. She looked sleek and graceful in her new dress of rabbit hides. She had even created a collar of what looked like a weasel. Her feet were no longer bare, though the moccasins were of the design of Crow, with a center seam down the middle of her foot, instead of the more comfortable seam affixing the soft upper buckskin to the tough protection of rawhide. And of course they held no adornment.

"And you," said his mother.

Running Wolf forced his attention away from Snow Raven.

"You had best remember who you are and who she is."

Running Wolf no longer saw fury in Ebbing Water's eyes. Now he saw anxiety.

"She is Crow. An enemy. And you have been asked by the chief himself to court his youngest daughter. What will she say if she sees you making moon eyes at a lowly captive?"

That straightened his spine. It was one thing to suffer his mother's ire. But the wrath of the daughter of the chief would put Snow Raven in real peril.

Running Wolf nodded his understanding and withdrew. The best way to protect Snow Raven was to keep his distance.

Chapter Ten

The tribe followed the scouts who would lead them to the herds of buffalo. Running Wolf had traveled near his mother much of the day, afraid that she might hurt Snow Raven and equally afraid that Snow Raven might hurt his mother.

He had intended to allow his captive to ride her horse, but his mother would not let a captive ride when many women of his tribe walked. She likely would not even have permitted Snow Raven to lead her gray mare, but was unaware that the horse had belonged to her captive.

The horse knew. That was obvious by the whinny when she had first discovered her mistress. Both her horse and Snow Raven had kept their relationship secret from Ebbing Water, but Snow Raven had thanked him twice. She had almost touched him again, too, but then she had glanced over her shoulder at his mother, preparing to ride the brown horse, and dropped her hands back to her sides. Running Wolf smiled, recognizing that Snow Raven also struggled with a need to touch.

His smile died under the slow realization that this would only make both of their situations worse. She would gain more enemies among the women and he would risk offending his chief.

No, his mother was right, her warning wise. He must distance himself from this little warrior woman. She was sly. Could she steal a man's heart as easily as she stole his horses?

He left them and rode along the line of families traveling southwest. When he passed the family of Spotted Fawn's friend, Pretty Thrush, she called a greeting and he scowled at the child for her impudence until he recalled his promise to Spotted Fawn. He groaned and then returned her greeting. In response the girl giggled. He rode ahead as quickly as he could without appearing rude.

That night his mother made a temporary camp. The sky was clear, so there was no need to erect the lodge. His mother sat squarely between him and their captive, watching. Running Wolf accepted a large bowl of the stew his mother had carried in her iron kettle from their last camp. It was hard not to comment on how little Snow Raven was given to eat, but there was less than

she had started with because his mother had
dropped the kettle.

He ate quickly and then went to see to his
horses. He did not return until late and found
only his mother sleeping between the buffalo
robes. His bed was made and empty. Where was
Snow Raven?

He tried to think where he would go if he were
hungry and had no robe to sleep upon. Had she
noticed the buffalo wallow? It was only a few
paces from their trail and not very far back. He
headed in that direction.

Buffalos liked to roll in the same places. Their
horns and hooves dug up the thick sod until there
was a deep indentation; in this way the hole grew
through the efforts of thousands of buffalo over
many lifetimes.

Running Wolf had seen as many as a hundred
buffalo all rolling in the dust in one place. They
liked to cover their coats with mud in spring and
dirt in fall. In the spring such wallows were alive
with frogs and snakes and birds. In the fall, when
water was scarce, animals came from all over the
prairie to drink the rainwater collecting there. The
wallow was a natural place to hunt, and Raven
was a hunter.

He stood and collected his bow and quiver.
If buffalo were close, there might be pronghorn
drinking or even wolves.

Running Wolf stilled at that thought and the realization that Snow Raven had no weapons and might be right now standing by the wallow alone at night. He broke into a run.

He had enough sense not to charge down the hill to the wallow, because if there were any game he would frighten them. He crept over the rise and gazed down at the half moon reflected in the water. The sun had not yet stolen all the water, though it had taken much. The muddy banks were wider than the lake.

He looked for Snow Raven and did not see her. He did not know if he should be relieved or annoyed. Then he noticed something beside him in the grass that ringed the indenture in the earth. He reached out and closed his fist around the patchwork dress made from many rabbit pelts. Beneath lay two Crow moccasins.

She was here.

His heart sped as he scanned again more carefully and found that some of the mud was moving. Snow Raven had coated herself from head to toe. Even her hair was covered. Was she planning to grab any animal that wandered too close?

Ducks were migrating now, and geese. If she was lucky, she might catch one when it landed. Though without a weapon, he was doubtful.

Part of him wanted to watch her hunt, but another part wanted to be near her. He slipped out of his leggings, loincloth, moccasins and shirt. Then he untied the feathers that decorated his hair. Finally, he gave the call of a whip-poor-will.

She stopped moving and listened. He called again. She turned in his direction and he signaled her with a sweep of his hand, kept low and parallel to the ground. She returned the gesture and waited as he slithered down the bank with his bow and arrows.

She lay facedown so he could see the moonlight illuminating the sensual curve of her back and the enticing round cheeks of her bottom. The mud only made her more appealing because he knew they both would be as slippery as otters.

He came up beside her and she gestured that she was watching something on the far bank. He saw nothing and waited beside her. He was hungry for her, but she was hungry for food. He could speak to his mother, of course, but that might just make matters worse.

They waited there, side by side. He heard the rustle before he saw the animal—a pronghorn buck stepped through the tall grass, nostrils twitching as he scented for predators.

Snow Raven had wisely put them upwind, and the mud would also cover their scent. The buck disappeared for a moment and Running Wolf removed his quill of arrows and slid both the bow and the arrows to Snow Raven. She looked at him with wide-eyed astonishment, but her fist gripped the bow and she notched an arrow.

The buck appeared again, leading six does down to drink. He had done well this fall, thought Running Wolf. Six females might mean six to twelve fawns come spring, if he was potent and his females willing.

Would she take the buck? He wouldn't. He would go for the smallest doe. Give the others a chance to mate and raise young.

She lifted the bow so that the grip was just off the mud. Then she cleaned the gut string with a slow sweep of her thumb and first finger. As the pronghorns made their way down to the water to drink, she tested the new weapon, drawing back the string and feeling the flex of the ash bow.

The mud was deep and the pronghorns' hooves made a sucking sound as they continued toward their objective. Snow Raven notched an arrow. One of the does paused and half turned sideways to their position, looking back the way they had come. Raven released the arrow. It flew across the water like a shaft of moonlight and into the doe's side.

The doe jumped and kicked, startling the others. Blood frothed from the antelope's nose and mouth. The arrow had missed the ribs and gone through both lungs.

A lucky shot.

But was it luck? Raven stood now. Showing herself to her prey. She was not greedy. She did not take another shot. The remaining pronghorns galloped up the incline and disappeared as their unlucky companion fell to her knees, rolled and died. But that was the way of life. One had to drink, and that meant facing predators who had to eat.

Snow Raven handed back the bow, and even though she was coated in sticky mud, he could see her form perfectly in moonlight. The mud seemed almost like war paint, as if she really was a warrior woman as he had first seen her. Only now she was a hunter.

"Thank you," she said, returning his bow. He wished she could keep it. It belonged in her hand.

His eyes seemed to stick to her just like the mud.

"That was a good shot." He motioned toward the antelope. "What were you hunting?"

"I saw a flock of ducks flying over the night sky and hoped they would land. But they flew on."

She started toward her kill and he followed her, but the mud was so deep they stuck up to their knees, just like the pronghorn. She stopped first beside the muddy water. He judged the distance and estimated the depth. Then he looked back to find her studying his body with the same apt curiosity as he had looked at hers.

His skin tingled, and he thought the heat suddenly coming from his body might dry the mud into cakes of dirt. He cleared his throat and her gaze flicked back to his face even as his body made a full show of arousal. Her gaze dropped and then swept upward again.

"You have seen a naked man?"

"Of course," she said.

He smiled. "How do I compare?"

She returned his smile, only hers was full of mischief. "You are much dirtier."

Yes, and his thoughts were just as murky as the mud. In a few more moments he feared he would not be able to think at all. He gripped his bow tighter to keep from reaching for her.

"And you smell like a frog." She laughed.

Her mirth was contagious, and he found himself laughing, too. "Me?" he said, lifting one muddy strand of her hair from her shoulder. "I think that is you."

She used a single finger to sweep over his collarbone and then down the swell of muscle at his chest. She drew back a glob of mud and sniffed it.

"You," she said.

"Can you swim?" he asked.

She nodded.

"Would you like to clean off?"

Another nod, cautious now. "But a woman does not bathe before a man."

He knew this, of course, but seeing her wearing nothing but a coating of mud made her look wild and more desirable, if that was even possible. Most women tied downy feathers and beads and ermine in their hair. And Snow Raven had no adornment. Yet she was the most beautiful female he had ever seen.

"I would bathe if you will give me the privacy to do so."

"You are my captive. If I say you must bathe, then you must."

She folded her arms beneath her breasts, effectively lifting the plump flesh upward.

She considered him, measuring his intent. Then she shook her head. "No."

"Stubbornness in a captive is a dangerous thing."

"In my heart I am still free."

"Snow Raven. You are a captive of the Sioux. Were I another man…"

"I have already been struck by another man and several women. I have seen what is done to the other captives here. So though you can kill me or beat me or set me free, you cannot force me to do this."

She left him with a hard choice. Submit to her will or force her to his. He imagined washing her body and felt his arousal twitch. Her eyes sank and then returned to meet his.

He imagined breaking her and watching her slink around the village like the other captives here. Or worse, watching her sway her hips, enticing any man who would bring her a bit of food or cloth. No, he was wise enough not to kill what he loved in her.

He bent his knees and sprang. She gave a little shout of surprise as he sailed past her into the water. When he surfaced he scrubbed himself clean and then exited the pond to retrieve his clothing. He slipped into his loincloth, leggings and moccasins. He did not look back as he shouldered the carcass of the pronghorn in one hand and his bow and quiver tin the other. Then he climbed the hill. Once on the crest he glanced toward her and then strode away. He walked the outer rim of grass until he laid down the pronghorn and studied the hole she had punched between two ribs. Had she really had such accuracy with an unfamiliar bow, lying on her side with only the quarter moon for illumination?

Behind him he heard splashing and forced himself not to return to watch her.

Instead, he sank to his knees before the antelope and stared up to the heavens, chanting a prayer of thanks, as any hunter should do, grate-

ful to the doe for the gift of her life. Finally he
prayed his thanks to the Creator for providing
all creatures and then added a song for patience
and strength.

When the last note of his song disappeared, he
retrieved his arrow and returned it to his quiver
as he worked with the doe.

He did not hear so much as sense her approach.
Her tread was light and graceful. Snow Raven's
skin now shown silver in the moon's light. The
rabbit-skin dress was back in place, but the length
still revealed much of her shapely legs. His body
gave another tug and he sighed.

"You will have a cape next," he said.

"I may keep the pronghorn hide?" she asked.

"You killed it. Of course it is yours."

"Your mother will not like that."

That was true. He had had words with his
mother over the rabbit hides, and he wondered if
his mother was now realizing why he had been
so generous with his first captive.

"It is yours," he said again.

"Then, I will give it to Little Deer."

"Who?"

"The youngest captive of your people. Her
dress is in ruins."

Your people. Of course, she saw them all as
other.

Why was she providing for another captive? He

wanted her to keep the hide, but he said nothing as he began skinning the doe and she gathered buffalo chips and dry sticks from the cottonwood grove.

"Would you like the liver?" he asked her. "Or the heart?"

"Both. I am so hungry I could eat the hide."

He remembered his grandmother speaking of a time when the people did just that, boiling hides and drinking the broth. Now there was plenty. He could not imagine a time when there would not be enough buffalo to feed them all.

She gathered the fuel. He butchered the meat. This time there were no prying eyes. He did not have to be war chief and she did not have to be captive. For this evening they seemed alone in the world and he felt comfortable and content.

He found himself wishing he could keep the sun from rising. Together they laid the tinder. From his pouch he drew his steel and flint. The days had been dry, so he was careful to clear the ground so a stray ember would not set the plain ablaze.

As the coals grew hot, Snow Raven raked the embers aside and set the meat roasting. He watched her, finding pleasure in her graceful movements. He was happy just being near her. Here he did not have to be a wise leader or a brave

war chief or court a woman he did not want. With
her, he could be himself.

She turned the roasting meat again, testing the
firmness of the flesh with a finger and then offering him the stick. He accepted it and waited
until she had her own.

They ate in silence. She seemed to be trying
to eat as much as she could hold. Afterward she
drew close to the fire. Nights were cold, and she
had only her thin dress to warm her.

He settled in beside her, looping an arm about
her shoulders. She glanced at him and then back
to the fire. She did not move away. He thought it
the most perfect moment of his life, sitting side
by side, her body tucked against his. She looked
toward the heavens.

"Do you see the Way of Souls?" she asked,
pointing at the band of white stars that littered the
sky, marking the path to the Spirit World.

He nodded. "One day, we will all walk that
way. My people call it the Ghost Road."

He felt her head move as she silently agreed.
"I have heard it called such, as well."

They sat there in silent contemplation for some
time.

"Your mother has walked this way," he said,
recalling that she had told him this. He worried
for a moment that his tribe might be responsible
for her death. He knew what it was to grow up

with such hatred in one's heart and did not want her broken in that way.

"Yes. Spotted sickness took her and many others. It is why we moved into the tall grass."

So their chief was caught between the white man's diseases and Sioux land. A difficult choice.

"I am sorry," he said.

"I was sick, too. But she left me here on the Red Road and went on ahead of me. See?" She turned her head and pointed to a place beside one eyebrow. "There is the scar here from one of the spots, and here beside my mouth."

He had not noticed the tiny blemishes before, but now he could see the small marks she revealed. They seemed to add to her beauty, giving her the imperfections that told who she was.

"Yes. They are small."

Snow Raven settled beside him again and gazed upward. "When she left I was angry for a long time. I would not do as my grandmother told me. I went into the woods and stayed there for many days. I did not come when they called. I did not follow when the tribe left."

Like a vision quest, alone, without food for many days. He thought of his own quest and the wolf that had given him his name.

"That was dangerous."

"I wanted to follow her. I waited in the woods

thinking that when the stars came down to touch
the lake I would be able to follow."

Like the story, he thought.

"I woke in a new snow to find a raven sitting
on the stump beside me. It watched me with hungry eyes, so I thought I was already dead. When
I did not rise to follow, it came back and called
again. Finally, I followed. The raven led me to
a pronghorn with a leg trapped in a hole, and
then I knew two things. I was not supposed to
follow my mother and that I would call myself
Snow Raven."

"I have heard of ravens leading hunters to a
kill. They are very smart and know that we will
always leave some meat for them."

"That is what I did. When I got back to our
camp, I found my father and brother waiting. Just
their tepee all alone in the empty camp. I told
my father I was a hunter and that I needed a
horse."

"What did he say?"

"Nothing, but he gave me a horse."

"How did your mother call you?"

"I do not speak that name. That girl is gone."

"I will call you Raven."

She nodded. "That is what my family calls me.
My father, grandmother and my brother."

"Your brother?" He had a curious suspicion.

"Yes. You fought him, knocked him from his horse."

"That was your *brother*?" His voice was louder than he had meant it to be. "Bright Arrow."

"Yes."

"So you are…the daughter of Six Elks."

"I am."

Chapter Eleven

No wonder she was so brave, Running Wolf thought. Six Elks was a legend. Until Running Wolf's raid, no one had ever defeated the old Crow leader. He was infamous for taking no captives and killing every enemy on sight.

A second realization rocked him. He had come so close to turning back and killing the warrior who fought for Snow Raven. If he had killed Bright Arrow, such a thing would have driven them apart forever. He met her gaze, seeing that she had known this all along, how near he had been to losing all hope of ever having her willing and wanting in his arms.

Did she also remember that he had spared her brother's life?

"Why tell me this?" he asked.

"So you will know why I cannot be like the other captives. They know who I am and they look to me for…courage."

"How do you know I will not tell my chief, use you to lure your father into battle?"

"He has not come because you have taken all they had. They will be lucky to survive the winter, and he is too wise to risk more men to recover me."

Her thinking was good.

She lowered her head and spoke in a much softer tone, all the bravado gone from her voice. "Also, you have earned the truth."

"How?"

"Sparing my brother. Allowing me to keep the hides I catch. Leaving me your stew bowl when your mother would not feed me. Allowing me to keep the pemmican I took from your food stores. Giving me a blanket. Letting me sleep inside your lodge."

He had done all those things.

"Do you trust me?" he asked.

"No. I am grateful to you. You are strong, but you do not need to destroy those who are weaker. I think you would make a good chief."

He reminded himself that it was a chance he would never have if he picked Snow Raven over his duty.

"But I would not stay with your mother if you marry Spotted Fawn," she said.

Was she asking to come with him? He hoped so, but then he was struck with a vision of Spotted

Fawn, the daughter of a chief, sharing his lodge with the daughter of another chief. He grimaced. The two women were so different, but he knew a young bride would not relish her husband's attentions to a captive.

"You might be safer with my mother."

"The morning your mother found me inside her lodge," said Raven, "when you went to bathe, she chased me out with a knife."

"Why did you not tell me this?"

"If you defend me, it will make matters worse."

Likely true, he realized, contemplating the problem.

"She wants you to court Spotted Fawn. She thinks your interest toward me is unseemly, that I am encouraging you."

He found that all he wanted in the world was to hold her in his arms. All other ambitions and all his plans dissolved like the mud that had caked their bodies.

What was happening to him?

"My mother hates all Crow," he said.

"And I am both Raven and Crow," she joked.

But he had no laughter for her humor.

"Raven, you have told me who you are. Now hear who I am. My father was killed by Crow. My mother says that she will mourn him forever and will not marry again. She has no other sons. My father's brother was also killed by the enemy and so could not take my mother as a second wife. This adds fuel to her hatred of the Crow."

She drew her knees to her chest and hugged her legs, rocking slightly, like a child seeking comfort. "Again and again, we kill and are killed. Only the hate lives on."

Their gazes met and held.

"Is that why you are war chief?" she asked. "So you can kill as many Crow as possible?"

"He was my father."

"And my uncle and the fathers and brothers of my friends. How many will be enough?"

He shook his head. "I do not know." In truth he had never thought to ask such a question. But then again, he had never sat under the stars with the daughter of a Crow chief. "I think only of my duty and the next coup."

"We were pushed from the mountains, you know?"

He was silent, staring at the coals as they collapsed upon themselves.

"The whites build their forts in our land and the diseases came."

"One day we will have to fight them, too," he said.

"Yes. I think so."

Raven caught his gaze once again. "I know of your mother's hatred. What of yours?"

"I do not hate the Crow or the Blackfoot. I

only defend what is ours and take what they cannot protect. This is all there is for me." Or it had been all. He scrubbed his jaw with his knuckles, feeling the scratch of the growing beard and the prickle of her questions. "I want only to lead my people with honor, earn coups for brave deeds and have stories of my battles told when I am an old man." Or that was what he had thought he wanted. Sitting so close to her, he wondered if life might offer more.

"You are war chief."

He nodded. "I have the honor."

"And your mother says you will be chief one day. Is that so?"

He lowered his head in modesty and to hide the confusion that tore at him. Why should he care what this woman thought of him? She should be nothing but a captive, a Crow.

"You have asked many questions. Now answer one of mine." He liked the way she met his gaze directly. "Why are you not married?"

She laughed, a musical sound of merriment that resonated inside him.

"I have shared a blanket with some of the warriors in my tribe. But none have yet offered a bridal gift."

Did the Crow women do as the Sioux? Did they stand outside their parents' tepee, wrapped with a blanket with their sweethearts, making plans for their future and… His smile dropped away. The image of her in the arms of another man raised only fury in him. He knew this was unreasonable and struggled to control his ire.

"Are you all right?" she asked.

"But you have not chosen?"

"No. None have made my heart soar." She cast him a long look, and he felt a surging of hope that he was the man that made her feel like a hawk in flight.

Is it me? he wanted to ask. Instead, he said, "For me, also."

"But what of Spotted Fawn?"

"A difficult situation. Her father encourages me. His new wife has not. Now I find that my friend has secretly loved her but been too shy to speak to her."

"Big Thunder, Weasel or Crazy Riding?"

She knew his closest friends. What else did she know?

"Big Thunder," he said.

"I see him hanging about her. She speaks of you and of him."

"Does she?" he asked. When really he wanted to tell her not to talk about Spotted Fawn. To forget her and the tribe and the world beyond their fire.

"I know she has no favorite, but is ambitious and thinks you would be a good choice. But she says you are too serious. She said she has never heard you laugh."

"I smile." *I smile with you because you make me happy.*

"Yes, but not often."

"When do you speak to Spotted Fawn?"

"I have not. But I hear her talk to the women at the river, when I carry water. Usually, they take no notice of me. Usually."

He lifted his brows. "Usually?"

"Red Hawk was there."

This got his attention. "At the women's bathing area? What happened?"

"He said that if I speak to his wife he will cut out my tongue. And if I touch her again, he will cut off my hands."

Now Running Wolf was simmering like the coals. Red Hawk had no right to threaten his captive. He wanted to go find this man and drag him from his lodge. Instead, he clasped Snow Raven's hand and thrilled at her sharp intake of breath.

"If he touches you, he will be very sorry." He lifted her hand and pressed his lips to the back of it.

This time, her smile reached her eyes.

"Red Hawk asked Spotted Fawn if she would like to come to his tepee for a meal. He said his wife wanted to talk to her. That night she told her mother that Buffalo Calf asked her if she would be interested in being Red Hawk's second wife."

This made him sit up straight. "What?"

"She told Buffalo Calf that it was an honor and she would have to consider that. But she told her mother that Red Hawk is too old and wrinkly. Though her mother said that he is destined to be on the council of elders and would be a good choice."

"Would you make such a choice?"

"I might." But she shook her head. "I understand it. Many women would. But I am different. Not so ambitious." She looked at him a long moment. "I would choose for love, and I would want a husband who will think of me before all else."

His fingers slid from hers. "That is not the way for a man. He must always think of his people first. His duty to his family is only part. He has a duty to the tribe."

"I know this in my head. But my heart speaks its own tongue. Perhaps this is why I have found no man. The man I take will know that if it comes to a choice between the two, he would choose me."

"This is a kind of selfishness. Only by the survival of the tribe do the people survive. A man must risk his life to save his people."

"Then, he should do no less for the woman he wishes to wed."

"Anything else?"

"He must make my skin tingle and my heart beat fast."

"Yes. On that we agree." He smiled.

"And he must be a skilled horseman."

"What if he could beat you in a race?" He grinned at the prospect of racing over the prairie after Snow Raven.

"That would be a start."

"Perhaps I will race you."

Her smile died and she looked at him with sad eyes. "We will never race."

He knew she was right. Women of his tribe used horses to carry and to drag their possessions. They never rode out alone, as he suspected Snow Raven once did. She knew her place, even if he had forgotten it.

He flicked a broken stick into the fire, feeling morose now, trapped like one of her rabbits. The more he struggled, the tighter the noose became.

She sat with perfect stillness, savoring the heat of the fire.

"You asked me of Spotted Fawn," he said. "I would tell you something I have shared with no other."

She straightened, giving him the gift of her attention.

"All these other women." He waved a hand in the direction of the tribe. "They bore me. They all bore me. I cannot imagine spending a meal with any of them, let alone a lifetime. Now I have finally met one who interests me and stirs my blood." He stroked a finger down her soft cheek. "She rides and hunts and does not speak nonsense, and she is you."

Raven pressed her fist to her mouth and regarded him in silence.

"I cannot have you, Raven. Not and do my duty. I cannot choose a captive as a wife and lead my warriors against yours."

"I understand."

"Do you? Before I met you I knew what to do. The ground beneath me did not heave and shudder. I never asked the questions that you ask, like when is the killing enough? I fear if I stay here with you I will not want to do what a man must do, that I will not want to ever go back. But I must."

She bowed her head and pressed her hands over her face. Her words were muffled, but he heard each one. "Even if you asked, I could not take you as my husband."

He narrowed his eyes. "You are a captive. Marrying me would raise your status, make you one of us. You have everything to gain."

"It would raise my status among my enemies and lower it among the other captives."

"Why do you care what they think?"

"Because they are Crow and I am Crow." She beat her fist on her breast. "Do you think you are the only one that risks losing who and what you are? I am the daughter of a chief. I am a Crow woman. If I married you, what would I be? No one. My father would have nothing to do with me. My brother? You might have to kill him in a battle. Do you know what that would do to me? I cannot. I will not."

"What do we do, then?"

She lowered her head and gripped her fists in her hair.

"I only know what I cannot do. I cannot be your woman."

The silence stretched. He wrapped an arm about her. She resisted the pressure of his embrace.

"In the darkness, one cannot see who is Crow and who is Sioux."

She relaxed against him, and he relished the feel of her warm body next to his. Why did this one have to be Crow?

After a time, her head sank forward, then bobbed back up.

He knew he must bring her back, because if he slept with her out here in the cottonwood grove one thing would happen, and even if it did not, others would think it had. He scattered the coals and covered them with dirt. Then he packed what meat he could carry in the skin.

He led the way back to their camp. Only once he was at the place where his mother slept did he recall that his mother had left only two sleeping skins. One for beneath him and one for over him. He dragged away the top buffalo robe and pointed to it. Snow Raven wrapped herself up in her blanket and the robe with her back toward him. He did the same.

It did not help.

All he could think of was that she was lying at arm's length and he could pull her to him and they could touch and lick and fondle until they both found release. He feared that even this would not satisfy him, for he no longer wanted just her body. He knew he would not force her because taking her would help kill everything that was interesting and good inside her.

Instead, he rolled to his back and looked at the stars a long time, searching for some way to have Raven and keep his place in the tribe.

Running Wolf opened his eyes to see Snow Raven kneeling at his side and putting the second buffalo robe over him. She swept back the hair from his forehead and pressed her lips there. He reached for her, but she was already gone.

The birds were singing around him as he

watched her walking with the six empty buffalo bladders in the direction of the stream.

Had any of last night really happened? Had she killed the pronghorn and had they sat arm in arm in the moonlight? His mother coughed and then made a startled sound.

"When did you catch this?" she asked, peeking inside the skin of the antelope at the tender ribs and haunches.

He answered with two words. "Last night."

His mother crawled from her skins. "We should give most of this away. Fresh meat on the trail is a blessing, but it will not last."

"Yes. Give it all away and give the skin to Snow Raven."

"Who?"

"You know who."

"Her name is Kicking Rabbit."

"No. It isn't."

Her mother's bright mood now darkened. "She knows her place here. Why is it you do not?" When he did not answer, she muttered, "We should give her away with the meat."

Now he was glaring.

"Will you ride with Spotted Fawn today?" asked his mother.

"I will ride with the men, as I always do. We should reach the herd of buffalo today."

In fact, they did see the buffalo. Running Wolf

was in the front of the line when they spotted the herd, covering the next hillside and stretching back as far as he could see.

"Tomorrow," said Iron Bear, "we will gather much meat."

On the ride back to camp, Weasel galloped past, whooping and shouting.

Was his friend as anxious for the hunt as he was? The truth—that he kept in his heart—was that he loved the hunts much more than the raids and far, far more than the battles. He was not afraid, but he gained no joy from killing enemies. When a buffalo died, it fed his family. But killing men was different somehow.

Raven's words came to him again. *When will it be enough?*

Big Thunder drew up beside him riding one of his traveling horses. Today his friend's face was all smiles.

"Spotted Fawn spoke to me yesterday."

He sounded pleased, and that made Running Wolf happy.

"What did she say?" He really didn't care one way or the other, but his friend seemed so excited.

"She said, 'Hello, Big Thunder.'"

It was all Running Wolf could do not to laugh. Where Weasel could not shut his mouth, Big Thunder rarely opened his.

"Did you answer her?"

"I did."

Running Wolf feigned that he might fall off his horse from shock, which brought a smile to Big Thunder's face.

"What did you say?"

"I said, 'Hello.'" He sat straighter and his chest lifted, reminding Running Wolf of a grouse fluffing his feathers.

"Well. That is good."

Big Thunder grinned. "I never spoke to her before. She even looked as if she would have said more, but I rode away."

"Next time, stop your horse."

Big Thunder's shoulders rounded. "What's the use? Her father wants you."

"Who does Spotted Fawn want?"

Big Thunder thought about that. "I do not know."

Running Wolf knew that choosing Spotted Fawn would help him with his ambition to rise to the position of chief. But he did not want to take the woman his friend desired, if you could call her a woman. And especially when there was no pull of attraction between them, no rising of heat, no yearning, no need and no fascination.

Only one woman gave him those feelings, and she was the one woman he could not take as wife.

His mother was surly at supper, despite the fresh antelope they shared. She gave Raven very little, and so Running Wolf stopped eating until his mother gave their captive a larger portion. His mother's animosity toward their captive simmered and Running Wolf worried. When his mother went quiet it always meant trouble.

Before sleeping she said, "I would think a man who lost his father to a Crow lance would know the enemy."

Running Wolf made no reply as he took to his sleeping robes. Who was right? Snow Raven, who questioned the killing, or his mother, who did not? Perhaps Raven knew her people were not strong enough to defeat the Sioux and so she tried to defeat his will to fight.

He tossed and dozed and slept poorly before rising fuzzy headed. This was a dry camp, so he could not wash in the river, but he greeted the sun and prayed as was customary. When he finished the short prayer of thanks he glanced around to see if his mother was about and was surprised to find her robes rolled for traveling and neither woman in sight.

He walked to the river where the women gathered water for the morning meal, but the only captives there were Mouse and a young one who held her torn, ragged dress on her shoulder. This must be the one Raven wanted to have the pronghorn hide. He was certain. Running Wolf also saw how thin and sickly they looked and felt ashamed.

He found Big Thunder preparing his best buffalo horse. This one was fast and could maneuver through the herd. He recalled the horse had been taken from a dead enemy that Big Thunder had killed in battle. Running Wolf paused to mentally count the number of horses he had stolen from the enemy or taken from those he had killed. Suddenly his precious feathers seemed to represent more than coups. They represented families whose fathers were not coming home. In battle he had never thought of anything but avenging his father. Each death was one more enemy gone. Each scalp lock a reminder of his valor. But had his opponents also fought to avenge a fallen member of their family?

When is it enough?

"What's wrong?" asked Big Thunder. "You look as though you have a stomachache."

"Have you seen my mother?"

"Yes. She was talking to Yellow Coat."

Yellow Coat was the French trader whose Christian name was Dubois. He was the only white allowed in their camp because he had married a woman from the Sweetwater tribe. He had come from the north, not the east, many winters ago, so he was tolerated, if not welcomed.

Most whites were killed on sight and from a distance. Since many carried the spotted sickness, they were treated like rabid dogs.

"Dubois is here?" asked Running Wolf.

"I just said so."

"Is Raven with my mother?"

"Who?"

"Kicking Rabbit," he corrected.

"Yes."

Running Wolf headed off toward the middle of the camp. What was his mother up to?

He found the women crowded about something. He pushed his way through until he reached a series of blankets piled with goods. White conical beads for breastplates and ornaments. Thimbles, tin cones, tiny vials of colored glass beads, string and brightly colored cloth, knife blades, ax heads and metal cooking kettles.

Running Wolf glanced about the gathering and saw many women admiring the goods. Where was Dubois? He found his mother first. She was grinning and nodding. Before her was a large pile of cloth, two red blankets and a cooking kettle full of white beads. She didn't have enough skins to trade for that many beads.

A shot of fear went through him as he found Raven kneeling behind his mother, her eyes down, her chin tucked so that she stared at the ground.

He walked straight across the blanket to reach them, scattering beads and cloth as he went.

"Oh, *mon Dieu*," said Dubois, his ruddy face

growing red. The man was short and round and as hairy as a bear, except his hair was more the yellow-orange color of a two-year-old buffalo. That was why the people called him Yellow Coat.

"What goes on here?" Running Wolf demanded.

His mother's eyes were bright with excitement but her smile seemed forced, as if she smiled only for the gathering of women.

"Look at the good trade I have made," she said, waving a hand over the stacked goods.

He did not look. Instead, he grabbed Raven by the arm and drew her up in front of everyone.

Dubois spoke in their language, but his accent was bad, so he used gestures, as well.

"Wait, friend. This one is now mine. Your mother has made a good trade. All this for one useless woman."

Running Wolf pulled Raven closer. "No trade." He emphasized the finality of his words by kicking the pile of goods across the blanket.

"But I have already made the trade," said Ebbing Water, her voice filled with astonishment.

"No."

"Why? Did you not give her to me?"

Running Wolf pressed his lips together to keep from raising his voice to his mother. She had him in a tight spot. He had given Raven to her, but only to keep Red Hawk from killing her. He knew now without a doubt that his mother sensed something was growing between her captive and her son, something dangerous.

"She is mine. You said so. Now I have traded her to Yellow Coat."

"No."

"The trade is already struck," said Dubois, beating his fist to his hand in emphasis.

Running Wolf could not think of what to say. He was not quick with words. So he acted, grabbing Dubois by the throat and drawing his knife. He pressed the point of the iron blade to the pulsing vessel at the trader's neck.

"You will take back what you gave my mother."

"Yes! Yes, I will." Then Dubois broke into his own language.

Running Wolf released him and took hold of Raven and his mother, pulling them away. But his mother would not go and tugged free.

"What will you do with her now?" said his mother. "Because I do not want her. If she is no good for trade, perhaps I will stick her with my knife, for she eats too much and works too little."

His mother did this to him in front of all these watching women. He was lucky that the men were not also here to witness this, as they were all preparing for the hunt. But they would hear of it. Such a tasty piece of gossip would spread far and fast. Their war chief fighting with the trader and his mother for a captive.

Her mother spat her words at Snow Raven. "She is Crow, and all Crow are better dead."

Running Wolf looked from his mother to Raven and then slowly about the gathering. All stared at him as if he was a stranger, and so he was, even to himself. What was he doing? He held Raven tighter, knowing what he should do and fighting against giving her up.

"Send her to the common women's tepee," said his mother. "That is all they are good for."

He looked about and his gaze caught on Spotted Fawn, the woman he should be courting. The woman Big Thunder was too shy to speak to. The woman who made his heart cold. Her mouth had dropped open and she looked as shocked as the rest.

"If you do not want her, then I will give her to someone who does." He turned from his mother. "Spotted Fawn lives in her father's home. Her sister and brothers have their own lodges while she takes care of her father alone."

"Iron Bear has a wife," reminded his mother.

"Whom she must answer to. Now someone will answer to her." He lifted his brow, praying that Spotted Fawn would accept this gift. He had no idea what else he could do that would not expose his shameful need for this enemy woman.

Spotted Fawn smiled. "I would accept her, if I have Ebbing Water's permission."

"Take her. But hear me, she is Crow and so will only bring you misery." She said this to Spotted Fawn but she looked at her son.

He ignored his mother's warning and pushed Raven toward Spotted Fawn.

"Go," he said to Snow Raven. She glanced back at him with eyes that told him what she thought of this. He had not freed her from the trader. He had only made her a captive to another.

But she went to Spotted Fawn without a word. He stood straight as the anger gripped him. He watched Raven take her place behind her new mistress. Why couldn't he pull her back? Why couldn't he tell his mother that he would not be ruled by her or by any other?

In that moment he recognized that Raven was not the only captive here. He was a prisoner to his ambition and the expectations of his tribe. He must choose a Sioux woman and have children and raise them to hate the Crow, just as he had been raised.

Now he knew that he did not want this. He wanted the impossible. He wanted Raven.

But he kept his face stern. Spotted Fawn positively glowed with pleasure and her eyes sparkled. It took him several moments to realize that by giving her such an elaborate gift he had as good as said aloud that he would court her. Next she would expect him to play his flute in the evening as the stars were growing bright and stand wrapped with her in a blanket outside her father's lodge.

"I thank you for the gift. Kicking Rabbit will be of much help as we make meat after the hunt." Spotted Fawn motioned to Raven. "Pick those up and follow me."

Raven glanced at him and then did as she was told, lifting the goods belonging to Spotted Fawn and trailing behind her new mistress.

It was better, he told himself. She was free of the trader and his mother.

The trader watched Raven go and then heaved a heavy sigh that made Running Wolf want to knock him to the ground. Running Wolf knew exactly what the trader had intended to do with his captive. It took a moment to recall that he had the same plans. But unlike the trader, he would not take her from tribe to tribe. Would Yellow Coat have eventually brought her back to her own people? What would her brother have traded to free her?

When Raven was out of sight, he turned his attention to his mother to find her glaring at him with a venom he had only rarely glimpsed. He knew what she wanted, what she'd always wanted—for him to kill Crow warriors. Only now, apparently, she also wanted him to kill women.

Well, he would not do it and he would not let her do it. Not with a knife and not by slowly starving her to death. Raven was better off with Spotted Fawn. Wasn't she?

Chapter Twelve

Raven followed Spotted Fawn to her lodge. As she walked, she fingered the tiny nick in her rabbit-skin dress, the one just below her left breast. This was the hole cut by Running Wolf's mother when she'd pressed her skinning knife so hard against Raven's chest that she had sliced the leather and broken the skin underneath. It was a tiny nick, but Raven had no doubt that Ebbing Water would have loved to thrust the knife into her heart.

What had stopped her?

Perhaps only that she would have to explain to her son. This was how Raven had awoken this morning. Ebbing Water's knife and her signal that Raven should be silent. Once they had moved clear of the place where Running Wolf still slept, Ebbing Water let loose a string of the ugliest curses Raven had ever heard. She'd called her every foul name she could think of and traded her away from her son.

Raven had followed Spotted Fawn with a heart that ached like an infected tooth. What had she expected, that Running Wolf would leap to her rescue and stand up to his mother before every woman in the village?

Only a fool would do such a thing. But that was exactly what she had longed for.

That made her the fool.

Spotted Fawn took her into the lodge of her father's second wife, Laughing Moon. Because of Raven's presence, Spotted Fawn did not simply duck into the opening to the tepee, even though the flap of hide was open. Instead, she called a greeting and announced them.

They waited until they were invited inside. Raven followed Spotted Fawn within and set the goods Spotted Fawn had gained where directed. Then she sat in the place of lowest rank, closest to the draft of the door.

Laughing Moon seemed delighted to have Raven. Both women chattered on about the meaning of this offering. Apparently a captive was an unusual present for a warrior to give his intended.

"She will be of much help tomorrow," said Laughing Moon. The chief's new wife was pretty and round in the face, with a high forehead and light brown eyes. Her young daughter, Gathers

Sticks, sat watching Raven with large dark eyes while her mother deftly braided her hair into twin ropes and smoothed the stray ends with grease scented with sage.

"And she can fetch water for us."

When Spotted Fawn turned back to Laughing Moon, Raven saw the smile vanish and her face go hard. It seemed the chief's young wife was not so happy as his daughter to have her here.

"I think that she should earn her place beside the fire."

Spotted Fawn turned and gave Raven a questioning look.

"She is still Crow, and I do not wish to have her slit our throats while we sleep."

Spotted Fawn lifted a hand to her neck. "If you say so, Laughing Moon."

Spotted Fawn waited until the work was done before sending Raven outside without a sleeping robe.

That evening she could hear the voices of the warriors as they met with the old chief in the council lodge that sat beside the lodge of his wife and daughter.

Raven sat in the dark, hugging her knees to her chest, wishing for the blanket she no longer had. Though the walk was short, Laughing Moon had been sent to help her husband home, for Iron Bear was feeble.

Spotted Fawn appeared a moment later.

"I give you this, so it is yours now." She held out a small buffalo robe that likely once covered a two-year-old calf. These yellow hides made the best lodges and were not often used for sleeping, but Raven accepted it gladly.

"Also, this is your water bladder and some dried meat." Spotted Fawn handed over the items and their hands touched.

"Many thanks. Small kindnesses are the greatest of all."

Spotted Fawn stood beside her lodge, looking down at Raven. The glow of her fire made the skin a lovely golden hue.

"Would you really slit our throats?"

"Not yours," Raven promised.

Spotted Fawn laughed at that. "A good start, then."

Spotted Fawn did not argue with her father's new wife, but she did manage to see that Raven had food and a hide to stay warm. Was she kind or just protecting her new possession?

Raven wrapped herself in her new robe. It smelled of cooking fires and leather and home. She fought back the sorrow that threatened to overtake her thoughts.

Laughing Moon appeared with Iron Bear, walking at his side, supporting some of his weight as he shuffled along, pausing to cough and spit.

Running Wolf followed behind them and walked within a few steps of her.

Neither Laughing Moon nor Iron Bear saw her. But Running Wolf did. Their eyes met, closing the distance separating them, and he held on until the tepee blocked him from her sight.

She shivered as she thought of the intensity of his stare and how hard it was not to follow him. What was this longing to be in his company?

She listened to the murmured voices. Spotted Fawn. Laughing Moon. The old chief. And finally Running Wolf. The night was bright with stars, and now that she had a sleeping skin she was warm enough. So why did she not lie down to rest? Why did she inch closer to the place where she knew he sat? It was pitiable, her efforts to be near him.

Still, he had saved her again today, kept that white devil from taking her from the village. She knew what that man had planned, had seen it in his eyes. The thought made her sick. But when she imagined doing that same thing with Running Wolf her body tingled and pulsed with need.

The council lodge flap opened and men stepped out. Raven retreated farther into the shadows between the two lodges.

Time passed. She dozed, coming awake from some unknown instinct. She looked up to see him standing over her.

"You," she whispered.

"I should not be here," he said as if to himself.

In response she threw back the buffalo robe that covered her, revealing herself to him. She heard his intake of breath as he dropped to his knees.

He wore only his breechclout, and she could see the soft leather stretching with his arousal.

"You saved me," she whispered.

"I captured you."

"I would have you capture me once more."

"We have no future, you and me."

"We have tonight."

Raven rose up on her knees to face him and looped her hands behind his neck. His arms came around her as she pressed her cheek against his chest. His heart beat strong and steady beneath her, and it gave her courage.

She reached to his hip to release the cord that held his breechclout in place. Her hands stilled as he stroked the soft skin of her hips, exploring her body, becoming familiar with the round curve of her bottom and the slope of her spine.

Raven rocked against him, her hips meeting his. Only the scrap of soft leather separated them, and it did nothing to disguise his need. She pressed firmly against his erection. He sucked in air between his teeth. Then he did capture her, his hands controlling, holding her in place, deepening the contact of their hips.

Running Wolf breathed in her scent as his blood zipped through his veins, faster than any arrow. Her hands now cascaded up and down his back in feathery caresses that drove him mad. He'd have to step away to release the barrier that separated them because she seemed to have forgotten her mission to free him. He struggled against his need to take her right here outside his chief's lodge, a few steps from the woman he was supposed to be courting. Should he take Raven away, somewhere they would not be disturbed?

He recalled stumbling on more than one couple in the tall grass when the spring afternoons turned warm and the insects buzzed from blossom to blossom. Now he was the bee and she the delicate flower. Would she open her petals and let him taste her nectar?

He longed to stroke between her legs to see if his touch excited her, but he let her explore his shoulders as her hot breath heated his flesh. She drew their hips apart and then thrust, bumping against his arousal. The signal could not be misconstrued. She wanted him and he needed her. Tomorrow, in the daylight, they must return to their roles of captive and warrior, but tonight he was hers.

Raven's hands looped about his neck and she leaned back, giving him a fine view of her breasts, full and round in the blue moonlight, her dark nipples tight and hard. He draped her over his arm, whispering to her secret words of wanting and of her power over him.

He wished he could spend each night of his life caressing her firm bottom and nuzzling against the soft pillow of her breasts. As he took one tight nipple into his mouth and drew, he felt the perfect bud draw tighter.

She was as malleable as hot clay. As he sucked, she fisted her hands in his hair, and made soft mewing sounds of need that drove him mad. He pulled her back to an upright position and she fell against him. He took a moment to release the knot at his hip and drew away the breechclout.

She stared first at his face and then her gaze slid down. He remained still for her perusal, but it was hard. He wanted to please her, excite her, drive her to madness and make her his own. But it all depended on her. Would she accept him?

Of course she had seen naked men. But had she seen one aroused and trembling with desire?

He certainly hoped not.

She reached, and before her fingers even closed around him, his erection jumped in anticipation. She gripped him with a firm hold and slowly pulled, letting him slide through her fingers. He closed his eyes to savor the soft velvet of her touch. She stepped toward him, pressing his pulsing flesh against the softness of her belly with her palm.

Was it that she was forbidden that made her touch so exciting?

When he opened his eyes it was to see her staring up at him with an expression of need. She smiled and he did, as well.

When she moved away it was to stretch out before him. Her body glowed, pale in the dark shadows of the lodge.

Her torso was narrow. Her stomach flat with a slight doming at her sex. He stared at the triangle of dark curls. Unable to resist, he dropped to his knees beside her and slid his hand over her hip and down into that nest of tight curls. She whimpered as his fingers slipped between her legs. Raven drew up her knees and then let them splay, welcoming his touch.

Running Wolf stretched out beside her, nestling close against the warmth of her body. She rolled to her side and rubbed her bottom against his erection as he stroked her slick, warm flesh. Raven rocked, pressing back to him and rubbing against his hand.

The mewling sound in her throat came again, and she could not seem to catch her breath.

He'd never taken a woman of his tribe. He had

never wanted a woman badly enough to make an offer to her father, until now. He was certain that Snow Raven was also a novice at this game, but somehow she was willing to allow him where no man had ever been. Perhaps, like him, he left her with nothing but a need too great to be denied.

He closed his eyes, knowing he should stop—knowing he would not.

They had no future. But they had tonight.

Chapter Thirteen

Raven lifted her head, offering her mouth, and he slanted his over hers. Her lips were soft and warm, her tongue pliant. He pulled her tighter. Running Wolf thrust his tongue over hers, showing her what he meant to do to her, tasting the sweetness of her mouth. Her cry of need muffled.

Did she know what she was doing? Did he? She was a captive, an enemy, and none of it mattered. All that mattered was his need to please her and to make her his own.

But taking her would not protect her. In fact, if any discovered them, it would place her in even more danger. How could he protect her from all the threats she faced? His mother, Spotted Fawn's inevitable jealousy, Red Hawk, who wanted her dead, and the men in his tribe who wanted her as a common woman.

His need put her at risk. He knew it, and his hand, the one that made her blind with need, stilled. He began to pull away and then *she* captured him, trapping him and guiding his fingers until they slipped inside her passage. His hands moved, one stroking the sweet slick folds between her legs while the other moved rhythmically inside her. All the while he rocked his hips against her, his erection pressing to her lovely round backside. But he waited, wanting her to know the joys of release.

She rocked faster. He matched the pace she set.

Then from her throat came the low moan. Raven arched against him, while deep inside her body the rolling contraction moved over his questing fingers. The next time she reached the crest of this mountain, he vowed to be inside her.

She went slack in his embrace and he held her, dipping to scoop her up in his arms. His first thought was to run with her, away from his tribe, away from his people.

But that was madness.

Despite what she had told him, that she wanted a man who would look to her needs above all else, he could not be that man. He could not abandon his tribe for a woman. True, he might someday move from his clan to the clan of his wife, but his wife would be Sioux. She must be.

Her breath still rasped, but her body was calm as he held her close.

How could he make Raven Sioux?

He recalled that Spotted Fawn had lost a sister. The baby had been born without a heartbeat. She could adopt Raven, bring her into her family. And if Running Wolf married her, he could also marry the sister of his wife. That way he could protect Raven and he could still make the chief happy, become the next chief himself.

He knew what she wanted, longed for. A man who would look to her needs before his own and before his people.

He could not. But he could protect her.

Raven opened her eyes and reached for him as he slid a knee between her legs. She spread her thighs for him, eager, he thought, for their coupling.

He reached between them, feeling the sweet slickness of her need. He would keep her, make her his in the only way he knew how. But would she accept him? Would she be pleased to become Sioux?

"Raven, will you stay with me?"

"Yes."

"Not just for tonight."

"If I was free, I would choose you, keep your lodge and bear your children, Running Wolf."

He closed his eyes at the meaning of her words, the ones spoken between a wife and her husband. She chose him.

She gave a soft moan of need and lifted her

hips so that his fingers sank deeper into her body. She threaded her fingers in his hair and tugged, bringing him closer.

She wanted him. He didn't care why. He would take her, protect her. Love her. And somehow he would bring her into his life. A captive. A second wife. He did not know. But he accepted her because he could do nothing else.

He moved his hands upward, and this time she did not stop him. He wrapped both arms about her and pulled her tight against the length of his body. His head fit beside hers and her back warmed his front.

"I will protect you," he said.

She gave a soft moan and she turned her head. Their mouths pressed tight, sealing their promises.

His hands roamed up and down, over her breasts, the soft skin of her belly and the strong, firm muscles of her thighs. She twisted so they lay face-to-face on their sides. Then she stroked his chest with featherlight caresses. He gasped as her fingers danced lower, collecting him in both hands and measuring the length of him.

He had been ready for her since the first moment he had seen her, but he wanted this to be perfect. He would not hurry. He would show the control he needed to so that she would know what life would be like with him, even if she must share him with another. She would be his favorite, though he could never say so aloud.

Her mouth was on his skin, kissing and licking. He groaned as he directed her mouth to his chest, holding her head against him. She hesitated only an instant before drawing his nipple into her mouth. The tug and draw sent an electric charge of sweet desire bolting through him, increasing his readiness and his need.

He leaned forward, nuzzling against the soft lobe of her ear as he fondled the swell of her soft breasts. She gave a low moan as he sucked. Her breathing grew labored and her expression strained. Her skin was flushed, her body all sweet surrender. In this, at least, she was willing to yield.

Raven trembled as she looked up at him, her eyes huge and dark. He could still see the need reflected there. She wanted him. He brushed back her long hair and then threaded his fingers through the richness of her mane, lifting her head, bringing her mouth to his. She exhaled the breath she held in a long sigh as their mouths joined.

He arched away, holding himself up upon his elbows, and ran one finger along the outer edge of one breast. She shivered and writhed. He made wide circles around her soft flesh, stroking, until her back left the ground in her eagerness to feel his touch. She captured one hand and pressed it firmly to her breast.

He watched her as he stroked the soft flesh on her inner thighs. She splayed her legs for him again. He looked down at her, open, wet and waiting, and his need surged like a horse galloping over open ground.

Raven reached up and gripped his shoulders, her fingers turning to claws as she scored his flesh all the way down his exposed back. The sensation sent chills down his spine and heightened his desire. He pushed one leg between hers and she spread her thighs farther apart. He reached between them to stroke the warm, damp curls.

She lifted her hips and tossed her head. He rolled between her legs, moving his hand from her aroused flesh to his, positioning himself to take her, feeling his own fingers slide over his erection as he lifted his hips, readying his shaft like that of an arrow. Poised and ready to shoot forward deep into her needy flesh.

Running Wolf did not dart forward, but lowered himself inside her with slow deliberation, a warrior claiming what he had won. His intrusion stretched her tender flesh so she seemed to be clasping him with her body. Each movement tested his will, for it was so difficult not to greedily take what she offered.

But a prize such as Raven's innocence was

more valuable to him than any coup he had ever won, for this was not something he took, but something she gave.

The barrier pressed against his needy flesh and he did not pause, just continued on with slow determination. He watched her face as her body yielded to this intrusion. Her brow knit for a moment and then she released her breath in a long sigh. She lifted her gaze to his and smiled as he settled as far inside her body as nature allowed.

And still it was not near enough.

They shared a moment of calm as he waited for her to give him some signal or sign that his claiming had not been too painful.

"Raven?" he whispered. "Are you… Did I hurt you?"

"No," she said.

He should have known that his warrior woman would not cringe now. Her courage impressed all, and in this moment she was no different—brave and eager.

He drew back and then moved forward just a bit. She groaned.

"Pain?" he asked.

"Pleasure." She stroked his face. "Don't stop, Running Wolf, do not ever stop."

Her heels dug into his flanks and suddenly he was the stallion she rode at breakneck speeds. He drove and she lifted to meet his stroke, her body squeezing his, causing the most maddening, wonderful, exquisite vibrations he had ever known.

Running Wolf's fingers danced over the wetness, his touch bringing a sharp, sweet stab of sensation between her legs. She felt the building tension that told her she climbed toward that magnificent shattering bliss.

Raven lifted her hips, bringing him tight against her. He rocked, in fluid grace. His glide and thrust drove her mad, and she tossed her head as her fingernails raked his skin.

The tension burst inside her, rolling outward like a thundercloud, sending vibrations of pleasure out from her center. She rode the thrumming pulse of gratification till the last sweet quaking dissolved into exhaustion. Her body trembled from fatigue, but now he bucked forward with a stifled cry of release. She felt the part of him that was inside her contracting again and again. She lifted her weary arms and held him tight as he fell half on top of her.

His breath came in hot blasts, sweet against her neck.

He rolled away so that he stretched beside her. The cool, dry air chilled the beads of moisture from her skin as they lay still. When she shivered, he drew her close and pulled the buffalo robe over them.

She had given her virtue to this man, willingly as he wished. She did not regret that, but her mind now jabbered at her like a blue jay in the woods. The other captives, they expected her to lead them, and she had agreed to go. But how could she leave this man? The very thought gave her physical pain.

"What will happen now?" she asked, more to herself than to him.

"What do you mean?" he asked. "All will be as before. I will protect you as I have said."

"Protect me?" she echoed.

The chill she felt now rose from within. Understanding came at last. Her feelings for him could not change what was, and like a sparrow in a tornado she tumbled where the wind blew her with no power to stop the storm.

Running Wolf tried to tuck her closer, but she stiffened in his arms. He lifted up on one elbow to look down at her and realized they were only ten paces behind the chief's lodge. Had he lost all reason? What if Iron Bear came out to relieve himself and found him here with this woman?

His brow knit as unease trickled through him. Had her words of last night, her reluctance, her proclamation that she could not be his woman because she was Crow and the daughter of a chief, had all that just been some trick, some bait?

Big Thunder's words came to him. His friend

had mentioned their bear hunt and reminded him that there was more than one kind of trap.

Running Wolf rolled away. Was she so calculating? It was hard to think so when she had been panting and purring beneath him. But she was a woman.

"What did you think? That I would bring you home to your father?"

Her silence was answer enough. When he turned to her it was to see her forearm thrown over her eyes as if she could not even bear to look at him.

"Big Thunder was right. But you will not trap this bear."

"I do not understand you," she said, and then lowered her arm so she could look at him. Her features were shadowed like the dark side of the moon.

"If I marry her, I can be with you."

"And what of me?"

"You will be safe in our household."

Snow Raven struggled to breathe past the shame and sorrow that rose up like floodwater. This was his solution. He would keep her safe by keeping her captive. This was not love, but just another kind of possession.

She would not live under the rule of the Sioux, even the Sioux who had stolen her heart. He would not bring her home. She must do it alone.

As her breathing slowed and she again became aware of the world beyond him, Raven glanced to the sky. The wind blew a sudden gust of cold air. They both stared at the clouds sweeping across the skies, blocking out the stars.

Running Wolf spoke. "A storm is coming."

"Yes." There was. And she did not know if she would survive it.

Chapter Fourteen

The tribe departed the next day in a cold rain, following the wide trail of the buffalo. By midday the scouts returned with news; the herd was just ahead and they would make camp here.

Raven helped set up the chief's lodge, and when it was up Spotted Fawn sent her to the stream for water. The rain clouds that had followed them all day now swept on without them. In their wake came wisps of steam rising from the warm, wet earth.

The mud tugged at Raven's moccasins, making her footsteps heavy. She glanced to the sky, following the flight of a hawk as it soared on the wind. Soon she must also take wing and be away. For the longer she stayed, the harder it would be to leave Running Wolf behind.

Raven found Snake first, trying to help Wren raise the lodge of the old widow. Raven lent a hand and soon the poles were up and the skin stretched tight. Snake set the last spike through the hide, holding it tight over the lodge poles, and Raven released her grip on the tanned buffalo hide.

"Thank you, sister," said Snake, wiping the sweat from her face.

Raven waved off the thanks. Little Deer arrived carrying a cradle board. Raven stared in astonishment and Little Deer laughed.

"He is not mine, sister. This one belongs to Snake."

Raven glanced at the infant. She felt slightly ill as the reality of the task ahead of her landed cold and hard in her belly.

The old widow, Pretty Cloud, carried a bundle of goods past them.

Wren waved a hand. "You can say what you like before her. She is deaf as a chunk of wood. They ought to call her Stooped Woman or No Teeth Woman. I have to pound her food before she can eat it."

Raven turned back to the problem at hand— Snake's child.

But Snake beat her to the question. "Should I leave him behind?"

"If you bring him, he will be the boy born of the Sioux," said Wren.

Snake rounded on her. "Do you not think I know this? Our people will hate him, these people will hate him. But at least there he will not be a captive."

"He will never be accepted," said Wren.

"What would you have me do, drown him in the river?"

Wren did not reply, but her lips pressed tight. Was Wren's sour face because she thought that this infant would slow them or because she so hated the Sioux?

Raven stepped between them. "What is the child's name?"

"I call him Stork."

She looked down at the small, round face of the sleeping boy. He was innocent in all this.

"A baby is born of his mother's tribe. That means that he is Crow and one of us. He will be no more to carry than a blanket or a buffalo robe."

Snake's strained face flushed red and tears welled as she stroked the face of her child. "Yes. He is Crow."

Wren lifted her hands in defeat. "Fine. But what of Mouse?"

Raven frowned in confusion. "What about her?"

"She is ill with her break with the moon." Snake motioned to the small lodge set some thirty paces away.

That was not too serious, thought Raven. The once-a-moon cycle of bleeding was natural, and required Mouse to remain in a separate lodge until her time ended. This was to protect the men and keep a woman from draining the power of his medicine from his person and weapons, while she drained of blood. But women had nothing to fear from a woman at this time.

"We can go to her," suggested Raven.

"Let her rest," said Snake.

"But…"

Frog stopped her words. "It is more than a break with the moon. I asked Turtle Rattler to see her."

Raven could not stop her jaw from dropping at this news. A medicine man did not treat one such as Mouse.

Frog nodded. "Yes, he saw her, because I asked it. He says her insides are bad and she cannot have children. He thinks she takes something to keep from getting with child. Perhaps that is what makes her sick. Mouse told him that she would rather die than have a Sioux baby."

Little Deer's eyes bulged. "Can a woman do such a thing?"

"Prevent a birth? Yes," said Wren, and then glanced to Snake's infant. "It doesn't always work."

Raven returned to the subject of Mouse. "Is it so bad?" asked Raven. It was rude to interrupt this way but she had to know.

"No one can bleed like that for long," said Wren.

Snake nodded. "It is very heavy and it stops for only a few days each moon now. The men will not take her, which suits her fine." Snake scowled and Raven recognized that with Mouse unavailable, Snake must be very busy indeed.

"You are lucky, Raven," said Wren. "If not for Running Wolf, you would be a common woman already." Wren looked to Little Deer and wrinkles etched her brow. "They'll wait for Little Deer to break her link with the moon so she can take Mouse's place."

Little Deer was only fourteen winters, according to Mouse, but would take her place with the common women. Raven needed to get them out of this camp before Mouse grew any sicker, before the baby got any older, before Little Deer was taken to the lodge of common women.

"No," said Raven. "We are all going. The scouts have found the herd. There will be a hunt and then a feast. We go on the night of the feast."

"Mouse is very weak. Maybe too weak to travel," said Frog. "Perhaps I should stay with her. I could take Stork, as well."

Snake looked at the older woman as if she had suddenly lost her reason. Her grip on the cradle board tightened.

"Should we leave Mouse behind?" asked Wren.

"No one is leaving me behind."

They turned to see Mouse step clear of the newly set lodge of Pretty Cloud.

"I will go when you go, and I will make it home or die." She looked at Snake and then to Snake's swaddled infant.

No one argued with this particular mouse.

Raven looked from one to the next. "We will see our mountains soon and join our tribes for the winter camp." Raven saw Mouse's head bow and she knew she thought of her husband and son. She squeezed Mouse's arm and their gazes met. "You will come to live with me in my grandmother's lodge, in the lodge of the chief of the Low River people."

Mouse cast her a rare smile and took her hand. "I hope I can repay this kindness."

Raven gave her hand a squeeze and released her. "It is no kindness to welcome one so brave to our home." She turned to the group, feeling protective and frightened and hopeful all at once. "The night of the feast. Be ready. Meet at this lodge when the men begin the buffalo-hunting dance."

The morning of the hunt, Running Wolf led the familiar formation. First came the soldiers, riding twenty across. This was his place. He had earned it with many successful battles and hunts. Big Thunder rode to his left and Crazy Rider on his right. Behind them were the hunters six deep riding five abreast. Behind the hunters came the people, ready to strip the carcasses of the fallen buffalo.

Running Wolf rode upon his buffalo horse to the top of the ridge, pausing for a moment to savor the anticipation of the hunt. There was nothing so thrilling as to ride at a full gallop into a herd of buffalo.

Unless, he thought, it was sharing a buffalo robe with Snow Raven.

He glanced back to the new camp the women had set. Already they stood behind the last of the hunters, skinning knives ready to harvest what their men could catch. Was she there with them?

Any moment they would sweep down the incline and the herd would run. His blood rushed in anticipation, for he loved the challenge and the danger of hunting these most mighty creatures.

He checked the leads that ran from the back of his saddle to trail behind him on the ground. If he lost his seat, he knew that he must catch the safety rope. Just a tug would bring his well-trained buffalo horse to an abrupt halt, even amid stampeding buffalo. Such training had saved his life once when a stumbling horse had sent him from his saddle.

This fall hunt would provide fresh meat for the entire tribe and, if their arrows were sure, enough meat to dry in preparation for the coming cold. He needed enough to provide for his mother and offer some to Spotted Fawn. He did not worry too much over Snow Raven's survival over the winter, for the chief would always be provided for.

Crazy Rider drew him from his musings of Raven. "This is my first hunt without Iron Bear."

Running Wolf nodded. It was a visible reminder that their chief could no longer provide for his own family, no longer ride. But he had two sons and the husband of his oldest daughter to provide meat for his family. Still, it caused more talk of who would take his place and when.

"If Running Wolf keeps collecting coups, he will be an easy choice," said Crazy Rider.

Big Thunder rubbed his nose and looked away.

"Do you not agree?" said Crazy Rider.

"I do agree. But there are those who think our war chief spends too much time in the company of the enemy. Red Hawk now tells all who would listen that you are as crazed as a bull elk and that this woman bewitches you."

"She is not a witch," said Running Wolf.

"But she is Crow. It is enough to ruin your chances."

Running Wolf did not offer a reply.

Big Thunder lowered his voice and leaned toward Running Wolf. "You are a leader, or that is what you told me you wished to be. A true leader leads by example."

Running Wolf glared.

"Are you really going to risk it all for this woman?"

Running Wolf pressed his heels to his horse's sides and rode to the top of the ridge, waiting as the soldiers followed, forming a long line.

The buffalo stretched out before them, covering the hill and valley. He waited for the call to charge and then realized the chief was not here to shout. He glanced about to see who would make the call and found the soldiers all looking to him.

Lead by example, he thought, and lifted his voice.

"Heka hey!" he shouted, and they all cried out in unison as they charged together toward the herd.

The women followed the hunters, using horses to turn the great carcasses from one side to the other. Skinning knives flashed in the sun and hides were gathered with the meat. Women tugged arrows from the bodies, each shaft assigning the prize to the hunter who had made the kill. Skinning the huge beasts was hot, sticky, messy work—women's work.

They labored late into the afternoon. At sunset they carried away what they could and left the rest for the scavengers. By firelight they cut the glistening red muscle into thin strips of meat. The persistent wind and dry air would draw away the moisture and leave the leathery meat that would last all winter as jerky or be pounded into powder for pemmican.

The next morning Raven's muscles were sore and her back ached, but she rose and gathered water before Spotted Fawn and Laughing Moon were even awake.

Tonight the tribe would feast. Tonight the Crow women would flee.

As she crossed the village she found the Sioux women already lighting cooking fires. In the center of the village sat the large open area where a pile of dry cottonwood awaited lighting this evening for the great central fire.

When she returned it was to find Iron Bear coughing so hard he turned purple. Turtle Rattler was summoned and gave their chief a tea to ease his raspy breathing. As always, the oldest captive, Frog, accompanied him. While the men, Spotted Fawn and Laughing Moon were occupied, Frog pulled Raven aside.

"You go tonight?" she asked.

Raven glanced toward Laughing Moon, who was lifting her husband so Spotted Fawn could pour the tea into his mouth. Then Raven spoke to Frog.

"Yes. Tonight," whispered Raven.

"I will stay here."

"What? No," she whispered.

"I have made a life here," said Frog. "And Turtle Rattler needs me."

"He has not married you."

"He has."

"Not to his people."

"In his heart and in mine. It is enough."

Raven blinked in astonishment, then gathered her wits. "When we go, they may take it out on you."

Frog lifted her chin a notch toward the shaman, who chanted over the old chief.

"He will protect me."

Raven glanced from Frog's confident expression to the shaman.

"If you change your mind, we will be gathering during the buffalo dance."

"I will not change my mind. Good luck to you," said Frog, and then returned to Turtle Rattler, kneeling at his side.

A Crow marrying a Sioux—their shaman. She could hardly believe such things were possible.

Chapter Fifteen

Raven passed the afternoon working with the buffalo skins. It was a tedious process, and she hated this work.

By the time the light faded and the drums began to pound, her back ached and her fingers were raw. Still, she washed in the river below the place where the Sioux women bathed. The captives exchanged looks but did not speak of their plans. There was no need. All were alert, anxious and focused.

The drums called the people to the gathering ground for feasting and dance. Raven's skin prickled with anticipation. Would they make it home?

She tried to rein in her nervous energy as twilight crept over the tribe, making the fire bright. There was so much meat that even the captives had their fill. The others watched her, and she ate a good meal, but less than she could hold. Little Deer, Snake, Wren and Mouse all did the same.

The Sioux women made a circle, without the captives, of course, and began a slow circle dance, their moccasins pounding the grass flat. Snow Raven inched farther from the central fire. There were smaller fires everywhere tonight. She watched the others gradually move to the shadows.

"There you are."

She startled to hear Running Wolf's voice. She forced a smile.

"Congratulations on a successful hunt. You have brought much meat."

"More than the women will be able to hang, I fear. Did you see my kills?"

She had, and congratulated him on his prowess.

She let her eyes devour him. He was safe.

"Did any fall?" she asked.

"No, but Red Hawk planted his lance in a mound of earth. I wonder if his eyes are bad. Also one of the young warriors, Little Feather, lost a horse to a bull's horns. Overall it was a good hunt."

He clasped her hand and tugged her away from the dancers, past the near lodges that ringed the central open ground.

"I have missed you," he said, and dragged her into his arms, his breath leaving him in a rush.

She closed her eyes and savored the sweetness of his embrace. What would it be like to stay with him, the way that Frog stayed with Turtle Rattler?

But the shaman had made Frog his woman, claimed her, married her.

"I have a plan," he said.

She knew she could not turn back. Without her, the others would have no chance. But still she grasped at his words like a hawk hungry for a mouse.

"What plan?"

"Spotted Fawn once had a sister."

Raven drew back, confused.

"I do not understand."

"Her sister died. She has lost a sister. That means she could adopt you, make you the daughter of a chief once more. Then as the sister of my wife, I could marry you, as well."

Her heart ached. This was his solution, to keep all he had—his position, power, status—and add her as a second wife.

She drew back and rested her forehead on his chest. "It is a very good solution."

The joy brightened his voice. "Do you think so?"

"Any captive would jump at such a good offer." But not her.

"It is the only way that I can keep you safe and have you as a wife."

"Yes. I see."

He pulled her back and studied her face. Did he see the sorrow that tore her heart to pieces?

"Oh, Raven. I am sorry. I know you want a man to choose you above all. But I am a war chief of the Sioux."

"Yes. A good warrior must protect his tribe first."

Could she have found a better solution? No.

Her answer was to leave the man she loved. And she was now preparing to do just as he planned to do, choosing her people above him. She could not blame him for doing the same.

She stared up into his handsome face. She could not have him, no more than she could follow her mother across the sky.

"No matter what happens," she said, "I will dream of you and a place where you and I are not enemies and can live together in peace," she whispered.

"We will live together. I will convince Spotted Fawn."

The girl was young, but she was not a fool, and only a fool would take a captive as sister at her husband's request. Did he not see that?

"I am lucky to have a war chief's protection, and know his love."

He stroked her cheek and smiled. "It is just the beginning for us."

"Yes. A good start."

Then she tilted back her head and leaned forward until her aching breasts met with the hard pressure of his chest, and still it was not enough. He touched her face, kissed her mouth and held her as if he would never let her go.

He threaded his fingers in her hair and fisted his hands, tugging tight so that a shiver of delight raced down her spine. She reveled in the look of need shimmering in his eyes and knew that her eyes were like mirrors brought by the white traders, reflecting back his passion.

She could not say goodbye to this man. But later, after they were gone, he would recall her words and know this for what it was: a parting.

The drums ceased and they paused to listen. The warriors gave a great cry and the drums began again.

"The buffalo dance," he said, his face animated, full of anticipation. "Come and watch me dance."

Chapter Sixteen

He pulled her along until they passed the lodges, and then his hand slipped from hers. Raven had to stop herself from calling him back for one last kiss.

He turned to her, grinning, as he entered the circle of men for the buffalo dance.

Raven looked past Running Wolf and found each captive staring back, faces drawn with worry. She nodded and retreated back into the shadows. One by one they would slip away. She thought of the bridles the women had made of their hair. They would not be strong enough. She must get strong bridles and saddles if possible.

She gradually moved back until she sat behind the chief, out of his vision. Then, when the men began to dance, she stood and walked away from the circle, carrying a horn cup as an excuse for her departure. She saw no one as they moved through the shadowy outline of lodges.

She knew exactly where Running Wolf and Iron Bear kept their bridles, so she took those. Then she took a good portion of the dried buffalo, Running Wolf's bow and quiver and all the arrows from the chief's quiver. She also stole the chief's knife. Finally she took both Running Wolf's hunting saddle and his war-saddle frame and what skins and rope she could carry. Laden with all this, there could be no other explanation of her purpose than her real one, so she skirted the lodges, moving in the darkness with a swift step.

The moon had not yet appeared, but she needed time to cut six horses from the rest. They needed only five, since Frog was staying behind. But it was wise to have an extra.

The boys who had the unlucky duty of watching the horses were all at the inner edge of the herd so they could hear and sometimes see the dancers. They whooped and sang in their own small circle, making such a ruckus that she could have been beating a drum and she doubted they would have heard her.

She began with Song, slipping a noose over her head and then bridling her within the herd. Her horse gave a soft nicker at her mistress's nocturnal visit. Raven set the small section of buffalo skin down upon Song's back as a pad and tied it beneath the horse's barrel. She did not place the saddle on her mount, as she thought the women who were inexperienced would need it more than she did, for they could grip the pommel for support. Mouse and Little Deer were small and could ride double tonight. She could not take any of the fast, smart buffalo horses because the warriors had all wisely picketed them before their lodges for safety from raids. She selected five more horses, saddling and bridling two and putting a lead on the final two.

She had the horses tied in a line when Mouse appeared with Little Deer and Wren. Wren carried several skins rolled and tied for travel. Each brought something for the journey.

"We brought robes against the cold," said Mouse.

"Four," said Snake, lifting the bundle in her strong arms.

"Frog is not coming," said Raven.

Mouse lifted her hands in a gesture of shock, and one of the horses shied. Raven settled the mare and tried to decide if she had time to change her out with a less jumpy horse. But already Snake came creeping along, a skin over her back so she looked like a horse until one realized that she carried a cradle board against her body. Seeing that cradle board and the anxious looks in the faces of the women made Raven realize the risk she took with all their lives.

They all stood shifting nervously from side

to side, anxious to begin. Beyond the herd, the drums continued to pound and the voices of the men reassured her that they were not yet discovered.

Snake helped Mouse up into the saddle of the second horse as Raven held Song's head and kept her still. Next Snake climbed awkwardly up onto the third horse and looped her infant boy's cradle board over the pommel of the saddle. Little Deer sprang up on the second horse behind Mouse, and Wren took the pinto at the back that also wore only a saddle pad of buffalo hide. With all mounted, Raven jumped across Song's withers.

All the women lay low over the horses' necks so as not to stand out among the herd. Raven guided the string of ponies through the others until she saw nothing before her but the open prairie and the waving grasses. The rising of the moon cast little light and the dark clouds swept across the sky. She hoped it would not rain again but then perhaps it would shield their escape.

She moved at a walk until they had crested a rise and settled down the other side of the hill. Once out of sight of the Sioux, she told them to hold on and began a trot that eased into a lope. She listened for a fall, but all the women clung like ticks on the ears of a buffalo.

It was a gamble. For the warriors would pursue them the moment they discovered their escape, and unless they found safety among their people, Raven had no doubts that they would catch them.

The race had begun. Would she find her people before the warriors of the Sioux found them?

She tracked their progress by the light of the moon and the racing clouds. The others were silent. The only sound came from the horses' hooves and the wind that blew from the north.

She headed southwest, knowing that her people would also be following the herds of buffalo that blanketed the grassy plains, as they did every year. The skins were necessary for food, clothing and shelter. Without them, her people could not survive the harsh winter. She wondered how her tribe's warriors would manage the hunt without their horses. She also wondered if she could find any of the Crow tribes before the Sioux overtook them, and then they would be saved.

The moon moved across the night sky and the women moved across the prairie. To the east came the first wisps of dawn fighting the storm clouds to break the day.

They had stopped only once, briefly, and then Snow Raven had made them walk their tired horses along in the darkness. She could see only a few feet before her and they stumbled along over the uneven ground, making a trail so wide that even a white trapper could follow it. All were thirsty, as they had carried no water. Foolish, perhaps, but the extra weight would slow them, and if they did not find help today they would be taken by the Sioux in any case.

Little Deer trotted up beside Raven to tell her that Mouse had fallen and refused to rise. Raven called a halt and found Mouse folded in a heap with the others gathered about her.

"Do you still bleed?"

"Only a little. But my thirst is great and my legs will not carry me."

"I will help you back onto your horse," said Raven, and then motioned to Little Deer. Together they managed to lift her to her feet. Seated Mouse clutched the horse's mane, and looked down at them.

"You should leave me here."

"No," said Raven.

She glanced out at the waving grass and the storm-filled skies. "Sometimes in the wind I hear the calling of my little boy. I know my husband has guided him to the Spirit World and that they wait for me there."

"That's enough of that talk. We go," said Wren. "They will be coming for us now."

The women looked back, but instead of the warriors in pursuit they saw low black clouds sweeping across the plain in their direction.

"Rain?" said Snake.

Wren shook her head and drew her baby, still

bound in his cradle board, even closer. "That does not look like rain."

"Snow?" asked Snake.

Wren nodded. "Perhaps it will cover our trail."

"Everyone up. We ride," said Raven. But she knew it was hopeless. The storm was too big and too fast. Soon she felt the sting of hail pound down upon them.

The hail grew to the size of her thumbnail. When it reached the size of a thrush's egg, she called another halt. They picketed the horses in a circle and the women all crouched on the ground beneath the buffalo robes for protection. The hail beat down upon them. From the edge of the robe Raven could see the white hailstones bouncing upon the ground and piling up upon one another.

When the hail finally slowed, they threw back the robe to find themselves surrounded by a Sioux raiding party. Little Deer screamed and Snake wept. Mouse turned to Raven and asked for her knife.

"Better to die here than there," she said, but Raven did not give it to her.

"Perhaps they will only return us to their village," said Wren.

"And perhaps they will only cut off our feet," said Mouse.

"Or send us all to the common women's lodge,"

said Wren. "Oh, I should have stayed with Pretty Cloud."

The men moved quickly. Raven knew their faces, but was surprised not to see any of the warriors she knew. These were the younger men, anxious to count coup and earn the rights associated. Did they not even warrant the attention of the senior men?

No, she knew those men had feasted and danced after their victory against her people. They would not go chasing after a few missing women.

Raven did not run, but waited with the others as their wrists were tied before them and they were placed on the horses they had stolen. The ride back to the tribe took less time than their outward journey. Raven was ashamed to see that she had carved a half circle, instead of the straight line she had intended.

The warriors announced them with cries of triumph echoed by the boys who shook their fists as they passed. What would happen now?

It was not until they reached the council tent that they were cut down and the horses led away. They were left outside the council tent in the mud to await their fate.

They watched the warriors come and go from the council tent. She watched Running Wolf exit the tent. He stopped and stared at her for a long time. Was that disappointment or fury? She could not tell from his grim countenance. But she recalled his warning on that star-filled night. If she ran, he could not protect her. The council now held their fate. Running Wolf turned and walked away.

"I will see my husband soon," said Mouse.

"Yes," said Raven. "Perhaps."

"Your mother waits for you there?"

Raven nodded, knowing in her heart that she was not ready to die. But this was not up to her. It was up to the circle of men now sitting warm and snug in their lodge, while their captives, wet and shivering, awaited their decision.

None came.

Finally Running Wolf appeared again and ordered the warriors on guard to take them to the tent of the common women. He told them to separate Raven and put her in the tent where a woman stayed when she had broken her link with the moon. She noticed as they were taken away that no man touched her, and she understood because they thought she bled.

Running Wolf was still trying to protect her, and though she did not appreciate being separated from the others, the knowledge that he still cared warmed her a little.

Later, as she lay wet and isolated in the dark, wrists still bound, she listened to Snake's baby cry in the night and then another voice crying and then another. Raven cried, too, quietly, alone in the night, while she waited and waited.

Chapter Seventeen

Running Wolf sat before his mother's lodge. He felt sick to his stomach and sick at heart. She had run. Hadn't he told her that he could keep her with him? That he could marry Spotted Fawn and she would live with them. In time she might even have become part of the tribe.

Now she had done this stupid, selfish thing.

But it wasn't selfish. He knew that. She had done all she could, risked everything, to bring the other captives home.

If she had been selfish, she would have taken her horse and run. He doubted that even he could have caught her, for he had seen her ride.

Now what was he do?

Big Thunder arrived and sat beside him on the buffalo-skin rug he rested upon.

"Red Hawk is still calling for their lives," he said.

Running Wolf sagged. "Are they considering this?"

Big Thunder lifted his eyebrows as if the answer was obvious. "She stole the chief's horse."

"He can't ride it."

"He plans to have it killed when he dies so he can bring it along to the Spirit World."

Running Wolf knew of only one other warrior who'd asked that his horse be slaughtered at his death. Most men were content to wait for their horse to arrive, or they had a quirt or dance stick made with the hair of a favorite mount and that was sewn inside the buffalo robe with them before they were placed on the scaffold. Often their favorite horse's mane and tail was cut short so their mount could mourn with the tribe.

Running Wolf started to rise. "I have to go speak with them again."

Big Thunder pressed him back down. "Wait until he leaves. You two cannot be at the same council fire together."

"I was polite."

"You were gnashing your teeth. If you keep on like this people will think you are crazy, or worse, bewitched by one of the captives." He gave Running Wolf a pointed look. "If any say such a thing again and others believe him, then none will listen to your words."

Running Wolf sank to the buffalo robe. "Has anyone said such a thing?"

"He has never stopped saying this. I said he was still mad because she unseated him. He was furious at me for that. But I said that you are protecting women, as we should all do, and that his actions seemed vengeful."

"And you have made an enemy of a man who may be chief."

"If he is elected, I will go and join the Crow," said Big Thunder.

That almost made Running Wolf smile.

"He has to talk himself out soon. The council is getting restless and wants him to give up the talking stick. I say, let him talk. It is the best way to see he never becomes chief. He is making everyone grumpy because they are getting hungry and stiff from sitting."

Running Wolf glanced at the sky that was changing fast from pink to blue. The captives had been returned early this morning.

"Has anyone fed the captives?"

"I don't know."

Running Wolf stood and poked his head in the lodge where his mother worked on a supper for them both. He asked her to bring the women food. She seemed as if she would refuse, but after a long silence, she rose and gathered pemmican from their stores.

She kept her voice low, so as not to embarrass him before Big Thunder. "This is a time for putting food aside for the starving moon. Not a time to give away what we have."

"I will hunt again before then," Running Wolf assured.

Big Thunder walked part of the way with them.

"Will you tell me when he leaves the council?" asked Running Wolf, anxious for another chance to push for leniency.

Big Thunder nodded and cut toward the council lodge while Running Wolf followed his mother.

They stopped before the lodge of common women, but she refused to enter. That left Running Wolf to bring them the food and water. The young guards looked horrified that his own mother would leave him to feed bleeding women. Both were still without their first coup and anxious to show their strength. He was their war chief, after all, and such a task was demeaning to say the least.

"A mother can make a man do what no other man would ever expect," said Running Wolf. "The same can happen with a wife or daughter."

"I'm never getting married, then," said Living Elk, watching Running Wolf's mother disappear.

"Do not say that. You'll insult his mother," said Spotted Horse.

"Are they still tied?" asked Running Wolf.

Spotted Horse looked to Living Elk, who nodded.

"Come help me, then."

Living Elk preceded him inside and freed each

woman so they could eat. Afterward Running Wolf walked with Living Elk the twenty paces to the separate smaller lodge where Mouse usually lived.

"Did you go in there?" asked Running Wolf. And better still, how would he get a moment alone with her?

"We just opened the flap and tossed her in."

And she had been lying alone and bound all day.

Running Wolf turned to Living Elk. "Tell Spotted Horse to watch the lodge of common women while you go and get me the hide of a wolverine."

"Wolverine? Why?"

Running Wolf exhaled his frustration. He was not accustomed to being questioned, and Living Elk realized his mistake. He turned to go but Running Wolf told him to stop.

"You can touch a woman who bleeds if you do it with the hide of a wolverine. Didn't you learn that?"

He shook his head.

He likely hadn't because Running Wolf had just made the entire thing up so he could be alone with Raven, whom he knew did not bleed. He'd chosen a wolverine because they were nearly impossible to trap, and so the furs were extremely scarce. It might take Living Elk a while to find what his war chief needed.

"I will find one," promised the young man. Then he set off toward the other lodge, presumably to speak to Spotted Horse.

Running Wolf bowed his head in shame. This woman had made him a liar. Still, he waited until he had ducked around the larger tepee before lifting the flap and entering the hovel of a lodge. The interior smelled of human sweat and musk and blood. His nostrils wrinkled and for just a moment he considered backing out, for though he knew Raven did not bleed, this place was soiled with the blood of other women, and he wondered if this might steal his power.

His hand went automatically to his throat and the medicine bundle that protected him in raids and battles. Then he called out to Raven.

"Here," she whispered.

He found her in an instant, struggling to rise, as she was still tied hand and foot. By feel he reached the bonds at her ankles and sliced through them. Next he cut the ones that held her wrists. She toppled against him.

"My legs and hands are asleep," she murmured.

He rubbed the blood back into them and fought the urge to sling her over his back and run for the horses. She could escape. He knew he could save her. And if he did this, all would know it was he who had let her go.

He would lose his place as war chief. He would

forfeit any chance of succeeding Iron Bear. But he would still be a warrior of the Sioux. He could still serve the next chief and fight his people's enemies. Was she worth the cost?

Raven stretched her legs and then flexed her hands. He drew her into his arms and held her and she rested against him.

"I am sorry," she said.

"Why did you go? I told you I would take care of you. I told you we could be together."

"Yes. But what of my people? What about the ones who are not adopted by the Sioux? Little Deer will be made a common woman any day and Mouse and Snake are already ones. What of Stork, her son? Will he be a warrior someday?"

He knew that the baby was half Sioux, but he was also half Crow. Where did such a boy belong?

"He would be accepted by your tribe?" he asked.

"His mother is Apsáalooke, so he is Apsáalooke. The Black Lodges tribe will welcome him and teach him to be a man."

Running Wolf knew Stork would never join this tribe, and if Running Wolf did not do something to stop Red Hawk's efforts, they would all be put to death.

"These women are not your responsibility," said Running Wolf, feeling as though he was talking to himself.

"They are. Can't you understand? They are *my* tribe. They asked me to help them. How could I refuse? And although I have failed them, if I have the chance again I would still give everything I have to save them."

She shamed him, for he knew he did not have the love in his heart for his tribe that this woman held for hers.

"I could save you. I could take you out of here now. Put you on my horse."

"I will not leave them."

"Alone you could make it." Even as he made this offer, he held her tight, fearing she would pick the others over her life. While he would pick her over anything and anyone.

He drew back.

"What is it?" she whispered, her voice telling him that she sensed some change in him.

"I cannot be chief."

"But you must."

"No. I would not have done what you have done. And even if I let you go, I would wonder if it was your tribe I faced. If it was your village I raided. It would make me weak."

"Not if I stay."

"You said you would escape again."

"I said I would help the others escape. If you marry Spotted Fawn and become the next chief, you can free them. Do this and I will be yours."

"I do not want to marry her. I want only you."

Raven shook her head. "Marry her."

"If you were not Crow, I would make you mine."

"I am Apsáalooke and I *will* be yours."

Running Wolf thought of her offer and her words. She'd just said she would give everything she had to save them. That included staying with him as a captive instead of riding free across the open prairie toward home. Did she love him so much or did she love her people so much?

If he cared for her, could he really do this to her?

If he didn't, he would lose her forever.

"Please, Running Wolf. Do you not see? This is a chance to help them. A different kind of coup."

He pressed his lips to the top of her head. "Yes," he said. "Yes, I will do what you ask. I will marry her and keep you safe. I will become the next chief and free your people. To have you, I would do anything."

She sagged against him, her breath ragged. He wanted to stay with her, love her. But not here in this place.

He released her and reached for his bag, offering her the food he had brought and waiting while she ate.

"I would keep you here until the council has decided. If they think you bleed, they will not touch you. It gives me some time to convince them to spare you and the others."

He offered her water and she drank thirstily.

"You will not leave this lodge until I come for you?"

"I promise."

Then he left her to return to the council. It was bright enough outside to see the other lodge and the shadow moving between them. Was that Spotted Horse returning with the wolverine?

He walked around to the front of the common women's lodge to find Spotted Horse guarding diligently. The young man straightened at his approach.

"Do you need anything?"

The young man shook his head and Running Wolf made note to bring this one and Living Elk on his next raid. Time for these young bucks to earn a feather or two. And he needed only a handful more to make his war bonnet.

Running Wolf returned to the council lodge after their dinner recess to find Weasel speaking about their war chief's bravery on the last raid. Red Hawk was not among the circle. Running Wolf frowned as a trickle of dread slipped through him.

He joined the circle, sitting between Yellow Blanket and Black Cloud, one of the council elders. Running Wolf glanced about to note that Big Thunder had not returned.

Weasel gave him a look that told him things were not going well.

"He is war chief and it is his decision whether to take captives or kill enemies. None who follow should question him. It is easy to question after there is time to think. It is harder to make the choice at the moment with what information you have. I would not want to follow any other than Running Wolf."

He passed the talking stick to the next man, Winter Horse, who held it for a moment as if considering whether he would speak. Running Wolf stared at the large open sockets of the coyote skull and the jaws that, even when tied shut, seemed to be laughing at him. Winter Horse passed the talking stick to the one beside him, Lone Feather, who spoke.

"Running Wolf is a good war chief. But he was different on this last raid. I do not know why."

The stick went next to Turtle Rattler, who also spoke. "We are gathered to speak about the captives and their escape. Are the two subjects related or are we drawn down a false path leading nowhere?"

Big Thunder ducked inside the lodge, followed by Red Hawk. They moved together and sat directly across from him between Walking Buf-

falo, an elder, and Yellow Cloud, a warrior. Red
Hawk and Running Wolf divided the circle in
half, with the elders on one side and the warriors
on the other. Big Thunder sat closer to Red Hawk.

A second row of younger warriors surrounded
the inner circle. Running Wolf looked around at
the faces. There were those who were also in
contention for chief: Yellow Blanket, the chief's
eldest son, Two Knives, Spotted Horse, Lone
Feather and, of course, Red Hawk.

Red Hawk was not favored by many because
of his lack of skills, the most recent being that
he'd counted no coup in the last battle and was
unseated by a woman in the last raid. More re-
cently he had faired poorly in the buffalo hunt.
Before this last raid, Running Wolf would have
said that the three favorites were Two Knives,
who preferred hunting to war, Yellow Blanket and
Lone Feather, who were both wise but old in a
time when many men wanted a young, vital chief.

And then there was himself.

He was under attack but must depend on the
warriors who trusted and respected him to speak,
for a man who must defend himself had already
lost. The talking stick went to his best friend, Big
Thunder, who looked at him directly and then
passed the stick along without a word.

Running Wolf felt a prickle down his spine.
Everyone watched as the stick made its way to

Red Hawk. He gripped it like a war ax and drew in a breath to speak.

Red Hawk had followed Running Wolf to the common women's lodge, and he told the gathering he had seen their war chief send away one of the guards so he could enter the place where women were unclean. This caused much shifting and troubled glances but none spoke.

Running Wolf sat as if a stone, for he knew what came next. Red Hawk was a poor rider, a worse shot and less than bold in battle. But he had an excellent memory and recited the words spoken between Running Wolf and Raven. How he was going to let her escape, but she would not leave the others, so they plotted for him to marry the chief's daughter so he would be the next chief and then free the enemy Crow. How he had said to her that he could not be chief because he would be a weak leader, unwilling to face and kill their enemy.

How this Crow captive had convinced their war chief to betray them all.

"Do you deny it?" asked Red Hawk.

When asked a question, a man could answer.

Running Wolf lifted his chin and replied. The shame was deep and red, but he was a man and a man admitted the truth. "I do not deny this."

The younger men forgot to be silent, and a buzz like a hornet's nest filled the lodge as Red

Hawk passed the talking stick to their chief. But Turtle Rattler stopped the coyote staff's progress.

"A young man who is brave in battle may be made foolish by a woman. All of us who are old were once young and remember this. An elk in the spring goes mad with love, crashing into trees, attacking any rival, even to the point of forgetting to eat and sleep. Men are little different. But when the spring has past the elk becomes what he was before and forgets his heated blood. I say that this woman must go, and when she is gone our war chief will forget her."

Running Wolf's skin dimpled in the warm air as an inner frost crept through him, freezing him to the spot. Suddenly he did not worry over his loss of honor or the certainty that he would never lead his people. Suddenly he feared for Snow Raven's life, and in that instant he understood that he loved her. He would do anything to save her.

The buzzing in his ears made it hard to hear for a moment. He concentrated, seeing Turtle Rattler's mouth move, but was unable to make sense of his words. At last he could understand again and his blood chilled.

"This woman must be killed. The others will then be as they have been. And as for Frog, who did not run, I think she should be rewarded and become Sioux."

Running Wolf started to rise and then recalled

his place and settled back down. Inside his mind he was running back to Raven, taking her to his horse and letting her go. Why hadn't he done that when he had the chance? He knew she could have reached her tribe.

But she would not leave her people, and he had still believed he could have her. His selfishness would cost Raven her life.

Turtle Rattler handed the staff to the chief.

"I withdraw my favor from Running Wolf, and he is no longer welcome in my lodge." He looked at Running Wolf now. "I hoped to see my youngest wed to a fine man. I still hope she will choose such a man, but I will not live to see this." He looked back to his advisers. "As to my successor, I make no recommendations but leave this to the council, who I trust will choose wisely." He had to pause here because the wind had left his body. His lips were now a constant and unnatural blue, and the whites of his eyes had turned the color of the yellow clay used to stain buckskin.

How many more days did he have left? Running Wolf knew he had disappointed the man who had treated him like a son and he had embarrassed his youngest daughter. The shame smoldered like the coals beneath the charred wood of a fire, burning hot.

Iron Bear regained enough wind to speak, but his voice trembled. "As to the captives, I begin with the one who remained behind. I agree with Turtle Rattler. She should be rewarded, adopted as a member of this tribe. The others I would put to death, for a captive who runs needs two to watch her, and that makes her a burden. As to the one they call Kicking Rabbit. This one may look like a woman, but her heart is that of a warrior. So let her die like a warrior."

"No," said Running Wolf. The word was just a breath, but he had spoken out of turn. Interrupted the chief. He stood to take his leave.

"Send warriors to watch him," called Red Hawk. "He will go to her and try to set her free."

Running Wolf found himself surrounded and escorted to the lodge of Turtle Rattler. Then a guard was posted. He knew he could take the man but he did not wish to add *murderer* to his list of failures. Once a man did that, he had left the Red Road. Such a man would never reach the Spirit World, but would be condemned forever to the circle of ghosts.

If they killed her, then he would die and they could be together.

Chapter Eighteen

The following morning, Raven was examined by Laughing Moon and Buffalo Calf, who quickly determined that she did not bleed. They dragged her from the small lodge into the sunlight, where she squinted and shivered at once. Her lodge was cold, but not as cold as it was outside.

Her eyes were still adjusting to the light when her wrists were bound by Living Elk under the supervision of Weasel, who looked apologetic, and Big Thunder, who looked as angry as a storm cloud.

"Where is Running Wolf?" she asked.

To this Weasel just shook his head and sighed.

Big Thunder answered, "You have destroyed him."

"What?"

Weasel spoke now. "Red Hawk was outside." He pointed to the lodge. "He heard you and Running Wolf. He told the council. Running Wolf is under guard."

"No," she whispered.

"Yes," said Big Thunder. "You shamed him and you have shamed the most wonderful woman in this entire tribe. If it is permitted, I will gladly kill you myself."

The look in his eye left her no doubt that he would do exactly as he said. He grasped her arm in a punishing grip and tugged her along to the front of the common women's tepee where the others stood, already tied in a line from wrist to wrist, so they looked like ponies ready for travel. Big Thunder tied her to the back.

"She should be in the front," said Weasel.

"If she had followed, they would not have escaped. Let her eat their dust for a change," said Big Thunder.

The line of captives was led to the central place before the lodge of the council of elders. The gathered assembly seemed to include the entire tribe. The people moved aside to watch them pass. They did not hurl insults or rocks, which surprised Raven.

It would have been better.

Now she did not know what to expect, but she found it took all her courage to put one foot before the next. It was hard to move forward when your mind told you to run. The other women hunched in a posture of humiliation and protection. The last defense of defenseless women. It made her angry.

"Lift your heads," she ordered. "You are Apsáalooke women, not dogs."

The women obeyed, straightening and lifting their chins. Raven felt a moment's pride in them. Then they were lined up to face the elders, now wrapped in their finely painted buffalo robes against the cold, frosty morning.

The people gathered to hear the decision of the council. Their once great chief, now stooped and forced to hold his eldest son's arm for support, stood before them. The captives stood, arms tied behind them. Laughing Moon and Buffalo Calf reported that only Mouse had broken her link with the moon.

Raven heard Buffalo Calf mutter, "Her link is always broken. Do you think it is from all the men?"

Ebbing Water shook her head. "You saw her breasts. They are full of lumps like the bites of a horsefly and some of the sores bleed. She is sick as a rabid dog. I don't know why they even took her along. Stupid. She can barely stand."

The chief lifted his hands and swayed. His son looped an arm around his waist to keep him from falling, and the entire tribe gave a gasp and then fell silent.

Iron Bear's voice was so weak it reminded Raven of an infant's wail. He coughed and wheezed and finally motioned to Red Hawk to step forward. The man was dressed in his finest war shirt. As he lifted his arms for silence, Raven stared at the fringe of hair on his sleeves, suspecting it was horsehair from raids, rather than from the heads of his enemies. Still, it was an ominous sign that Iron Bear had chosen this man, her enemy, to speak for the council.

"These women are not like our women," said Red Hawk. "Once they ate our food, tended our sick and saw to the needs of our young men." He looked at Raven as he spoke. "Some have even tried to forget that they are enemy. But I do not forget. They steal our horses like Crow warriors. So they will die like warriors."

There was a gasp from the tribe, for all knew that captive warriors were tortured in the cruelest of methods, their bodies mutilated over days so they could not pose a threat in the Spirit World.

Frog, the only one of them who had elected to remain behind, fell to her knees and wept. Her sobs echoed loud in the still morning.

Little Deer fell forward in a faint, taking Wren to her knees.

7

7

Snake held her baby in her bound arms. "What of my son?"

Red Hawk's mouth twitched. "He will not grow to be a warrior. One less to kill later on."

Now Snake fell to her knees with Wren beside her. Both wept. Only Mouse, at one end of the line, and Snow Raven, at the other, remained standing.

Raven looked to Running Wolf, who stood between Spotted Horse and Yellow Blanket looking pale and grim. But he did not speak in their defense, and the way he was flanked by the two warriors made it appear he was now a captive, too. What would they do to him?

He was yet a member of the council of elders, so he could speak, but he could not vote. Whatever he had done inside the lodge of the council to save her, it had failed because Red Hawk had known what they had said last night.

Now her people were doomed to the most painful of all deaths and an afterlife where they would carry the wounds inflicted upon them through eternity. Would her own mother even know her when she stepped from the Way of Souls to the Spirit World?

Little Deer cried and Snake held her child and rocked. Only Mouse's eyes were dry.

Mouse spat and muttered, "Better to die than live a whore."

* * *

Spotted Fawn stepped from the gathered women and spoke to her father before the tribe.

"Many of these women are loved. What will Pretty Cloud do without Wren?"

"This captive should have thought of that before she left her," said Ebbing Water.

"And Kicking Rabbit is mine. Running Wolf gave her to me. It is not fair that you take what is mine."

Clearly, none had yet told Spotted Fawn what had been said. Perhaps none on the council would ever tell her. Still, Raven worried that she would be shamed, for such gossip would not remain secret for long.

"She ran," said Laughing Moon.

"But I want her back," said Spotted Fawn. "She is my friend."

Raven felt the stab of guilt for having slept with the man Spotted Fawn intended to wed. Raven had even considered allowing Running Wolf to take her as his second wife without even consulting Spotted Fawn. Raven knew that Spotted Fawn did not love Running Wolf. She was infatuated with him and with several others, truth be told.

Still, she deserved better.

"No longer," said Red Hawk. "The council has decided."

"But my father has the right to make such decisions without them."

It was true, but unwise for a chief to make decisions without the support of his advisers.

"Daughter, come here." Iron Bear lifted his free arm, and Spotted Fawn stepped beneath the shelter of her father. He now stood, supported by his eldest son on one side and his youngest daughter on the other. When had his daughter grown taller than the chief?

"Take them to the common women's tent and place a guard on the entrance. None go in without the council's permission," said Red Hawk.

They were roughly dragged to their feet and hustled away. Raven found herself tossed inside the tent. Stakes were driven into the ground and each woman tied to one, with her hands behind her back, except Snake. She was first struck because she would not release her baby's cradle board. One of the warriors took Stork from her and passed the cradle board to another outside.

The warrior staked her with the others and she screamed and screamed until her voice grew hoarse.

Outside the drums began to beat.

"They are going to begin today! Now!" cried Little Deer.

Snake began to rock and babble in gibberish.

Raven stared at the closed flap of the lodge.

There must be something she could do to
save them.

And then she knew.

She was not sure if her idea would work, but
she knew that she must try.

By the afternoon, all was ready. The drums
pounded a steady beat. The stakes were driven
deep into the earth so that the struggling women
would not escape as bits of their flesh were cut
from their bodies. They would receive water to
keep them alive for a day, perhaps two. But eventually the pain and the loss of blood would be
too much.

Running Wolf had not been selected to admin-
ister the punishment, thank the Great Spirit. But
he would be here to witness it under guard unless he could stop it.

His efforts to speak to the council members
individually had failed. The chief refused to see
him. So he stood beside his mother, wondering
if he should kill the captives to spare them this
torment. It would be a mercy. But the thought
of driving his knife into Raven's flesh made his
palms sweat and his stomach heave.

"You look ill," asked his mother. She pressed
the back of her hand to his forehead. "Sweating."

"My heart is sick."

"Best she die here. She has already cost you

too much. Once she is gone you can begin to repair your reputation."

He did not think he'd so quickly recover either his heart or his reputation, and he found that he did not want to live in a world without her. But he could not follow her, because to take his own life would keep him from the Spirit World.

He looked to Red Hawk, who had volunteered to be the one to torture Raven. He looked gleeful, excited, his eyes dancing brightly. At last, Red Hawk's revenge was near.

The captives shuffled forward, each flanked by two warriors. The rope between them was cut and they stood facing Iron Bear, each before the four stakes where their wrists would soon be bound.

Iron Bear lifted his arms and the drums ceased. He looked even more ill than this morning, and now both his sons, Two Knives and Curling Horn, flanked him. His third son, Takes to the Sky, had died, Raven knew, in the raid where Mouse had been captured.

"The Crow captives are to be killed as warriors, and as warriors, they are permitted to speak before us. Do any have words?"

Raven looked about, waiting for the others to say anything they might choose, but realized that all looked to her. She returned her attention to the council and then to Iron Bear.

"I am the daughter of Six Elks."

There was a murmur that grew to rabid conversation all about her. Two Knives lifted his hands and Yellow Blanket called for silence. Iron Bear had been seated on a raised platform covered with fur because, Raven assumed, he could no longer stand.

When the gathering had quieted, Raven spoke again.

"I am my father's daughter, though he raised me like a second son. I am a warrior and I have counted coup against this man." She lifted her bound wrists and extended one finger at Red Hawk.

He brought his arm across his chest and slapped her. She rocked and staggered, but she did not fall. Blood now dripped from her lip.

Big Thunder stepped up beside Red Hawk. "She is permitted to speak."

Clearly Red Hawk did not want her to tell this story.

"She is a Crow. They are liars. No one believes her words."

"But she speaks the truth," said Running Wolf. "I saw her unseat you."

There was a long silence. Then Red Hawk spoke again. "No one will believe the words of a man who betrays his people."

"What about my words?" said Big Thunder. "Do you have reason to doubt me?"

"Or me," said Weasel.

"Or me," said Yellow Blanket.

Red Hawk's face turned scarlet but he said no more.

Yellow Blanket motioned to Raven to continue.

"I am a warrior and I am the daughter of a chief. I would make a fine servant to any chief."

"She makes a plea for her life?" said Red Hawk. "No! This one will die. The council has decided."

This time it was Iron Bear who spoke. "Silence. Let the warrior woman speak."

Red Hawk looked murderous, but he clamped his lips together and Raven thought that he would not interrupt again.

She spoke in a loud voice, so all could hear. "I stole Iron Bear's horse. I took it because I wished to bring this fine animal to my father. This horse is worthy of a chief. But I was wrong to do this because this horse must go to the Spirit World with his master. He must have his weapons and his blankets on the trip to the Spirit World. And he should have one with him who has sworn to serve him. I would be that one."

The interruption did not come from Red Hawk, as she expected, but from Running Wolf.

"No. She cannot." He seemed not to realize that

she would die either way and that being smothered or having her throat slit would be an easier death than the one the Sioux had decreed.

Their eyes met and she silently begged him to understand. Then she looked about to see if there were any other objections, and her gaze fell on Red Hawk.

He stood with a disgruntled expression and arms folded tight across his chest. Did he see his chance to take personal revenge slipping away?

"I have never heard of such a thing," said Iron Bear.

Turtle Rattler spoke now, his voice pleasant and loud enough for all to hear. "I have heard of such a thing in the time before I walked the Red Road. Perhaps some of you are old enough to recall. A wife who lost her husband in a terrible accident, a drowning. When her husband died, she cut her hair and blackened her face as is customary. She also cut her legs and arms, and this is also expected. She went a step beyond and cut away two of her fingers." He lifted his hand. "Many of you have seen this done. But this woman was not finished. All this still did not let the pain and sorrow drain away, so she took up her knife again. And she cut very deep and joined him on his scaffold and went with him."

Some of the oldest members of the tribe nodded as if in memory of this.

"But one cannot take one's life and expect to walk the Sky Road," said Two Knives.

Turtle Rattler shook his head. "That is for the Great Spirit to decide. Did she take her life or only give the fullest measure of her devotion to her husband? Who can say?" He looked at the chief now. "I only say that it has been done. I do not say that I have ever seen a captive sacrificed, but I have never seen one offer herself, either."

Raven watched the chief consider this and was afraid he would reject her. If he did so, the others would die. So she spoke again.

"You have said that I am brave. And you are brave. Such a man deserves a strong servant in the Spirit World.

"I, the daughter of Six Elks and Beautiful Song, granddaughter of Winter Goose and Tender Rain, Truthful Woman and Night Storm, will lie beside him on the funeral scaffold. I will travel the Ghost Road, and once he has crossed to the Spirit World, I will serve him and his first wife, Elk Teeth. This I will do, if he agrees to free the other captives and lead them home."

The tribe waited in silence for their chief's response.

Iron Bear rose, swayed and then found his footing.

"I am honored by your offer and I accept. On the day I pass from the Red Road and place my

feet upon the Sky Road, this one will be with me.
When I take this journey, Running Wolf will lead
the others to their people. He will not return until
he has taken a dream quest. When he returns he
will be welcomed. These are my words."

Chapter Nineteen

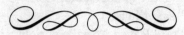

Snow Raven went with the others to the lodge of the common women and the infant Stork was returned to his mother. Their bonds were cut and they were permitted a fire and food. Snake opened the flap door to find two warriors guarding the lodge.

"What?" asked one.

"We have not eaten since yesterday," she replied. "My baby needs food and water."

"And you will get it. Now close the flap."

She did.

"You saved our lives," said Little Deer.

Raven smiled, pleased to know Little Deer would live, not as a common woman, but as a wife and perhaps a mother.

"It should be me," said Mouse.

Raven scowled at her and shook her head.

"Why?" said Mouse. "Everyone knows I'm dying. None of the men will touch me because they think I am unclean. And my husband has already taken my son ahead to the Spirit World."

"You are not the daughter of a chief," said Snake. "It would be a disgrace for a chief to take a common woman to the Spirit World. Especially one who bleeds. Oh!" Snake covered her mouth with her hand. "I understand."

"Yes," said Mouse.

"No," said Raven. "Snake is right. He would not accept you. It is my honor to go with him."

"Who asked you?" said Mouse. "Do you know what I was thinking while they were weeping on the ground?" She thumbed at the other women. "I was thinking, at last, I get to hold my boy, kiss my husband, see my parents. I am ready to leave this world, for I am sick of it."

"It doesn't matter what you want," said Snake. "He has chosen Raven."

Mouse folded her arms across her chest. "If I could take my own life, I would."

"Well, you cannot," said Snake. "Not if you want to see your husband and son again."

"You heard Turtle Rattler. He said it has been done," insisted Mouse.

"I have no interest in what a Sioux woman does. We are Apsáalooke, Children of the Large-Beaked Bird. Our ways are our ways. Frog may wish to become Sioux. I do not."

Little Deer crept close to Raven and took her

hand. "I, for one, would like to thank the daughter of Six Elks for her sacrifice. If she had not done as she did, right now we would all be screaming as they cut us to bits instead of arguing. This is not how I would have her remember us, bickering like old women. We should all thank her and honor her."

Snake began to cry, and Stork, seeing his mother cry, began to wail, as well.

For the rest of that day and all the next, no one bothered them except to bring them food, good food. Fresh meat that they roasted on their fire and wild rice in an iron kettle and dried cherries that they had soaked in water until they were sweet and chewy once more.

Raven savored these meals and her time with the others as she wondered how many more days and nights she had before the chief died.

It had been two nights since Snow Raven had made her terrible bargain, and in that time Running Wolf had gone to every member of the council, but none would support his cause. He had tried to persuade them that it was a mistake to send Iron Bear to the Spirit World with an enemy. But none would intervene.

The scaffold upon which Iron Bear would rest until his spirit left his body behind had already been raised.

Turtle Rattler had not left the chief's lodge for two days, and Running Wolf was not permitted to enter. Spotted Fawn came to speak to him and said that her father would not wake and now lived in a dream state between the living and the dead. She also said that Big Thunder had told her what Running Wolf had said to Raven in the women's lodge, and although she might have been very happy with Raven as their servant, all that had now changed.

She took hold of Running Wolf's hand and walked him away from her father's tent. Their path seemed aimless as she spoke to him.

"You are still a brave man with many coups. But if I married you, the women here would think me a fool for choosing one who chose me for such a reason."

Running Wolf felt he had done this woman harm and she had done nothing to deserve such treatment. "I am sorry for any pain I have caused you."

"It will be less than yours. This I know."

They walked a little more.

Running Wolf began to see that the only way to save Raven was to take her by force. Time was running out. He needed to ready his horse and weapons. He prayed to the Great Spirit he might take her without killing any of his own men.

"Do you really love her so much?" Spotted

Fawn stopped before the lodge of Big Thunder. He had had his own lodge for more than a year now, though he had not made any offers for a wife. Because he loved this woman, Running Wolf knew. And Big Thunder loved his friend, as well. Perhaps he loved him so well Big Thunder would have stood aside and allowed her to choose for herself without her even knowing he loved her.

"I would do anything to save her."

"Even risk your life?" asked Spotted Fawn.

He nodded.

"What about your people? Is it not your duty to follow the decision of the council of elders and as your chief commands?"

He could not answer, as he thought back to what Snow Raven had once said to him.

"Raven told me that she wanted a man who would put her first, above all else. I told her that only a fool would do such a thing. That it was a warrior's duty to serve his people. But now I find I am a fool."

"You could be exiled."

"If I am with her, then I do not care. When she came here, all I could think of was how to keep her. Now I realize what I should have been doing was thinking of how to keep her safe."

"Her before all else, is that right?"

"Yes."

"That is also what a friend should do. Keep another safe, even from himself."

He cocked his head, not understanding what she meant.

"That is what Big Thunder would do for you. Keep you safe."

Running Wolf felt a sharp blow to his head followed by a splitting pain. He turned to see Big Thunder holding a club. Running Wolf lifted his hands to his head and tried to form his words, but everything was spinning now and his knees gave way.

"It is for your own good, friend."

Running Wolf woke on the ground to find his arms bound to his legs. Was it dark outside or was he blind? Running Wolf wrestled himself out from under a buffalo robe and looked about, recognizing the lodge of Big Thunder. The light inside the lodge was dim, as if there was a storm, but he heard no rain.

Was he alone?

He wiggled and his arms tingled. It was a moment before he realized that it was not his head pounding, but the drums. Running Wolf straightened.

"Untie me."

There was no reply.

The lodge door flap flew open and Big Thunder peered in.

Big Thunder's head filled the circular opening. "It has happened."

Running Wolf did not have to ask what he meant. Iron Bear was dead. Big Thunder did not say so directly because it was improper to speak the name of the dead and it could be dangerous, for calling a ghost was never a good idea. They were referred to only indirectly.

"Laughing Moon and Spotted Fawn are preparing him for his journey."

"When?" he asked.

"Now."

Running Wolf struggled. They would kill Raven any moment now. He had to get up. He tried twice before realizing that he was tied hand and foot.

"Laughing Moon insists that we wait one day to be sure he is really gone, but they are to prepare his servant and his horse now."

Now. Why hadn't he set her free when he had the chance?

"Let me up, Big Thunder!"

The tepee flap dropped back into place.

Chapter Twenty

❧◈❧

Raven and the others received word in the afternoon that the chief had died and that they were preparing his body. She was to prepare for her journey, as well.

"When?" asked Mouse.

"Tonight," said the guard.

She was not afraid, though she was sorry she would not see her father and brother again.

She spoke to Little Deer and made her promise to tell them what had happened. She wanted them to show her where to find her bones. She knew her tribe collected the bones of important members and placed them around the scaffolds of their leaders. It was an honor to have her bones treated in this manner.

The following morning, Ebbing Water and Buffalo Calf arrived and all the women were escorted by four warriors to the river to bathe. It seemed they did not want the chief's servant to try another escape. But she was content with her bargain. It hurt only when she thought of Running Wolf and the life they might have shared.

"Are you frightened?" whispered Snake.

"No. Just sad. I wish I could tell Running Wolf once more that I love him and that I am sorry."

"I will tell him for you," said Snake.

Raven smiled. "Thank you."

The men turned away as the captives stripped from their ratty garments. The only one among them with a decent dress was Raven, with her patches of rabbit skin, and Mouse, who had earned enough skins from her admirers to make a fine elk-skin dress. It was hard to believe now, but her figure was once curvy and lush. Now she was small, like Raven, but not so strong.

Raven helped her draw off the dress, careful of the fine beadwork across the front. That was when they all saw the terrible sores that Mouse had kept hidden from them.

"She still bleeds," said Buffalo Calf. "I for one will not touch her."

"What if this illness is catching, like the spotting sickness?" asked Ebbing Water. "We might both wind up like that." She pointed at the gaunt woman.

"They can paint themselves," said Buffalo Calf. "Surely they know how to paint their faces black in mourning." She looked at them.

Mouse spoke. "We do." She motioned to the middle of her chest. "Black to here." And then she made a cutting motion at her elbow. "And to here. Do you wish us to cut our hair?"

The two Sioux women exchanged looks. Mouse had never spoken to either of them before.

"Yes," said Ebbing Water.

"Very well. We will do so as a show of respect for the one who has left."

What was Mouse up to? wondered Raven. She was never so polite as this. The other women did not object and so Raven nodded, as well.

The women dried their skin and were allowed to dress. Mouse put on her dress decorated with the double strand of red and blue beads and her high moccasins, removing the open sores from the sight of their captors. Raven was brought up the bank first, and two of the four warriors walked her back to their lodge, leaving the others to finish dressing.

She was alone in the lodge several minutes and it occurred to her that they might be taking them away. Would they not even allow her a last goodbye?

Raven tried not to let her fear eat her up. But her impending death combined with this forced separation made her throat burn.

The flap lifted a moment later and the women entered one after another.

Snake noticed Raven's panic and moved swiftly to her.

"Raven?" said Snake.

"I thought you'd gone. I thought they'd taken you already."

"We are here," said Mouse.

Raven hugged Snake and then Little Deer. The others gathered near, giving her comfort with their presence. Mouse tended the fire. She looked more lively than usual, Raven thought, which was good because the journey would be long and taxing.

Another meal arrived. Her last, Raven realized with a start.

She tried to eat with the others, but her stomach cramped around the food.

"Perhaps this is a journey one needs to take on an empty stomach."

That made Snake cry.

"You will need the food," said Raven. "I will not."

"You need strength more than any of us," said Mouse. "And I have something that will help."

Mouse rummaged in a pouch that hung from a peg on one of the tepee poles and withdrew a smaller pouch. "Turtle Rattler gave me this."

"What does it do?"

"Eases stomach upset."

Raven knew her upset came from anxiety and not from her break with the moon.

"I do not need it."

"Would you lose the contents of your stomach before them?"

Raven did not wish that. And she did not want to be rude. Mouse was already steeping a tea from the herbs.

She hesitated.

"I will have some, too," said Little Deer. "My stomach is bad."

Mouse nodded and crushed the herbs into two horn cups. Little Deer accepted hers and Raven took the other. She drank and then lowered her cup.

"Bitter," she said.

Mouse smiled and nodded.

Ebbing Water returned, but would not enter the lodge. She spoke from outside, kneeling at the open entrance. She passed them a skin of water, a bone container of rendered fat, two bags and two buffalo horn cups.

"This one," she said, lifting a bag, "is the charcoal. Mix it with the fat and water." She dropped that pouch before them and lifted the second. "This one is white clay ground very fine. Mix it the same way."

"We know how to mix paint," said Little Deer.

"Fine. That one." She pointed at Raven. "Her

hair, face, arms and legs will be all white. Laughing Moon requests that you paint the symbol of the bear on your hands and face."

Raven nodded. "This I will do."

Ebbing Water dropped a skinning knife among them. "To cut your hair. Do not cut her throat or we will kill you all."

She left them and there was silence as they all stared at the knife.

"How will they do it?" asked Little Deer, her voice a mere whisper.

"Suffocate her in the skin with him."

Raven blinked at the harshness of her words and felt light-headed. She reached out a hand to steady herself.

Mouse grasped the knife and lifted it toward Raven. She took a hank of Raven's long thick hair.

"What are you doing?" she asked. Her vision was double now and she felt dizzier.

Mouse sliced Raven's hair so it fell even with her chin.

"What?" Raven tried to push Mouse's arm away but her movements were clumsy.

"It's working," said Little Deer.

The other women stared at her like a nest of owls.

"What?" Raven found her words slurred.

"Sleeping draft," said Mouse.

Raven blinked. Was this to ease her death? So

she would be asleep when they blocked the air from her lungs?

"But...sh-she drank." Raven tried to point at Little Deer but her arm was too heavy.

"She only pretended," said Snake.

"Strip her out of that," said Mouse.

They quickly pulled Raven's dress over her head, and when they had finished she sagged. Wren held her upright but Raven's eyelids were so heavy.

Only when Mouse removed her own dress did it occur to Raven what was happening. She struggled to keep her eyes open.

"No," she whispered. They ignored her and easily managed to get Mouse's clothing on to her, dressing her as if she was a child's leather doll.

Raven watched in horror as Mouse let loose one side braid after another, raking her fingers through her long thick hair. Snake then took over. When she had finished with Mouse, she had two thin braids at each temple in the unique style Raven wore her hair. Little Deer removed the feather from Snow Raven's hair and tied it into Mouse's.

Snake sliced off the rest of Raven's hair and then did the others'. They painted their faces and arms black. Raven tried and failed to avoid Little

Deer's quick strokes as she rubbed the charcoal paint onto Raven's face.

"Help me," said Mouse.

Raven saw that Mouse had already coated her hair, face and arms with the ghostly white paint.

But that was for her, thought Raven.

Wren used the black to create a bear's paw on Mouse's hands and feet. Then she added one more to her cheek. The effect was chilling. With the paint and her hair now in the style distinct to Snow Raven, it was impossible to see this was Mouse.

"Do I look like her?" asked Mouse.

"You do," whispered Little Deer.

"Good." She smiled at Raven. "Do not mourn me, my friend, for I go to see my husband and son. I made no bargain, so Iron Bear will have no servant in the Spirit World."

They all gasped at the mention of the dead.

"What?" Mouse tossed her head in defiance. "Do you think one ghost can haunt another? Soon I will be past his reach and theirs." She pointed toward the door.

Then she turned to Raven.

"You have shown me how to be a warrior. Now it is my turn."

Raven opened her mouth but no words would come. She stared at Mouse, her teeth now as white as the death mask that covered her face. The bear paw drawn on her face began to move, widen, until it was a great yawning hole and Raven fell into blackness.

Chapter Twenty-One

Big Thunder returned after sunset to find that Running Wolf had escaped from his bonds and was just emerging from his lodge. Around one wrist dangled the remains of the braided leather rope Big Thunder had used to secure him. In his fist he held the handle to the war club his friend had used to knock him unconscious.

"I should have staked you to the ground," said Big Thunder.

"Out of my way." Running Wolf raised the club to strike but Big Thunder moved back.

"It's too late. She is gone."

Running Wolf broke into a sprint.

He reached the lodge of the chief to find the flap down and Laughing Moon sitting before the entrance. No one, not even a wife, would sleep in the lodge of the dead. At a glance he saw that Laughing Moon had not yet cut her hair or

painted her face black. That meant she still had
duties to perform.

"Where is she?" he asked.

Laughing Moon's gaze moved from him to the
lodge. "There."

He opened the flap and looked inside. He saw
Iron Bear first. He lay on his back in his war
shirt, his body unnaturally still. Beside him lay
his weapons and pipe. He was already half sewn
into the buffalo robe that would protect his body
from attack by predators of the air. None of the
birds could puncture the hide of a buffalo, and
the ground predators could not jump high enough
to reach the scaffold.

Running Wolf's gaze flicked across the fire
to the second body. She lay inside a second robe,
sewn up to her neck, the flap down to reveal her
face. Her face had been painted white and the
symbol of the bear covered one cheek. Her eyes
were closed, but her mouth was open and her
tongue swollen and black.

They had strangled her.

Rage filled him. Who had done this?

But he already knew. Red Hawk would have
volunteered. Running Wolf felt the need to put his
own hands about the warrior's neck and squeeze
until his tongue bulged.

Running Wolf looked at her long hair now
covered in white paint, the small braids at each

temple neat and secured with the cord she always used.

"No," he whispered, and began to crawl inside.

Someone grabbed him by the arm and tugged. He lifted his fist to strike and saw Weasel and Big Thunder. His friends. His friends who had let them do this and who had kept him from saving her.

"I will never forgive you," he said to them.

"I hope you have many years to hold your anger, for I would have you angry and alive," said Big Thunder.

"The captives are waiting," said Weasel.

"Captives?" He did not know what Weasel was talking about; he could not think past the black rage before his eyes and hollow emptiness in his chest.

"Iron Bear agreed to free them and assigned you to lead them home."

He remembered now. The reason Raven had traded her life was to save them, her tribe. She had acted like a warrior and true leader. She had given everything to free them.

The least he could do was see them home.

"We will go with you," said Crazy Riding.

"No," he said. "I will go nowhere with you."

"But you will take them?" asked Weasel.

He nodded. "First, I tell my mother goodbye."

Running Wolf walked on legs of wood across

the camp. He felt the silent stares of the people. He did not speak or look at them. They were dead to him. He had made his choice. He had wanted her and they had taken her because she had a warrior's heart.

At his mother's lodge he collected his weapons, bridle, saddle and food supplies. Ebbing Water appeared from the river. Running Wolf saw that tonight she had to carry her own water.

"I am going," he said.

"Yes. Be careful of the Crow. As soon as you sight them, let the women go and you ride swiftly home."

"I am not coming back."

"After your vision quest. After that you can return. You can rise as a great leader, just as you were destined."

"I am not coming back."

"But you are my only son. What will I do without you?"

"Marry again, Mother. It is that or become like Pretty Cloud. You are not too old to have more children. You have kept my father's memory alive too long. You filled my heart with your hate and it has cost me all."

"I am still here. I still love you."

"You did not love me enough to help me keep her."

"Because she tried to take you from me," cried

his mother, and she fell to her knees. "Do not leave me."

"I go. You will not see me again." He swung the saddle frame over one shoulder and went to the herd to select from his mounts. He chose his horses, including Eclipse, his warhorse, and Song, the horse of the bravest warrior he had ever known.

He rested his forehead on the large flat cheek of her mare.

"She is gone, my friend." His voice cracked and he thought he would cry, but then he saw the people gathering, watching him in silence as he prepared his horses.

Big Thunder fixed a travois behind the last of the line. The two long poles were attached by harnesses to either side and crossed above the animal's withers. The two beams were roped together behind the horse, making a platform long enough to carry household goods, children or in this case the one captive who was so ill she could not walk or sit upon a horse.

Mouse, he knew, was dying. Yet somehow she survived, while his Raven was flying to the Spirit World.

Weasel began to saddle Eclipse.

"No," said Running Wolf. "I ride this one." He pointed to her horse.

Weasel hesitated and then moved the pad

and saddle. Others joined in. Soon they had six horses, including the one dragging the travois and one packed with robes and a lodge. He was ready for a journey with four captives and an infant.

They came in a line, three walking, one limp body carried by two men. Each woman's face had been blackened to honor the chief, but in his mind they honored Snow Raven.

The ill woman was placed on the travois and tied down so she would not tumble from the platform as it bounced over uneven ground. He barely looked as the women were assisted into place upon the horses. The one with the infant removed the cradle board from her back and hung the strap over the pommel of the saddle. Her baby's face was also black, though he seemed to be sleeping. The walking horse would rock him as they journeyed from this place.

He looked to the scaffold on the hill, empty now, but soon she would rest beside their chief.

"They are ready," said Big Thunder.

"And I am ready."

"Until we meet again," said Big Thunder.

Running Wolf nodded and pressed his heels to his horse. The women followed, some leading their horses, some riding. He did not look back.

He walked her horse up the rise toward the scaffold and paused to take in the sight, memorizing this place, promising to come back for her bones. He saw a horse lying beneath the scaffold, the creature's neck slit and the wound already buzzing with flies. The chief's buffalo horse, he knew.

Song caught the scent of death and shook her head in a restless bobbing motion. She was anxious to be gone from this place, and so was he.

Raven woke to the gentle rocking motion. She opened her eyes and saw that everything was black. Was she dead?

She looked for the Sky Road but this was not the sky before her eyes. The air was stuffy and smelled of tanned leather and buffalo. She had a powerful thirst.

She could not be dead if she was thirsty. What was that sound, that murmuring sound like the humming of bees over blossoms?

Snow Raven moved her head and felt a sharp pain behind her eyes. She closed them again and rode the wave of dizziness that followed. Better to drift back to silence than to suffer the thirst and the pain. She felt her body dissolving away as she floated up in the air like a speck of dust in the sun.

She woke again to the stifling heat, her face dripping with sweat and the sweltering shroud still covering her. She struggled and this time managed to toss away the buffalo robe covering her face. She lifted her hand to wipe the sweat from her forehead and it came away black.

What was happening?

Someone pressed her hand down. She stared up at the stranger walking beside her. She glanced behind her to see the hindquarters of a horse, walking along, dragging her upon a travois. She tried to recall what had happened but it was fuzzy.

She had been waiting for something.

Death, she recalled.

But this was not the Way of Souls. She looked at the woman again. She had cut her hair short and her face and arms were black.

"She's awake," said the woman, and Raven recognized the voice. It was Wren, the one who lived with the old woman, Pretty Cloud.

Another woman stepped into view—Snake, she realized. Where was Mouse? She was the one who should be riding in the travois, not Raven.

And then it came rushing back. The tea, the dizziness. Mouse telling her she was going to see her husband and son.

"She tricked me," Raven said, but her tongue was thick and her words slurred.

"Get her some water," said Snake. Wren disappeared from her view. "Don't talk now. He might hear you."

"Who?" She formed the word but nothing

came from her mouth. The need to sleep dragged at her but she pushed it away.

"Running Wolf. He is leading us home. But we don't know if he will continue if he finds out what she did. He might take you back. He might take all of us back."

Was she gone, then? Raven looked up at the blue sky, picturing the road of stars that could only be seen in the night sky. They took her at night, yesterday? She stared at the sun and said a silent thank-you to the dove who had tricked a raven.

Someone helped her rise and held the horn cup to her lips. She drank thirstily and felt better. Her body still seemed to be moving in slow motion, but her mind was clearing.

"The one who did this. She is gone?"

Wren nodded, fat tears rolling over the black paint on her face.

"Then I will cut my hair." She fumbled, and then found her hair cut short.

"They told us to cut it for the chief. But we are in mourning for our sister," said Snake.

"She saved my life," said Raven.

"Yes. And she left you a message," said Snake. "She made me repeat it."

Raven waited, anxious and fearful of what Mouse had said. She'd held much hate against those who had killed her husband and son. Would her last message be one of revenge?

"She said that she loves you, loves all of us, and that we should remember her as a young mother with a fat, healthy son and a good husband. That she would be that again when she crossed the Way of Souls. She said she would see us all one day, but between now and then, we should live in happiness and joy."

That caused Raven to weep. Soon they were all weeping as they walked along on a path that would take them home. Was Mouse home already?

The horses continued along through much of the afternoon. Raven wanted to get up and walk, but they insisted that she must stay hidden. When the horses stopped, she knew that this would no longer be possible.

What would Running Wolf do when he recognized her? Would he be the man who loved her or the warrior who must do his duty to his people?

Chapter Twenty-Two

Running Wolf saw to the horses, hobbling most, staking Song and Eclipse beside the lodge the women erected with a swiftness born of experience. Then they erected a second.

It was disconcerting to see them going about the mundane chores of setting the camp while still in their mourning black. Firewood, water, preparing the meal. All seemed so ordinary. His circumstances were anything but.

He was commanded by his chief to take these women home and then to pursue a vision quest before returning to his people. Did he want to return?

Once he had thought all he desired was to lead his people in war and in peace. He had thought to be Iron Bear's successor. Soon the people would choose. The council of elders would make the selection, but only after consulting with wives and warriors alike. The choice was an important one, and the chief must have the support of all.

His name, he knew, would not even be mentioned. If they asked him to assume the post, he would refuse. He was too broken inside. He had made his choice. Raven over his people.

And he had lost both.

The appointed leader of the women, the one with a son, the one Raven called Snake, came to speak to him.

"We ask to remove the black from our faces and bathe in the river."

He nodded. He did not care. They would see to themselves and he would see them fed as he took them across the plains to the lakes and mountains that were the home of the Crow people.

If they had not ventured into Sioux territory, he would never have met her. His life would have gone on as before and he would have been forever blind to the kind of love that took everything and gave everything.

Would he have been better off?

He did not know. He did know that he would not have traded one minute with Snow Raven for a lifetime as the leader of his people.

The sound of splashing at the river told him that the women were having their bath, scrubbing away the grease and charcoal that marked them.

In time their hair would grow out as well, and there would be no outward sign of their captivity.

But inside, they were marked. He did not think it was right, taking captives. Women were not like horses, to be stolen from their homes in the night.

The screams reached him a moment later. He leaped to his feet, thrust his war club into the waistband of his leggings and scooped up his bow and quiver. He had the bow strung as the others shouted.

This time the shouts were for him. "White men! Four! Riding with rifles."

What woman had thought to tell him not only the source of the threat but their number? The voice was familiar, but that was not possible.

Running Wolf cut the tether that held Song to the picket and leaped onto her back. He rode toward the women, ready to protect them with his life.

An instant later he saw the men. All wore the dark blue uniforms of the fighting white men. Two sat on horseback on the far bank, rifles across their knees as they laughed at the half-dressed women scrambling in the opposite direction. The other two charged into the water as if hunting game.

Did they think these women had no protector?

Running Wolf notched an arrow and shot both men before they even knew he was there. Both men in the river continued toward him, advancing on the women who had reached the near bank. One reached for the closest female, still in the water—Little Deer, he realized. The second man leaned far out to grasp the other, dressed in the dress of Mouse, but not Mouse.

Running Wolf's eyes must have deceived him, because for an instant he had thought…

He gave a war cry.

The closer man pulled up, glanced back toward his fellows to find them both lying on the ground with arrows through their hearts. These whites who came to their territory were becoming more of a menace than either the Crow or Blackfoot. Running Wolf aimed at the nearer man, but the white pivoted and his horse turned as they made their retreat, so he swung his arrow to the man still advancing, still reaching for his prize.

He recognized her now. He did not know how it had happened or if he was only dreaming. But there was no doubt.

The woman in Mouse's dress was Snow Raven.

She turned toward her pursuer as Running Wolf reached for another arrow. Before he had it notched, she grasped the man's extended arm in both of hers, placed one foot on the horse's shoulder and pushed. The combination of his lean and her kick took him too far off balance. Running Wolf aimed but held fire as the white man toppled into the water with Raven. When he came up, Raven was on top of him and Wren had his rifle.

Raven rolled away and Wren danced backward with her prize. The man stood, drawing his knife. He had time to look once more at the two women before Running Wolf drove the arrow cleanly through the intruder's chest. The arrow passed through and out the other side and the man fell backward into the water. The current took him as his horse watched his master float past.

All the women stared at him, watching, waiting. Little Deer, Snake holding her infant son, Wren and Snow Raven. He did not understand how that could be her in the dress that belonged to Mouse. Mouse had been ill, too ill to walk.

All this time, he had been dragging Raven on that travois. Which meant Mouse had taken her place and…

Now he understood the silence and the worry in their eyes. What they had done was dangerous, improper and so brave.

He stopped trying to think.

He swung down from the horse—her horse— and set aside his bow. Then he walked down the steep bank. She met him halfway.

He opened his arms to her and she clasped him about the middle. As he held her, he closed his eyes and thanked the Great Spirit for anything and anyone who had kept her here with him.

"I never thought to see you again," he whispered. His fingers raked through her thick, short hair and he laughed through the tears. "Why did you not tell me?"

"I did not know. They did not tell me, either. One moment the drums pounded and then next I woke on that travois." She drew back to look at him. "Are you not angry?"

"No. I am grateful for anything that brings you back to me."

The women gathered about them. Little Deer spoke first.

"It was Mouse's plan. She said you would forgive Raven. She knew because she said her husband would have forgiven her anything."

Snake pointed to the dead men. "What do we do with them?"

Running Wolf released Raven and then immediately dragged her to his side again. "Strip them of everything. Collect their horses and leave them for the carrion. I will scout. When I return we will travel through the night. This place is too close to the twin tracks of the wagons."

Raven started to move away but he pulled her back.

"You come with me, Little Warrior. We will scout together."

He retrieved the reins to Song and handed them to her. Then he returned to the camp to saddle

Eclipse, his warhorse. Finally, he collected his lance and handed Raven his bow and quiver.

"We will have to get you your own bow soon."

Together they left the camp to search for more white soldiers.

Running Wolf thought that he had never seen Raven look so happy as when she rode her horse, unless it was when she was in his arms. They rode in a large circle, finding new wagon tracks closer to their lands than they had ever been.

"They pass through and frighten the buffalo. But I have never heard of them attacking women before," said Raven.

Running Wolf sat beside her studying the tracks from his horse. "They are becoming bold, and there are more of them. They cover the trail like ants walking in a line. Turtle Rattler said that they are building wooden lodges with high fences to the south. That does not sound like a people passing through."

Raven looked along the twin tracks that traveled as far as she could see. "They have already built such forts in our mountains. Perhaps they are a bigger threat than our enemies."

Running Wolf considered that as wind blew through the tall grass. Night was coming and the cloudless sky promised a cold night.

"We must get back to the others. We will move

north before we continue west," said Running
Wolf. "Are you strong enough to travel?"

"They gave me something that made me sleep.
I am well rested. But you have a lump on your
head the size of a duck egg."

He cocked his head and gave her a questioning look.

She smiled. "I felt it when you took me in your
arms."

"I look forward to when we make camp again,
so I can take you in my arms again."

She smiled at the promise. "That time cannot
come soon enough."

He fingered the knot. "Big Thunder gave me
this to keep me from coming for you."

"Thank the Great Spirit for him, then."

"Race you back to the others?" he asked.

In answer Raven pressed her heels to Song's
sides and her mare leaped into a graceful gallop.
He did not let her win, but he did enjoy the view
as Raven and Song raced through the twilight.

They found the women packed and ready to
travel. They moved slowly north, away from the
white road that cut the plains. They stopped to
rest when the new moon set sometime before the
breaking of the dawn, and then moved forward
again until they reached the cover of the woods
that marked the territory disputed by his tribe
and Snow Raven's. He wondered if she knew how

close they were to the place where her tribe's fishing camp had stood.

The lake was close, but her people would now be farther south as the cold crept over the land.

He called a halt at one of the streams that led to a great lake, and the women quickly erected the two lodges and prepared a simple meal. All ate wearily. Raven gave him a regretful look before joining the others in the women's lodge.

That was not how he had imagined their reunion when he had held her in his arms beside the river. But she was a free woman now and no longer his captive.

Perhaps she no longer loved him?

When he entered his lodge, the chill in his bones had nothing to do with the frost that covered the grass.

Chapter Twenty-Three

Raven left the lodge of the women as soon as she had assured them that she had not seen any other white warriors. They would be safe until tomorrow, because all knew that the whites who walked across the land in wagons did not travel at night.

She saw the open flap and smiled at his signal that he welcomed visitors. Still, she called a greeting from beside the entrance and heard the rustle of his bedding. She shivered in anticipation, and with the air that chilled her skin, knowing that he would keep her warm.

Running Wolf bid her enter with the formal reply, but his words were deep and his voice gravelly. She ducked inside and barely had her bearings before he dragged her against him and fell back upon the soft cushion of buffalo robes beside the small cozy fire.

She laughed at his eagerness. He was right. Words could wait, but this, this need to hold him, breathe in his scent and taste the salt upon his skin, this was essential.

Just the flexing of his arm as he stroked her head sent a lightning bolt of desire streaking through her so that she pulsed with each heartbeat. Between her legs, she was slick, eager, wanton. What had happened to the chaste maiden who found no man worth encouraging?

He was her hunger. Her thirst. He made her blood heat and her body tremble and all he did was brush his thumb over her bottom lip.

But he would do more, so much more.

She leaned over his prone body and smiled down at him. He was so beautiful. She tried to memorize his face, each line and sharp angle. His mouth glistened as he smiled and then licked his lower lip. Seeing that tongue and thinking of how it had felt against her skin made her shiver.

"Are you cold, little bird?"

"No. Aroused."

That made his eyebrows lift. He sat up, taking her with him. He reached for the hem of her dress. An instant later she understood why men prefer their women in dresses, for the garment easily went up and over her head. He tossed it beside the fire and grinned a challenge.

"Now you," she said.

He leaned to one side, offering his hip. She tugged at the knot that fell away.

He'd have her in his bed tonight. But what of tomorrow?

Don't think of that now, she cautioned. This was not their marriage bed. Her wanting and his wanting did not stop the obstacles that separated them. Knowing they faced uncertainty only made her more desperate to have him.

She did not know what awaited them. She only knew that they had tonight. Tonight he was her husband and she was his wife. Their tribes would not accept them. But they had accepted each other.

She raked the strong muscles of his chest. He returned her hungry stare and she felt her nipples tighten and ache. She reached with both hands, greedy for the feast of his body. He lay back to let her explore. She stroked his arm first, just a brush, but his skin stippled at the contact and she smiled. Both hands grazed the skin of his chest, traveling lower as that most needy part of him twitched and lengthened.

She took him with one hand as she pressed her lips to his chest, then lowered her mouth to the center line of his body until she was just above the thick dark hair that curled around his shaft.

He dragged his fingers through her short hair as if uncertain whether to stop or encourage her. She used her tongue to touch the tip of him and he groaned, his hips lifting from the ground.

His scent and the velvet softness of the skin that sheathed his hard erection… All were tantalizing. She used her mouth to explore the entire length of him again and again as her fingers danced over his inner thighs, his taut hips and his ribbed stomach.

Without warning he grasped her by both shoulders and lifted her up and away as if she was a child straying too near the fire.

He kissed her neck and the shell of her ear, taking the lobe into his mouth to suck. A flood of moisture accompanied the welling of sensation as his tongue darted in and out. He blew on the wet skin and she shivered with delight as she gasped and clung.

He laid her on her back and she locked her heels against his firm buttocks, pressing him forward as he resisted, coming up on his forearms and then rolling to his side next to her. From this position she was the bounty stretched open before him. He gobbled her up with his gaze and then followed with his hands and mouth.

Her head dropped back and her eyes shut to savor the sensation of his touch. When he splayed his hands over her breasts, a moan rumbled deep in her throat. He lapped and licked his way from one plump breast to the other as she lifted up to meet his hungry mouth. Running Wolf moved leisurely down her aroused body until she thought she understood why the elk ran after the females until they succeeded or died of exhaustion. What a wonderful way to die, she decided, here in his arms, as his own precious love.

She wanted him to touch her everywhere. Tonight she did not listen for the sound of discovery or worry what others might say or do. Tonight she was free to lose herself in her lover and give to him all she would receive.

Running Wolf was the only man who completely enthralled her. It was with a welling of melancholy that she understood that one night or a thousand would never satisfy her need for his touch. Why could she not have him for now and always?

What about the Spirit World? Would she still be bound to the allegiance to her tribe, even there?

She looked between their bodies, reaching between her legs first to wet her fingers on her own slickness and then, grasping what she wanted, stroking his erection. He gave a quick gasp of breath and set his jaw as if fighting the need to take her.

Her slippery fingers glided over his taut flesh so that he swelled even larger in her hands.

"Bend your legs," he ordered, and she did.

Running Wolf pressed her back to the robes, taking a long look at her lovely form, knowing that he was the man she had chosen against all reason. They must be mad.

Her creamy flesh glowed light against the black hair of the buffalo. He memorized the sight of her, treasuring the gift of this night, already regretting what would come when they were found by the Crow. She was worth it, he thought. What better thing was there to die for? Duty? No, that was an illusion. If he died now, it would be for love.

Her clever fingers continued to stroke. He swept her hands away. He would not be rushed. He collected her wrists and pinned them above her head in one hand.

"You are still my captive," he said.

"Always," she murmured.

"And I am yours."

Her fragrance drew him like nectar. He had to taste her.

She reclined now, giving him a fine view of her breasts, aroused, budded and full. Raven waited, naked and wanting, for him. He found the sight the strongest of temptations, and he hadn't even tasted her yet. But he could smell her arousal, the musk that made him dizzy with anticipation. She let her bent legs drop to either side and lifted her hips, showing him her slick, pink flesh.

Her gaze drifted from his until she stared at his engorged sex. Only once in his arms, and already she was no timid maiden. Now her look was bold and certain. She knew what she wanted. But he would not give it to her just yet.

She pouted now, her full bottom lip thrust outward. He leaned down and took it between his teeth and tugged. Her inhalation was sharp. He released her and smiled down.

"Why do you not take me?" she asked.

"Patience. There is more to show you."

Now she looked curious; her lovely brown eyes glittered with intelligence and speculation. His insides twitched. She was an eager learner. What would she learn from him now? He already anticipated her using what he would show her on him. Would they have the chance? How many more days and nights did they have?

Already they were in the territory disputed by both tribes, the land that had long been Crow before their numbers had fallen as the Sioux's had grown.

"What will you show me?" she asked.

He lowered himself to press his mouth to her neck and then moved in a winding path down her body, loving her curves and hollows. Pausing to taste and lick and suck until she writhed beneath him, making urgent sounds of need. He traveled slowly, but with a destination in mind, reaching the soft wet flesh between her splayed legs.

He settled there, wrapping his arms under her, controlling her hips and lifting her up to meet his mouth. He sucked that tiny bud of flesh as she twitched and thrashed, trying to escape and draw closer. He relished the soft panting and tiny trembling moans she made when he dipped two fingers inside her. He sucked and licked and grazed the tender nub with his teeth. He rocked her against his mouth, mimicking the motion of a man and woman, and she threw back her head. She tossed her head from side to side, her fingers clenched in the hair of the buffalo as she cried out. The first contraction squeezed his fingers in a rolling wave.

She moaned and bucked, holding herself open to him as he continued to lick her wet cleft. He would do anything for her. Did she know that? Her cries faded and he laid her gently back to the ground. His body now demanded release. She gave another little moan as he rocked his hips against hers.

He rubbed his slick mouth on her stomach as he scaled her body, licking the dimpled navel and the hollow beneath her ribs. She lifted an arm in welcome and tangled her fingers in his loosely braided hair.

When his lips reached her throat, she had already begun to undulate in a sinuous dance, her hips bumping against his thighs.

She kissed his neck now, her fingers raking his back, her nails grazing his skin. She smiled an invitation at him with her eyelids heavy and her pupils large and dark.

She raised her legs and locked her ankles about his back and used one hand to position him. He dropped in a swift fall, like a diving hawk, until their hips locked and he was sheathed inside her. He paused a moment, his forehead resting on hers. Nothing in the world had ever been sweeter than this.

Then he drew back only to drop against her again. A moment later he understood the advantages of riding a woman who could ride. She was firm and soft, strong and yielding.

Perfect.

The sight of her flushed face and parted lips made his stomach twitch. He wanted to bring her pleasure again, wanted them both to fall into that madness together. But she was so hot and so wet and it had been so long. He growled as the need gripped him, rocking harder.

Raven threw back her head as a long, rasping moan broke from her lips. A moment later, he felt the rippling contraction squeezing his aroused flesh. He gasped and plunged deeper into her willing body.

She cried out as the contractions hammered inside her, her pleasure releasing his. He came in a hot rush of throbbing waves of pure pleasure that shot from his core and blazed outward. He

arched as he pulsed inside her. Both lay motion-
less for a moment, locked in this sharing of the
ultimate pleasure.

Raven relaxed first, collapsing to the earth. He
toppled next, half upon her, landing at her side,
their breathing labored as their bodies came to
sweet stillness. Raven stretched and made a humming sound down deep in her throat. He chuck-
led at the sound of pure feminine contentment.

The air hung heavy with the sweet scent of
their joining. Their breathing quieted. Raven shivered and he reached for one of the large buffalo
robes, dragging the covering over their cooling
bodies. She nestled close and slipped one leg over
his thighs. Then, still but for their heartbeats and
the steady draw of their breathing, they rested at
last in each other's arms.

Knowing that this could not last made it all
the sweeter. She lay beside him, her body sated,
and they slept.

Before dawn Snow Raven woke; her mind
rolled like waves on the lakes before the storm.

"What will happen now?" she whispered.

"I am bringing you to your people."

"But what will happen to you?"

He did not answer. She tensed. What if they
hurt him? She pressed an open hand over his
heart.

"My chief asked me to go on a vision quest before returning to my tribe. And this I will do. But it may be many seasons before I return."

"Why?"

There was a long pause.

"Because I wish to stay with you."

The delight and surprise tingled through her and she lifted to one elbow to look down at him in the light of dawn.

"Stay?"

"Is it so uncommon for a husband to join the tribe of his wife?"

"Not so uncommon if you were Apsáalooke. But you are not. What if they will not accept you?" Other possibilities sprang upon her. Captives were adopted in some cases, but mainly if they were children, and only then to replace a loved one. More often they were killed or enslaved. "It's too dangerous. I do not want you to do it."

"How else can we be together?"

"I will come back with you. You can marry me."

"You cannot return to my tribe, ever, because you are supposed to be dead."

She had forgotten that. Two people alone could not survive. They needed a tribe.

"It must be your tribe. There is no choice."

"I could be your slave," she said.

"No. They would kill you this time." He took hold of her hand. "There is only one question you must answer, Snow Raven. Will you let me protect you with my life? Will you marry me?"

"I will."

He kissed her hard and drew her against him so her cheek rested on his wide, strong chest. Her husband, she thought. But for how long? How could she keep him alive?

"But you are a war chief."

"No longer. Raven." He drew back, sat up and faced her. Before speaking again, he grasped both of her hands. "Once you said you wanted a man who would see you before all else. I was not that man. But now I am. I am yours first. I will do my duty to my tribe and I hope that will be your tribe, but your needs and your safety come first. If your people will accept me, I will fight their enemies, your enemies."

"That might be your own people. Your best friend."

"I know this. When I thought I had lost you, I recognized that you were right. My love for you clouds all else. Though I hope I do not meet my brothers on the battlefield, I will fight them to keep you safe. You asked me to choose. I have done so."

"I pray to the Great Spirit that never happens."

Outside their lodge, Raven heard the sounds of the women rising and striking the other lodge.

"We must go," she said. Into an uncertain future. Raven held him and felt the strength of his arms about her. He would protect her from all enemies. But she must protect him from her brother and father.

She prayed they would have a few more days together before that time came. But that did not come to pass. Not long before they set out, they were spotted by an Apsáalooke hunting party.

"What tribe?" asked Snake, shading her eyes with her hand.

"Low River," whispered Raven, recognizing the shield instantly. The red arrow was distinctive even from this distance. "That is my brother, Bright Arrow."

Chapter Twenty-Four

Raven did not know if she should call to her brother or hide. All she had wanted had now happened. She had managed to spare these women's lives, and with Running Wolf's help, they had found her people. She was free.

But she was not free. She would never again be that lighthearted, foolish girl riding through the forest.

"I should go to him," she whispered.

The other women looked to her and then to Running Wolf.

"No," he said. "He may not let you return. I will go."

"They will kill you," she said, absolutely certain that her brother would shoot a lone Sioux warrior on sight.

What should she do?

"Together," she said. "All of us."

The women straightened their dresses and smoothed their blunt-cut hair as best they could.

"You must help me keep Running Wolf safe," she said. She did not receive the rousing chorus of affirmation for which she had hoped. In fact, they stared sullen and silent. Clearly they did not share her sentiment toward their guide.

She looked from one to the next. It was Snake who finally spoke.

"He was there when we were taken four years ago, and while he did not visit our lodge, he did not try to see we were adopted. He and all the others except Spotted Fawn and Pretty Cloud treated us as enemy. Why should we do otherwise?"

"Because he will be my husband."

Little Deer gasped and Snake choked. Wren stared in mute astonishment.

"Your father will not allow it," said Snake.

Raven tended to agree with her. Her father had lost a brother to the Sioux and her uncle had lost his scalp. It might be on the war shirt of any of the older warriors of Running Wolf's tribe. Her father had taken them to the lake that was past the point they had ever ventured before. Had he done so to escape the whites and their new fort or to provoke the Sioux?

Was their presence here no small skirmish but a well-planned invasion?

Raven looked from her brother, far across the

prairie, to the women. "You all may go. I ask no more of you."

Little Deer stepped forward. "We would have all died screaming if Raven had not made a bargain for our lives. She was willing to die for us and all she asks is that we help spare this man's life."

"This enemy," said Snake.

"It is so," said Little Deer. "And I will do this and anything else she asks. She is our leader by our election. She was safe until we asked for her help. Spotted Fawn would have adopted her. She could have lived in his lodge and been a second wife. Who will say this is not so?"

None of them spoke.

Raven saddled Song and Running Wolf drew on his shirt and took up his shield. Raven knew her brother would recall the symbol of the wolf emblazoned upon it.

Together they rode slowly toward the party of five Crow warriors. She saw that her brother rode an unfamiliar mount, a small chestnut stallion with a wedge-shaped head and powerful hindquarters. His favorite warhorse, Hail, still lived within the Sioux herd. Had they traded with the other tribes for these, stolen them in raids or captured wild horses? As she drew nearer she recognized her brother's companions. There was Little Badger, shirtless as usual, and beside him rode Turns Too Slowly, his long braids reaching his waist and his forelock carefully roached and waxed so it stood up like a deer-tail headpiece. Raven felt the welling of joy at seeing them again. And there was Feeding Elk, Broken Saddle and Young Bear.

Her happiness was dampened by the growing unease, for surely they had recognized her horse. With her hair cut and her loss of weight, she did not know how much she had changed, but she thought she saw the moment her brother was sure it was her because his neck, stretched to its limit as he stared across the open space between them, shortened as he moved from standing in his stirrups to seated upon his saddle. He tossed his lance a few inches, changing the grip in preparation to throw.

"Get behind me," ordered Running Wolf.

At almost the same moment, her brother's order reached her.

"Move away from him, Snow Raven."

She did not move behind or away. She nudged Song so that she stood before Running Wolf.

"You embarrass me," he called. "Let us meet as men."

"No. I have seen how men meet." To her brother she called, "I am well and we come in peace. Will you give this man safe passage to our father?"

"I will not stop him," said her brother.

Raven let her shoulders relax slightly. She glanced back to see that Running Wolf still held his shield at the ready. When she looked back to her brother she noted he still held his spear ready to throw. Raven stopped her horse. The women who had chosen her to lead them continued on until they were standing before the warriors of the Low River tribe. They told their tribe names and begged for help. They said that Snow Raven had helped them escape the Sioux snakes.

Raven heard Snake say that the warrior was Running Wolf, war chief of the Sioux, and that the dying chief had made him promise to bring them home.

The men seemed confused by this, judging from the nervous dancing of their horses.

Bright Arrow called to her again. "Is he holding you?"

"No."

"Then, come to us."

"No."

He motioned for her to come.

"Safe passage to our father for us both. Promise."

In answer he threw his lance so that it stuck into the ground between them, vibrating with the force of the throw.

"Come, then," said Bright Arrow.

There was little choice. Raven nudged her horse forward and Running Wolf proceeded at her side.

"Why didn't you let me kill him?" said Bright Arrow.

"When we get home, I will tell you."

The other women returned to their camp to strike the lodges and pack their belongings. Young Bear accompanied them and seemed to be taking a special interest in Little Deer. Raven sat between her brother and Running Wolf, upon her horse, Song.

In all the times she imagined this reunion, it was never so cold or so tense.

She began to fear that Running Wolf was right. Her people would not accept a Sioux warrior in their midst any more than the Sioux would accept a Crow maiden for their war chief's wife.

For better or worse, the camp of the Low River tribe was only a short ride through thickening pine. Raven knew this place and recalled the river where they had camped many times when the south wind gave way to the west wind.

Feeding Elk rode ahead and so her entire village was there to greet them. But there was no drum to announce them, or cheering or dancing. All stood and stared as Raven returned to her people.

Only one woman stepped forward to meet her.

She was crooked and her hair was as white as a summer cloud, but she opened her thin arms to her grandchild.

"Welcome home, Little Warrior."

Raven slipped off her horse and rushed to her grandmother's embrace. The skin drooped from Truthful Woman's arms, but her grip was strong, and Raven was so happy that she was alive and here.

"Now it feels like home," she whispered.

When her grandmother released her, Raven saw her father approach. She smiled and then realized that her father looked past her. She turned to see Running Wolf had dismounted and now stood with the rein of his stallion in one hand and his shield lowered to his opposite side.

"Take him," said her father, Six Elks.

"No," she said, but it was too late. Running Wolf was surrounded. He did not fight as they took him to the ground and pinned him there.

Raven grasped her father's arm.

"He brought me home. Father, he kept me alive."

He ignored her. "Tie him."

She left her father and tried to reach Running Wolf as he was yanked upright with his arms bound. But her brother swept her over his shoulder. She yelled and kicked, but they marched Running Wolf away. Once he was gone, her brother dropped her back to the ground and followed the young warriors.

Her father spoke to Truthful Woman. "Talk to the others and report to me all that has happened."

Raven watched her grandmother turn to Little Deer, Wren and Snake, now carrying Stork safely in his cradle board. She welcomed them and motioned them to follow her. All of the women in her tribe trailed away after them, leaving her alone with her father, two of the elders and Thunder Buffalo, their medicine man.

"Father, you must listen to me," Raven said.

"I will. Come to my lodge."

She listened to the men shout.

"No! You will tell them not to hurt him."

"The last I checked, I was still chief here."

"Please, Father. They will kill him."

Her father said nothing to this but she recognized the look of hatred in his eyes.

"*He* did not kill Iron Heart," she said, speaking her uncle's name aloud.

Her father looked shocked. "You do not speak his name."

"Will you stop them?"

Her father looked away.

"Then, I will stop them." Raven ducked inside the lodge of her father to find her bow and quiver hanging on their usual peg, as if awaiting her return. She grabbed them both and set off at a run.

When she reached the warriors, it was to find them lowering Running Wolf's feet onto a bed of hot coals.

She shrieked and shot a warning arrow into their midst. The men scattered and Running Wolf, arms and legs tightly bound, rolled away. She used the iron tip of one arrow to slice through the bonds at his wrists before the young men in her tribe regrouped and closed in.

She pointed a finger at her brother. Then she aimed the arrow at him. "You promised him safe passage."

"Yes. Safe passage to the village, and he has arrived safely. My promise is done."

She renotched the arrow and drew back the bowstring, readying death for any foolish enough to approach.

"Look what they have done to her," said Bright Arrow. "They have made her lose her mind as well as her hair so that she protects a snake."

"She cannot shoot us all," said Feeding Elk.

She aimed the arrow at him. "But I can kill you."

"You would kill one of your own people over this man?" asked Turns Too Slowly.

"I would kill all of you for this man," she said.

"She is one of them," said Young Bear.

"I am not."

"Rush her," said Bright Arrow. "She won't do it."

They closed in and she realized that Bright Arrow was right. She couldn't do it. She released the tension on the bow, gradually bringing it back to rest. Then she tossed the bow aside, keeping hold of the metal-tipped arrow.

"He is right," she said. "But I will do this." She lifted the sharpened point and pressed it to her throat, feeling the point puncture the skin at her neck.

"No!" said Bright Arrow, lifting a hand to halt the others.

"Step back and leave us," she ordered.

Feeding Elk moved closer. "Do not be foolish, Little Warrior. There is no need to fuss."

She pressed harder and the arrow drew more blood. She felt it, hot and sticky, as it rolled down her neck.

Someone grasped her wrist and dragged the arrow from her throat. She turned to see it was Running Wolf. He looked at her with regret.

"You above all others," he said.

The next instant they were on them, dragging them down and apart. She reached for Running Wolf and missed.

Chapter Twenty-Five

"Let them up."

Raven knew the voice. It was her father and his men obeyed instantly.

"Separate them."

Raven was dragged kicking and screaming from Running Wolf, who made no sound as they marched him away. Would they kill him the moment he was taken from her sight?

Raven spent the day in her grandmother's tent, under guard, eating little and waiting to be summoned.

Her grandmother tried to reassure her. "If they were torturing him, you would hear the drums and his death song."

Raven shuddered. "Why does my father hate them so much?"

"He lost a brother."

"And you lost a son, yet you do not seek revenge."

Her grandmother smiled. "I am not a man. Men are different. They have trouble moving past death. Women bring life, so for us it is part of the wheel. Life, death, rebirth—a baby is born, an old woman dies."

That made Raven hug her grandmother, who looked well enough but was already past her six-tieth winter, ancient by any standard. Still, she had most of her teeth and could manage her lodge with little help with the lodge poles. After what Snow Raven had been through, it seemed a great accomplishment to have lived so long and seen so much.

"What will I do when they ask me to say what has happened?" asked Raven.

"You were ready to protect this man with your life and follow him into death. You must protect him with your words. Show our leaders that there is a way to let you live with him in peace."

"But he is Sioux. That cannot be changed."

Her grandmother did not respond to that, but she rose slowly to her feet. "I must go see our medicine man."

"Is one of the women sick?"

"I will return and go with you to speak to my son. He may not like what I have to say, but he will still hear his mother."

Raven waited with the other former captives, as impatient and twitchy as a rabbit in an open meadow, until her grandmother returned. They were kind and tried to distract her with stories, but the stories turned to hope for their homecomings and this made Raven more anxious.

Finally, as the sun began its descent, her grandmother returned, walking beside their medicine man, Thunder Buffalo.

"These women must come to the river and bathe away the taint of the enemy," he said to Raven. "You must go with them. After, I will bring you to the council."

"Is Running Wolf alive?" asked Raven.

Thunder Buffalo did not answer. He often ignored questions, especially from her. But her grandmother nodded her answer.

"Have they tortured him?"

"He is captive. Nothing else is decided," said Truthful Woman. Her grandmother stroked her cheek. "I went to look at him." She gave Thunder Buffalo a smile and then returned her gaze to Raven. "While I was there I gave him my special berry juice. At first he did not want it, afraid of poison, perhaps. But I told him who I was and we talked. He is very handsome, your young man. I also brought him some elk stew."

Thunder Buffalo made a growling sound in his throat.

Raven hugged her grandmother. "Thank you."

She patted Raven's arm. "It is nothing. Come, now. We must all bathe."

All the women of the tribe were there to accompany them. They were thoroughly washed. Thunder Buffalo instructed from the bank that the women all be submerged three times and, when they surfaced, he proclaimed them clean. All taint of Sioux was gone and the baby, Stork, was now free of any Sioux blood and was Crow again.

This last proclamation made Snake cry tears of joy. Thunder Buffalo then left the women to dress. Raven dried with a soft bit of deer hide and then pulled on her rabbit dress.

Women from her tribe came forward and gave each new arrival a fine two-skin dress. The dresses had each been dyed a bright color. Truthful Woman stepped forward with a new dress for her granddaughter.

"I made this while you were away. I knew you would return because you came to me in a dream and asked me how to make a dress." She laughed and pointed to the rabbit skins that Raven had made into some semblance of a garment. "Now I see why. Not bad for a first try, and with such small pelts, that would challenge anyone."

Her grandmother extended the bundle to her. Sitting on the folded dress were two leather moccasins, the tops of which were completely covered with beautiful quillwork of a black medicine wheel divided into the four directions, each with its associated color—white for the north, blue for the west, yellow for the east and red for the south.

"Oh, they are too beautiful to wear," gasped Raven, already reaching for the fine-looking footwear.

"You must look your best tomorrow," she said.

Some of the happiness went from Raven as she realized she would be wearing them when she spoke before the council and possibly the entire tribe.

"And this," said her grandmother, gripping the dress by each shoulder and letting the folds open until she held the dress out for Raven to behold. It was the finest garment Raven had ever seen.

Her grandmother had rubbed berry juice into the tanned leather until the entire garment was the deep red color of a ripe cherry. The dark color served to make the even rows of elk teeth across the upper chest stand out in sharp contrast.

Raven fingered one rounded white tooth. "You must have been saving for years."

Her grandmother nodded. "And I gave you a long fringe."

She met her grandmother's eye. Most dresses had a short fringe, so the long strands of leather did not catch when carrying firewood or dangle in the fire when cooking. War shirts, or dresses made for special occasions, had a longer fringe.

Raven hugged her grandmother, the dress now pressed between them. When they separated, Raven held the dress.

"You must teach me to sew like this. And quill-work, too."

Her grandmother laughed. "Oh, ho! Who are you and what have you done with my little warrior?"

Raven laughed, forgetting her worries as she slipped into the new garment.

She did not say she preferred her leggings and long shirt, because she found that she wished to look like a woman when she returned to the tribe tonight and tomorrow when she faced the council.

Their hair created a problem, but there was enough to gather at each side of their heads, and the stubby ends were covered with additions to resemble hair. Wren's hair now included thick ropes of mink tails and Snake's braids were made of horsehair woven and tied with tufts of the soft feathers of a hawk's belly.

Raven's hair received a sheath of deer hide that was tanned on only one side, so that the strips resembled hair left free. She thought Little Deer looked lovely with the shells tied to her hair and the strips of green leather woven at each side of her head in twin braids.

Once adorned, the women were escorted to the gathering place by the Low River women, who sang a welcome along the slow procession. Raven wished she could enjoy the ceremony, but instead she looked at each lodge, searching for the guards that would be posted to watch the captive.

As twilight stole the color from the day, the drums began to sound and the entire tribe gathered about the large central fire. After the women sang, the young men took over. They were followed by the older married men on one side of the fire and the older women on the other. They danced in separate lines.

When the young women danced, the returned captives danced, too. Raven was asked several times to join, but her heart was as heavy as her feet and she waved off all attempts to include her. Snow Raven knew that the celebration would continue for days, and she hoped that the high spirits of her tribe would reveal itself in mercy toward Running Wolf.

In the past, captives were killed, enslaved or adopted. One of the warriors, Soaring Hawk, had even taken a white boy into his family when he found his parents dead in their wagon. She had heard that he and his wife, Silver Cloud, loved the boy, who was thought to be fourteen winters when he arrived. He replaced the son they had lost to sickness and the boy was fond of them, but when he became a man and a warrior, he asked to return east and so Soaring Hawk had brought him to the wagon trail, where he had joined a group of blue coats traveling toward the sun.

Snow Raven's family had lost many loved ones. Her mother and her parents to illness; her father's brother to war.

Her brother approached and she wondered if, had she not returned, he would ever have taken a captive to replace her as sister.

"Tomorrow, the council will see you," said Bright Arrow.

"Where is he?" she asked.

"I cannot say." Bright Arrow motioned with his head and they walked away from the dancers, stopping outside the circle of light. He waited until Raven was away from the gathering before he stopped walking.

"Have you lost your mind?" he asked.

"No."

"Then, why choose him?"

"He makes my heart sing."

Bright Arrow groaned and looked to the heavens.

"Why couldn't you choose warriors from the Black Lodges when we camped beside them last winter or one from the Shallow Water people? The warriors of the Wind Basin tribe are brave. They would protect you with their lives."

"Perhaps they would, but Running Wolf has

already protected me. It is only because of him that I live."

"But he is snake!"

Raven tossed her hands in frustration. "Do you think I do not know? Do you think I am doing this thing to be difficult?"

Bright Arrow's shoulders sagged. "I do not understand."

"Because you have never loved."

Bright Arrow looked insulted. "I have been with a woman."

"That is not love." Raven lifted her gaze to the sky, now awash with lavender and orange. "I tried to resist, because I knew this path would be difficult. But I have chosen this road and will walk beside him in this world or the next."

Bright Arrow shook his head like a dog who sits too close to the fire. At last he motioned her on.

"Come. We have to return."

"I want to see him."

"That is not wise."

"Where is he?"

Bright Arrow placed a hand on her shoulder and pressed down so she felt the weight of his grip. "You cannot escape with him."

She knew that.

"I will see him. You can take me or I will find him myself."

"You may find him, but you will not see him."

She gave him a belligerent look.

"If you try, the guards have orders to tie you like a captive."

Raven considered that as an option.

"In a separate lodge," Bright Arrow added, as if reading her thoughts.

Her brother was war chief. But he still followed the order of the chief, their father. If she wanted to see Running Wolf, she must convince him. And she would need influence.

"Where is Grandmother?" she asked.

The dancing went on into the night. Raven found her grandmother, who agreed to go speak to her son the following day. So Raven searched the camp and found the lodge where Running Wolf was detained. She was not allowed to enter but was somewhat relieved to know that he was safe for the moment. She called to him and received no reply, so she called encouragement and promises, which she had no idea how to keep.

She spent a restless night in her grandmother's lodge, waiting for her father to return. According to Truthful Woman, Bright Arrow now kept his own tepee and was courting a woman from the Black Lodges tribe.

It was customary for a man, once married, to live with his wife's tribe. Truthful Woman was

Wind Basin and her husband, Night Storm, was born to the Black Lodges. Their sons—her father, Six Elks, and his brother, Iron Heart—were both Wind Basin. It was only after her father married Beautiful Song, Raven's mother, that he became one of the Low River tribe. When her husband died, Truthful Woman had come to live with her son.

Raven and Bright Arrow were both Low River, but if Bright Arrow married this Black Lodges woman, he would become Black Lodges, as well. It would not matter. Bright Arrow was brave and capable. She believed he would earn his place as war chief very quickly, just as her father had risen quickly to chief of the Low River people. And if she could convince her father to allow her to wed Running Wolf, he would become Low River.

Raven tried to think of ways to get her father to accept Running Wolf, but when the birdsong reached Raven's ears, she had no answer. She could see her breath in the cold air, and though the lodge was full of light, she heard none of the usual sounds of prayer songs being sung outside the lodges by the men. Everyone was still wrapped in their sleeping skin against the cold and the late night of dancing.

Raven snuggled down in her bedding, exhausted from worrying half the night. Was Running Wolf warm enough?

That thought brought her upright. She stirred the coals to life and rekindled the fire. She was up and out and drawing water before her grandmother had even stirred.

When she returned from bathing by the river, carrying the water, she found her grandmother inside the lodge, grinding dried tubers into flour. The husks of the dried turnips had been woven into a long rope for easy transport and her grandmother's rope was so long it stretched around her working area and back to the peg where it was stored.

"Bring some buffalo berries," said Truthful Woman, speaking as if all were normal and Snow Raven had not been away.

It was comforting and disconcerting all at once.

Raven retrieved the requested item from her grandmother's food stores and handed it to her. Then she wound the rope of tubers as she would a lead line and hung it back on its peg. Her grandmother stirred water into the mixture to bring the berries back from their dried state to something plump and juicy.

"Will Father join us?"

"Hmm. I don't think so. Some of the Black Lodges are staying here and my son is spending some time with his uncle."

"I did not know Brings Horses was here."

"You have been busy."

Truthful Woman served the meal in a turtle-shell bowl, and Raven lifted the spoon carved from buffalo horn and ate hungrily.

"It is good to see you have an appetite. You will need strength today, for it is a difficult job to convince men to do anything."

Raven paused in her meal. "Will you bring food to Running Wolf?"

Truthful Woman showed her another bowl full of porridge. Her brother arrived in time to finish the remainder of the meal, for though he had a lodge, he had no woman to cook for him.

"Will you speak to Father with me?" Raven asked her brother.

"You do not want my help. I still want him killed."

Her grandmother patted Bright Arrow. "Do you not want your sister's happiness?"

"Not if it means she will humiliate herself with a snake." He looked at his sister, his face a mask of confusion. "You will not tend fires or clean fish or make clothing. You insist on riding, hunting and fighting like a warrior and now you bring this man to our camp." He raised his voice. "It is too much!"

"We are who we are. And we love who we love," said Truthful Woman.

Bright Arrow grunted and returned his attention to his porridge.

Six Elks called a greeting to his own home, and all discussion ceased as he entered the lodge with his elderly uncle.

"From the volume of your voices, the entire tribe will know what is too much, son."

Bright Arrow gave up the place across from the entrance instantly and Truthful Woman added more water and flour to her iron kettle to begin a second batch of porridge. She offered the helping she had set aside for Running Wolf to her son and he accepted it and passed it to his uncle.

All was quiet except for the turning of the smooth stick Truthful Woman used to stir the porridge and the scrape of the horn spoon on the turtle shell.

Raven wanted so much to explain to her father that they must not harm Running Wolf, but her fear stopped her. What if she presented her opinion badly? What if it did not matter what she said because, like her brother, his mind was fixed?

Her father had raised her to hate the Sioux. Everyone had suffered loss from battle or raid, but her father harbored special detestation for their enemy since the death of his brother. She knew this only from her grandmother, who had said her son had once been carefree and careless but all that had changed when his brother had left.

Six Elks finished a first helping of porridge and her uncle a second. Raven found herself clicking her thumbnail with the one on her opposite index finger in a nervous repetitive action. Finally they lowered their bowls. And both men turned their attention to Raven.

"So, daughter, what is it you wish me to know about our captive?"

Where to begin? So many things seemed important. She wanted to leap into the conversation, but she collected her thoughts. She had rehearsed half the night, but now that she had his attention she was mute.

"Have you changed your mind, then? Come to your senses and realized that you are safe now?"

"No. I am more afraid now than when I was first taken captive because then I only feared for my own life. But now I fear for his."

"He walked into our hands. Once an elk walked into our camp. I'm sure you know what happened to the elk."

Raven began again. "When I was first captured, Running Wolf kept the man who attacked Grandmother from killing me. This man tried to kill me several times. Running Wolf protected me and outwitted this man at every turn. He kept me from being used by the men of his tribe, he kept me from being sold to a white trader and, when we were freed, he brought us home. These are not the actions of an enemy."

"If he is such an ally, why did he not bring you all home months ago?"

"Because like all warriors, he followed the orders of his chief."

"What is it you want us to do, daughter?"

She tore off her thumbnail with her teeth and then gnawed on the ragged tip. Why was it so hard to say aloud?

"I wish you to give your permission for me to marry him."

Her grandmother stopped stirring the porridge. Her brother choked on the hot tea he had been sipping and her father and uncle stared like owls.

Finally her father laughed.

"For a moment I thought you were serious."

"I am serious, Father. I love him. I would give my life for him."

"He is a captive," said Bright Arrow. "We kill captives. Let me test his strength. Let us see if he dies with honor or if he yips and howls like a coyote with his coat on fire."

Raven gripped her hand into a fist. Her grandmother placed a hand upon her arm.

Her father dismissed both Bright Arrow and Raven's request. "He is not Crow. You cannot marry him. But he has brought many of our women out of enemy territory and he did not kill my son when he had the chance. Still, he is Sioux."

Raven bowed her head to think. Her father had not spared him. Neither had he condemned him.

Then she resumed her attack.

"If he goes, I will go with him."

"He is not going. I do not free captives."

Truthful Woman spoke at last. "I have heard that my granddaughter protected the warrior from her brother and his men. I have heard that she was willing to go with him to the Spirit World rather than let him die." Her grandmother touched the healing scab on Raven's neck, and then turned her attention back to her son. "You have heard this, too. Did you also hear who stopped her?"

Six Elks made a face. "I did."

"This is a selfless act. Most men would have used her as a weapon to help them escape. But he saved her even from herself while knowing he would lose any chance of escape."

Six Elks's scowl deepened the creases across his forehead.

"Such a man does not deserve to be a captive," said Truthful Woman.

Her uncle spoke. "Truthful Woman is right. He should not be a captive because all Sioux are better dead. Making him a captive is dangerous. Who would want a warrior as a servant?"

Raven crept across the circle to her father and

took hold of his hand between her two smaller ones. She thought of all the requests she had made, both insignificant and outlandish. Her father had denied her nothing. But this…this she feared he would not grant.

"Spare him," she begged.

Six Elks looked to his uncle. "What are your thoughts?"

"No warrior with any honor would live long as a captive. Even if he did survive the winter, which he will not, he would try to escape. You will have to guard him constantly or let him go and then hunt him down and kill him. It is a lot of trouble. Just kill him now."

Raven gave a strangled cry and fell across her father's lap, wrapping her arms about his waist and weeping.

"If I were a captive, I would kill myself," said Bright Arrow.

Her father patted her shoulder as she wept against him. "Perhaps he will escape and we can just let him go."

Raven sat up. Before she had wiped her eyes, she realized that she would rather see him go than have him live here as a captive. Then he could keep his honor and go on his vision quest and return to his people. He could start again. He would have everything he had before.

Everything except her.

She had said that if he went, she would go with him. But she could not. She could never return to his tribe without revealing Mouse's deception.

Would he forget her in time?

She used the heels of her hands to swipe away the tears.

"Yes," she whispered. "Let him go."

Her father looked long at his daughter without speaking. At last he rested a hand upon her cheek.

"I will recommend this to the council. If I can persuade them, then he will go and you will stay."

"Thank you, Father."

Chapter Twenty-Six

Raven knew this was the best chance for Running Wolf. He would live. He would rejoin his people and, in time, he might forget her. Perhaps marry Spotted Fawn and reach his destiny as a leader of his people.

But even knowing all that, her heart was dead. It beat but it might just as well have been a burl in the wood of a tree. She would survive. She knew she would.

Her grandmother and her father showed her that the living continued on even after a loved one was lost. But in her father's case, the loss had changed him, made him more solemn and more angry. She felt herself changing, hardening like the cascading water that froze in blue strands in winter.

That day the council met, and at night the people prepared to continue the welcoming of the return of the captives. Tomorrow men would be sent to the other tribes to report who had survived and who had died in the four years since the first of the captives had been taken.

Raven watched the council lodge, waiting for the leaders of her tribe to emerge. For a time she sat with the other women around the outside of the lodge. Most of what was said could be easily heard.

She was not a patient sitter.

Unlike the other women, she had brought nothing to do with her hands. Truthful Woman handed her a small pouch. Inside were flint and steel and a soft bit of leather. By the time midday arrived, Raven had three new arrowheads napped.

Truthful Woman held a finger in the air and the women stopped working.

"They are coming out," she said. The women made no show of hiding. They continued to sit in a ring outside the lodge. Listening to the conversation saved time. If they heard what was said, their husbands would not have to say again the words spoken. The council members would return to their lodges for a midday meal and listen to the opinions of their families, especially their wives and mothers, before returning to their talk.

The council members filed out followed by her brother, the war chief, their medicine man and several other warriors who had been asked to join the council and render opinions.

"Grandmother, do you think they will follow Father's request?"

"Opinion seemed mixed. Now they gather the thoughts of all."

"If they will not free him, what will I do?"

"Your father offered a suggestion to me about your young warrior this morning without knowing he had done so. I have been thinking it over since."

"What suggestion?" The panic crept up into her throat again.

Her grandmother gathered her quillwork and rose. "Come now, it is time to make the meal, and if you are to be a wife, you must learn to cook."

A wife? The best she could hope for was that Running Wolf regained his freedom. She would never be a wife.

Raven gathered her arrowheads and hurried after her grandmother.

"Do you think I should go with him? Perhaps find another tribe of the Sioux?"

"No, daughter. A man comes to his wife's tribe, not the other way around."

"But, Grandmother, you heard Father. He will never be a Crow."

"I did hear your father. But in his words I heard room to wiggle, like a weasel through a very tight spot. Did you know my husband called me Little Weasel? It was his pet name because I was so good at getting through tight places."

Raven grasped Truthful Woman's arm. "Please tell me. What do I do? I will do anything you say."

"First we see what the council decides. You have never seen a male captive in our midst. But I have seen many. Sioux, Blackfoot, even a Cree boy. But that was past. Perhaps you would like to help me feed your young man."

"Should we not speak to Father?"

"We should feed him, but do you think your father is unclear as to your wishes?"

"No."

"Then, you do not need to talk."

Raven helped her grandmother prepare a stew and a flatbread from the remains of the flour that Truthful Woman had ground at breakfast. Bright Arrow and Six Elks ate first and did not linger. Raven choked down a small portion of stew because her grandmother refused to go to Running Wolf unless she did so. She carried the kettle across the camp. Her grandmother spoke to everyone they passed. Raven was in a hurry and she found the delays tiring.

"It will be dinner before we get there," she whispered.

Truthful Woman cast her an indulgent look. "These women are speaking to their men about *your* young man. They will be more inclined to help you if you are not rude to them."

Raven, properly chastened, took her time to speak to each person they met from there on, accepting welcomes and catching up on the news she had missed.

She was careful to include one example of how well the Sioux had treated her. They let her hunt. They gave her food. Her warrior's mother taught her how to pack a household, which she had never done here. And helped her learn to prepare buffalo for drying. She told them that she had prepared several hides on her own. So now she felt better ready to be a wife.

"His mother treated her like her own daughter," said Truthful Woman.

Her grandmother told of how this brave man had rescued all the captives, not just the woman he loved, and brought them home. "And he saved my granddaughter from the one who stole my beads. He killed four blue coats who tried to molest our women. And even when captured, he rescued my little warrior from herself." She touched the wound on her granddaughter's neck. "I remember being so in love. This Sioux brave is a good match for my granddaughter. They have the same heart, brave and free. It is not just any man who would understand a woman who would own her own horses and hunt buffalo."

They finally reached the far edge of the camp.

"Do you think that helped?" asked Raven, looking regretfully at the cold, congealed stew.

"Opinion is more important than truth."

"They should call you Opinion Woman."

She smiled. "Yes, they should."

Again the guards would not let Raven enter, so she waited outside as her grandmother fed Running Wolf. When she came out, she spoke to one of the young warriors.

"I released his legs and left the gag off. He said he will not escape."

Both men stared at each other and then back to Truthful Woman, mother of the chief.

"You should not do that."

"My granddaughter would hear his voice to know he is well." She turned to Raven. "Go on."

Raven glanced about to see that several women of her tribe stood near, listening. She didn't care. Perhaps her words would help him.

"Running Wolf," she called to the lodge. "I am here for you. I am going to get you out of this."

"My heart is glad to hear you," he said. His voice sounded hoarse. Was that from the gag?

"The council is considering setting you free because of your bravery in bringing us all home."

There was a long pause.

"I would not leave you."

Tears burned her eyes.

"But I would have you live."

There was no reply. Her grandmother pulled her past the guards and women toward home. The women of the tribe watched her pass, weeping as she went, and they said nothing before returning to their lodges and their husbands.

The council reassembled in the late afternoon after a meal and some rest time. There was plenty of time to talk. When they returned to the council lodge, more women gathered. Truthful Woman made the rounds with Raven, telling of how she loved this young man. How it would break her granddaughter's heart if he were killed. How she tried to end her own life to stop the young warriors from making sport of him. She showed them the scar on her neck.

When the council settled to work, the women buzzed for a time and then listened to the men.

"Grandmother, do you think the women are with us?"

"Yes, my darling. Women love a love story, especially an impossible love story like yours. They are with you."

But as the afternoon turned toward evening, the council talk turned toward the danger of freeing a Sioux. How he would reveal their position. How a captured warrior was not set free. They had the war chief of the Sioux.

"Grandmother, they are against him."

Her grandmother looked disappointed. "They forget the voices of their women and think only of war."

When the council filed out, Raven's defeat was complete. They had only to speak the words condemning him to death. But the decision was already made. She rose and turned to go.

"Where are you going?" asked Truthful Woman.

"For my bow. They will not test his courage while I live."

"Stay," ordered her grandmother. "You are too like them, ready to fight before the negotiations are over."

"But they have decided."

"They have only decided not to free him. Things must be done in the correct manner."

Something in her grandmother's look made Raven take notice.

"Grandmother, what will you do?"

"I will do all I can."

Her father moved to a place by the fire, and the people of the tribe gathered in a large circle, their faces illuminated by the orange flames. Six Elks lifted his arms and the fringe of his shirt swung gently. He wore his war bonnet, displaying his many coup feathers.

He looked powerful, and Raven felt the deep respect her people held for her father. She glanced from one face to another, thinking of which among them had lost a friend, a brother, a wife or a child to the Sioux. When she had finished her study of the circle of faces she felt more hopeless than before. The council would not let him live.

"Your leaders have thought about this captive over many pipes. While it is true he saved the life of my daughter in battle and, according to her words, on at least two other occasions, it is also true that he is an enemy. And one does not let an enemy live. We are chased from the mountains by whites and we are killed by the Sioux when we enter the prairie. The whites have guns and terrible diseases. At least the Sioux fight with honor and with rules we understand. This warrior knew what would happen when he came here. It is the opinion of the council that he be made a captive and treated as such. We will not let him free."

Raven sagged against her grandmother. A male captive would receive the harshest treatment. He would be humiliated at every opportunity. By her intervention she had saved his life and robbed him of the chance to die with honor.

Her father's voice continued, "As with any captive and with respect for what he did to save my daughter, I will ask this question to our people. Is there any among you who have lost a loved one who wishes to replace that person with a full-grown enemy warrior?"

He waited. The people murmured. For just an instant, Raven thought her father would take Running Wolf, since he had lost a brother. But then he looked directly at her and she saw the hatred for the Sioux burned too hot for him to do this, even for the daughter he loved.

No one spoke. No one would be senseless enough to adopt a warrior.

"I will."

Raven's head whipped around to see who was speaking and saw her grandmother. Raven's mouth dropped open, and she turned back to her father to see his expression thunderous.

Raven moved closer to her grandmother, taking her by the elbow and nestling close for support.

"Grandmother, do you know what you are doing?" she whispered.

"I am doing all I can. You were willing to die for him. That is recommendation enough for me."

Six Elks looked across the fire to his mother. Truthful Woman straightened and still did not reach Raven's shoulder.

"I have lost a son. He was brave and strong and noble. Now I have no husband and so will need a son to hunt for me."

"I hunt for you," said Six Elks. "Your granddaughter hunts for you."

"My son was Black Lodges and so I adopt this

warrior, Running Wolf, and make him one of the Black Lodges people."

"You are leaving us?" asked Six Elks.

"Unless you can convince me that my son will be welcome here. My younger son will not be of the Low River people." She looked at her granddaughter. "Unless he marries a Low River woman."

Raven hugged her grandmother.

"Mother, please. He is dangerous and this is no game."

"All men are dangerous."

The women around them laughed.

"And all life is a game. As in any game it is well to know when you have been outplayed."

Her son said nothing further to his mother. Now he spoke to his people, calling for the drummers to play, and the celebration continued well into the night.

This night Raven danced and danced as the joy in her heart filled her entire body.

Chapter Twenty-Seven

The drums lulled Running Wolf to sleep and roused him from slumber. Had he been here three days or four? He could not recall. But he had memorized each imperfection in the skin of this lodge.

He hoped the old woman would come again, because she brought him more than food. She brought him news of Snow Raven. His little warrior was safe. She was with her family. She was fighting the men of the council for his life. Obviously she had managed something, for a warrior in his camp would have already been in the midst of a long and painful death. A brave man might last four or five days and never utter any sound but his death song.

Yet he languished day after day in this lodge. His legs were good, for he could move them, but his neck and shoulders throbbed from the unrelenting position, sitting up with his back braced against the cursed rough-hewn pole with his hands tied together and to the pole. He had tried to keep the blood flowing to his arms, but eventually they went numb from the elbows down.

The drumming seemed to be getting closer. He straightened, listening. The sound of many voices, singing, chanting and shouting, reached him. What was this? He did not know but he did know that the time he had dreaded and prayed for had finally come.

The death song sprang to his throat and he released it, letting go of all the love and pain. He prayed to see Snow Raven again and prayed to die a good death as the guards entered the lodge and cut him from the pole. He was hustled outside and the women took over, pushing him along. He searched the sea of unfamiliar faces for her but she was not there.

They pushed him forward, their many hands guiding him as they laughed at him. He expected a fire, a low, hot fire of coals for roasting. Or four stakes where he would be tethered spread-eagle.

What he didn't expect was to see the entire tribe assembled upon the banks of the river.

The men stood on his left and the women on his right.

Where was Raven?

And then he saw her, standing knee-deep in the river with the old woman who had brought him food. His arms prickled and burned with each movement, the pain intense as the blood now flowed to his hands. He clamped his jaw closed and allowed the women to guide him to the river-bank. There they tugged away his shirt and untied his leggings until he stood in only his loincloth.

The women released him and shouted for him to wade into the water. Their voices reminded him of a flock of crows all calling at once. He did as they bid him. Did they plan to drown him, then?

Another man entered the water. He wore only a loincloth, and his wrinkled flesh showed he had survived many winters. He carried a staff topped with the body of a golden eagle. Strands of bone and claws hung from the talons of the eagle. His chest had been painted in blue with the symbol of lightning. Upon his head sat an elaborate headdress fashioned from the horns of a buffalo and feathers with all but the tips stripped of their finery. Weasel tails hung from the bottom of the headdress in long white cords. It was a fine bonnet with much medicine and he knew this person, though not the chief, was someone of great importance.

He thought from the symbols of power and the necklace of eagle claws that sat above his medicine bundle that this man must be their shaman.

The man lifted his staff and all the chanting and drumming ceased.

He raised his voice to be heard by all.

"This one comes to us an enemy. But the river will wash him clean." He placed a hand on Running Wolf's head.

Running Wolf had time to look at Raven and see her smiling face. A possibility dawned and he held his breath, allowing the medicine man to dunk him into the water three times. When he was allowed to stand, he found the women cheering.

The shaman lifted his arms again.

"This man is now an Apsáalooke of the Black Lodges people. All traces of the enemy are washed away and even his blood is pure. He is the son of Truthful Woman. We welcome him to our midst."

Could it be true?

He faced Raven, only now noticing that she wore a stunning dress of red buckskin, adorned with elks' teeth. Her short hair gave the illusion of length because of the artful way it was arranged. He went to her and reached for her, but the old women stepped in front of Raven. The women around them laughed.

"My son," said the woman. "I welcome you home."

So this was the one crazy enough to adopt a warrior. Did she really think that dipping in their river would make him less Sioux?

"I would like you to meet the daughter of my other son. She is of the Low River people." She presented the young woman at her side. "This is my granddaughter, Snow Raven."

Running Wolf smiled, feeling suddenly that being a member of the Black Lodges might be exactly what he wanted to be. Raven kissed him on each cheek. "Welcome home."

Someone shouted from the bank above them. "Truthful Woman! How is your son to be called?"

Truthful Woman turned to the women above them on the bank. Running Wolf saw nothing but joy and acceptance on the faces of the women. How was that possible?

Truthful Woman laid a hand on his shoulder.

"This is my son, Iron Wolf."

The tribe cheered and the drum began again, echoing the beating of his heart. Raven took his hand and led him forward to meet his new people. He had always known he would take a wife. But he never imagined he would have to travel so far to be with the woman he chose or that he would marry, not out of duty but out of love.

A moon passed and the seasons turned. The wind changed direction again, foretelling the coming cold and the snows. The Apsáalooke tribes gathered together for their winter camp and the captives reunited with their families. Stories were told and retold of their daring escape.

Iron Wolf was brought before the council of the Low River tribe to recount all that had happened. Raven could not speak before the council, but she could speak to guests in her father's lodge. So the council met there and she retold all that had come to pass.

Iron Wolf began to play his flute and Raven came out to stand with him in a blanket while her grandmother made dinner. Afterward all went inside the lodge because Iron Wolf was her son.

It was a tangle for Iron Wolf to ask his adopted brother to marry his daughter. Iron Wolf had only Black Lodges blood now and was therefore free to court any woman in the Low River tribe.

A few women even made their interest known. He was a handsome warrior, after all, but Snow Raven let it be known that he would be her husband before Six Elks had accepted the offer for her hand.

Snow Raven and Iron Wolf were married before the tribe, their hands symbolically bound together to signify that they walked, worked and followed one path from here forward. Iron Wolf promised to protect her with his life and Snow Raven promised to provide them a home. Her father, Six Elks, made no objections as their shaman, Thunder Buffalo, listed the items that Iron Wolf had offered for Snow Raven.

Six horses, taken from the Sioux, including Song, Raven's favorite horse.

Six bridles woven from the hair of the former captives.

Two Sioux lodges.

Five buffalo robes.

And the list went on. The captives had offered Iron Wolf every single item they had stolen or been given by the Sioux people in exchange for the servant Iron Bear had taken with him on the Sky Road.

Raven knew her father still hated the Sioux, but hoped that her new husband might someday change his mind. The ceremony to wash away all Sioux blood had satisfied him for now, and all would accept this adoption because their shaman had told them her husband was now Apsáalooke.

Her grandmother presented Raven with her own cooking pot and promised to show her how to use it. That brought good-natured laughter all around.

Next her father stepped forward. Raven feared that his words might spoil this perfect day. Before the feasting, it was customary for the father of the bride to speak to the groom. He did not always do so publicly.

Six Elks lifted his hands for silence. The tribe looked to their leader.

"Our newest member has delivered four of our people back to us, including my daughter. He led them from enemy territory and to our tribe. According to the words of my daughter, he saved her life at least twice. For these acts of bravery, I present him eight coup feathers."

Raven's chest filled with pride as her husband stepped up before all to collect this honor.

Six Elks continued, "It is my belief that this one will be brave and true and soon will have enough feathers for his own war bonnet."

Iron Wolf nodded his thanks and returned to his wife's side. She wanted to touch one of the feathers, but knew that a man's feathers, like his weapons, were not to be touched by any but a warrior.

The people came forward to congratulate the new couple, but her father lifted his hands again.

"There are two more feathers to give."

The people looked about from man to man, trying to recall a new act of courage, leadership or prowess.

"This first eagle feather goes to one who saved my own mother from capture by the Sioux."

There was a gasp and then a murmur and then a cheer as the people realized he spoke of his daughter. It was uncommon but not unheard of for a woman to earn a feather. All she had to do was save a life, defeat an enemy or perform some other act of bravery.

"Snow Raven, come forward," said her father.

She could not see past the blurring of her vision as water filled her eyes. She was so proud she thought she might swell up and burst.

He extended a perfect eagle feather, tufted with a fluffy white underfeather and the shaft wrapped with red trade cloth tied with cording.

The honor felt light in her hands.

Her father held up the second eagle feather, this one carefully stained with a single red bar at midshaft, indicating it marked a warrior's second coup. "And this feather is for leadership of your people and the sacrifice you were willing to make for their sakes."

The people cheered and howled their approval as Snow Raven accepted the second feather and held them up for all to see.

It was a long time before the people quieted enough for her to speak.

"I am honored."

Six Elks placed his arm about his daughter's shoulders.

"My daughter has returned a warrior!"

Another cheer filled the air. Snow Raven hugged her father and then returned to her husband, who hugged her.

Thunder Buffalo, the shaman, lifted his staff and the people settled. "Tonight, after the feast, I will tell the tale of Snow Raven's bravery and how the captives tricked the old Sioux chief. Oh, I have many new stories to tell!"

Raven held tight to the hand of her new husband as her heart wept with gladness. She had all she ever wanted and more. A home, a husband and the coup feather of a warrior.

Her grandmother took their hands, leading them to the feast set out in their honor.

"Do you see my son and granddaughter?" she called to the people they passed. "They are warriors of the Large-Beaked Bird people."

All they passed offered the words of blessing, "Walk in beauty."

At the center of the gathered tribes, Iron Wolf stood beside his wife and held her tight to his side. They feasted and danced and finally gathered by the fire as Thunder Buffalo stood to tell the story of the bargain made by Snow Raven, the sacrifice made by one who now walked the Way of Souls and the dangerous journey of the captives back to their people. Finally, he told of two warriors, now husband and wife, who had gambled their lives for their love and won.

* * * * *

Don't miss Sarah Morgan's
next Puffin Island story

Some Kind of Wonderful

Brittany Forrest has stayed away from Puffin Island
since her relationship with Zach Flynn went bad.
They were married for ten days and only just
managed not to kill each other by the
end of the honeymoon.

But, when a broken arm means she must return,
Brittany moves back to her Puffin Island home.
Only to discover that Zac is there as well.

Will a summer together help two lovers reunite or
will their stormy relationship crash on to the
rocks of Puffin Island?

Some Kind of Wonderful
COMING JULY 2015
Pre-order your copy today

MILLS & BOON®

HISTORICAL

AWAKEN THE ROMANCE OF THE PAST